I0614087

Overruling Judgment

by

Liz Ellyn

Overruling Judgment

Cover Art by *Lisa Dawn MacDonald*

The Wild Rose Press, Inc.
PO Box 708
Adams Basin, NY 14410-0708
Visit us at www.thewildrosepress.com

Publishing History
First Edition, 2023
Trade Paperback ISBN 978-1-5092-5080-6
Digital ISBN 978-1-5092-5081-3

Published in the United States of America

Ian started talking. Of course, he initiated control of the conversation just like he dominated legal negotiations. "We understand that you aren't inclined to choose either one of us. We aren't pressing you to do that now." The tenderness in Ian's voice and the concern in JD's eyes alarmed her.

Sasha's chin began to quiver as a feeling of doom swept through her. Tears welled up in her eyes. "Are you both here for closure's sake?"

"Fuck no!" JD swore, clasping her hand more securely. "I have no desire to end things with you."

A tear slid down her cheek. Sasha started biting her lip. Did JD think she was going to choose him over Ian? Her head started to spin. Nausea brewed in her belly.

Ian leaned in closer. "Neither of us wants to end things with you. Well, I suppose our case is a little different." Ian extended an open hand. Her free hand itched to reach out and accept Ian's offer. Uncertainty made her hesitate.

"I'm totally confused." Sasha looked back and forth between the two. Neither of their faces gave her a clue. What were they suggesting?

Dedication

Gratitude to all those, past and present, that encouraged
and supported me along the way.

Chapter 1

Sasha

Despite her best efforts, the damn door betrayed her and squeaked loudly. Sasha winced. All hope of an inconspicuous entrance was ruined. Her classmates turned towards her in unison. She froze as nineteen pairs of eyes stared at her. But then she found JD's upturned smile greeting her. No longer caring about anyone else besides JD, she regained control of her legs and dashed to her seat.

JD addressed the room as if he had not been rudely bothered. With his back to the class, he faced his easel and demonstrated how to use underpainting prior to applying color. Without the class's focus of attention on her, Sasha let out a deep breath.

Sasha tried to pay attention to JD's demonstration, but she struggled to focus on his easel. Staring at him was much more captivating than whatever he was doing on the canvas. His ass looked delectable under his well-worn denim jeans. A threadbare spot below his pocket tantalized her. Damn, he had a great ass.

He pushed up the sleeves on his thermal cotton shirt, revealing his naked forearms. These were not the arms of a starving artist. The corded muscles flexed as he flicked the paintbrush against the canvas. She caught a glimpse of the colorful and engaging work, but was again distracted by his beautifully masculine body. The man was seriously built. His shirt stretched tightly over his broad shoulders. The flex of the cotton delineated his bulging lats on his back.

As JD continued to paint, his shirt slowly began to free itself. Inch by inch the shirt creeped up and out from his jeans until it finally escaped the constraint of his waistband. A thin line of skin peeked out at his lower back. Just enough space to insert her tongue. The shirt continued to sway like an exotic dancer. The man should have been posing naked for the art class rather than teaching it. It should have been considered a crime to cover his body with clothes.

Salivating, she swallowed her desire.

Sasha's eyes were fixated south of JD's waistband when he turned around. She quickly shifted her gaze upward, but saw him smirk at her. Her face heated. She adjusted her eyes toward his easel and calculated the odds that JD had caught her staring at his ass. She covered her flushed face with her hand. What she really wanted to do was bury her head in the sand like an ostrich.

JD addressed the class, "Did everyone bring in an item as the subject matter for your oil painting? No worries if you didn't. There are lots of cool things around the room. Artists can find inspiration anywhere. Even a dirty paint can, covered in splatters of paint, can be inspiring. Or, check out some of the sculptures that my other students fired up in the kiln. Maybe the shape or color might catch your eye. If you find it interesting, go with it. Anything is better than a boring bowl of fruit."

Sasha reached in her bag and removed a box. She carefully opened the box and unwrapped a Matryoshka doll. She unnested the wooden Russian dolls, placing them safely on the table out of range from any paint splatter.

She hopped off her art stool, but halted when she noticed her workspace was ready to go. There was a clean pallet, brushes, a pallet knife, and a handful of tubes of oil paint in a variety of colors. Everything she needed to get started was already ready at her disposal. She didn't need to go to the back of the room to gather the necessary art supplies like all the other students in the class. Sasha raised her fingertips to her brow. The unsolicited assistance saved her precious moments of work time.

Searching around the room, she saw JD working with another student. She refrained from gawking at the dream-inspiring man and returned her focus to her pallet. Popping open a couple of tubes of paint, she dabbed and swirled some orange and red together on her pallet. She added more red paint to the mix. Pursing her lips, she squinted at the color before her. It wasn't quite right. She added a bit of yellow. When she finally achieved her desired hue, she smiled and nodded her head.

Sasha started with a narrow tip flat edged brush and attempted to sketch out the relative placement of the dolls on her painting. Her head bobbed back and forth between the easel and dolls as if she were watching a tennis match. Like the soft touch of a drop shot, she dabbed the paint, approximating the relative sizes of the dolls.

Pausing, she assessed her progress. Sasha inhaled deeply. The woodsy smell of men's cologne eclipsed the pungent smell of paint. The hair on her arms rose as goosebumps spread. She closed her eyes and drew in another deep breath. The scent flooded her senses. She stifled a moan of pleasure that threatened to escape.

"How's it going over here?" Damn, his voice was even better than his scent. It sent delightful shivers down her spine and tingled in all the right places. "Love the color." His breath tickled her neck.

Sasha turned to face JD. She attempted to say hello and thank him for setting up her station, but her tongue failed to work. Instead, she sat there, mute.

JD edged nearer to Sasha and pointed to her pallet. "I like that you break rules." His close proximity made her heart race.

Was that intended as a double entendre? She cleared her throat and stammered, "Don't get me wrong. I love the dolls, but the muted colors are rather dull. The beige and the brownish green feel sad. That wasn't the feeling that I wanted to express in the painting."

He smiled. "Tell me. What were you?"

His smile was infectious and she mirrored the sentiment. "Love, which is why I focused on using warm tones. The colors remind me of my grandma sharing the ooey-gooey goodness of fresh-from-the-oven chocolate chips cookies with me."

"Chocolate chip cookies are the best. Nice choice. Art is all about inspiration," JD nodded. His enthusiasm for art resonated in every word. "Can I ask? Why the doll?"

"My grandmother gave me the doll when I was born. It was originally my great-grandmother's, whom I was named after. It's nice to have a physical symbol of her as well as her name." Sasha sighed as the pleasantness of the memory filled her with joy.

JD slipped his hands in his back pockets and relaxed

his posture. He didn't seem in a rush to move on to another student. "Your great-grandmother was named Sasha? That's a lovely name."

It was a very personal question, but she unreservedly shared. She corrected his assumption, "Actually, Sasha is a nickname that my father and mother called me."

"That's a pretty nickname. I've had some crappy ones over the years." He chuckled.

She flirted back, "You've piqued my curiosity. Tell me." Did others simply refer to him as Gorgeous?

"Some other time. I don't want to waste yours. Can I offer you a few suggestions?" He pushed up the sleeves on his shirt.

She would listen to anything he had to say as his deep voice melted her insides. She stared dreamily. "You're the teacher. So yes. And, I would appreciate it."

A small laugh fell from his lips. "Take a photo of the dolls, now. It will be easier setting up next week. Reproducing the layout can be frustrating."

"That's great advice. I tend to have a problem losing track of time." She shook her head unapprovingly. "I'm sorry for being late to class today and interrupting."

"No worries." He shrugged.

She wasn't convinced.

"I mean it. Don't worry about it. This is a stress-free class." He dismissed her explanation with a flick of his hands.

She smiled and nodded, though she envisioned other ways to relieve stress with JD. They didn't need stretched cloth canvases for painting; using their naked bodies would be a lot more fun. She imagined him guiding the bristles of his brush down her neck and along the curve of her breast. Her cheeks heated. The sexual tension between them had been intensifying over the weeks. Her smile turned devilish.

He pulled her from her divergent thoughts. "I wouldn't suggest this to other students in the class, but you have a gift. Laying down cool colors underneath the warm ones, gives your work a lot more depth."

She looked intently at JD, judging the veracity of his compliment. Nothing indicated that he was lying. She smiled and thanked him.

"Do you mean like this?" She picked up the blue paint and began to squirt some on her pallet.

The sound of a gavel striking twice rang loudly from under the tabletop.

She stiffened. Her hand clenched tightly around the tube and blue paint shot out all over the pallet. "Dammit!" She reached for the pallet knife but accidentally hit the paint pallet with her other hand. "Fuck." She grabbed a towel and wiped her hands but smeared the paint, making the problem even worse.

Sasha cringed and carefully extracted the phone from her bag. Amazingly, she avoided painting the inside of her leather purse.

There was a message from her boss that she needed to come to the office immediately. "Fuck!"

She mentally listed all the things she needed to do to get into the office: clean up her space, pack up her doll. Also, wearing yoga pants and a ponytail was not acceptable attire for the office.

Her breathing accelerated and her hand began to shake. She dropped her phone on the floor.

"Hey, what's wrong?" JD's voice suspended her panic.

The words flew out of her mouth. "I need to get to

my office ASAP. There's some kind of emergency."

A comforting hand landed on her shoulder. "Listen, I got your stuff. I promise to take good care of your great-grandmother's nesting dolls." He gently removed the paint tube from her hand. "You go. Take care of whatever you need to do at work."

"You sure? I feel terrible leaving you with such a mess." She didn't wait for an answer. She clumsily rose from her seat and made another attempt at cleaning the paint off her hands with a dry towel.

"Absolutely, Sasha. Go. I'll see you next week." JD beamed.

"Thank you so much." She stepped away and then turned back. "JD? You set up my station today?"

He winked at her.

"I owe you one." She scurried out of the room.

Sasha dashed to her car and popped the trunk. She exhaled at the sight of the spare business suit. Looking to the sky, she whispered, "Thank goodness." While she breathed a bit easier, she ground her teeth. The learned practice of suit stashing was still a bitter memory that she would never forget. A fellow first year attorney had spilled coffee on her before a big meeting. She'd doubted that it was truly an accident.

Inside the rundown university restroom, Sasha scoured her hands forcefully. No matter how much muscle she put behind the effort, the paint remained. She scowled at the offending blue pigment and grunted in frustration. As time ticked away, she eventually conceded.

She stripped out of her casual clothes and placed them neatly on the sink. She kept her socks on her feet, fearing direct contact with the grimy floor. Teetering precariously on one leg, she stepped into her skirt. But while attempting her balancing act, her shirt slipped off the cracked porcelain sink. She quickly reached to catch it before it landed on the dirty floor, causing her to wobble. Fortunately, she managed not to land on her ass. When she was done, she chucked each sock in the trash after slipping her bare feet in her heels. She never wanted to touch *those* again.

Finally, she twisted her loose ponytail into an acceptable professional bun. Gathering her belongings, Sasha bolted back to her car.

Heading into work, she tried to mentally prepare herself to meet with her boss. Her knuckles were white from gripping the steering wheel tightly. Mr. Lane had stolen the highlight of her week. The art class was her respite. She shook her head, shooing away her mood like an annoying bug buzzing in her vicinity.

At a stop light, she opened a new mindfulness app on her phone. She followed along. She had been working to develop her skills at masking her emotions and was careful to chuck the chip on her shoulder before entering the lobby of the firm. Any type of unacceptable emotion in the office would inevitably be seen as a weakness. Even worse, it would be interpreted as female fragility.

She stopped in one of the firm's bathrooms and did a last-minute, quick once-over before she crossed the threshold of her boss's office. She blotted at the sweat that beaded on her brow and offered herself an encouraging smile in the mirror.

Striding as quickly as possible without actually running, Sasha approached her boss's office where the door was open.

Mr. Lane spoke before she even had the chance to

say hello. "Don't bother sitting down. Jacob Stein's second-year assistant, Ms. Coleman, ended up in the ER with a ruptured appendix. Stein needs extra help this week. He asked for some assistance, and as his grandfather is a named partner, I couldn't refuse. I expect you to be a team player and help him out."

Sasha kept her answer brief, "Of course. Whatever I can do to help." Getting her work product seen directly by someone higher up in the firm was a great opportunity.

"Stein's office is on the floor above. I will let him know that you are on your way." Her boss broke eye-contact as if he were done with the conversation so she turned toward the door to leave. Just before she breached the doorway, he warned her without even bothering to look away from his computer, "By the way, don't forget that the quality of your work reflects on me. I expect you to work your ass off for Stein."

"Of course, Mr. Lane," Sasha mumbled in a nonresponsive manner. When it was clear that her boss had nothing more to add, she headed to the elevator bank.

Sasha pressed the button for the third floor. Once she stepped out, Sasha looked around as she was unfamiliar with the area. She moved slowly until finding the office with the right name plate.

Wiping her sweaty palms on her suit, she knocked on Mr. Stein's open door. He was sitting behind a desk much larger than Mr. Lane's. An impressive name and title apparently warranted impressive office furniture.

Mr. Stein stood to greet her and shook her hand. It was a pleasant change to how her boss brushed over any resemblance of courtesy.

A man sitting in a chair with his back to the door

stood as well. He turned and stared down at her. His chiseled face and light brown eyes seared through her. She prayed her knees didn't fail her. It had been months since she had last seen that face. Sasha bit the inside of her cheek. The metallic taste of blood seeped over her tongue. She straightened her back, but he still towered more than a half foot over her five-foot, five-inch frame.

Mr. Stein's handshake pulled her focus back to him. He gazed a little longer than necessary at her hands.

"Nice to meet you, Mr. Stein. Please excuse the paint on my hands. In my haste to get here quickly, I only had time to use soap and water." What would he have said if she smelled like turpentine?

Mr. Stein gestured to the other man in the room. "This is Ian O'Malley."

Ian extended his hand without hesitation. She placed her hand in his. The feel of his fingers wrapping around hers sent a warm quivering sensation through her body. "Pleasure." She agreed wholeheartedly. Touching him was staggering. Thoughts of the indulgences they'd shared ignited her arousal.

Mr. Stein curtailed her mischievous thoughts. "I'll let Mr. O'Malley explain to you what you will be doing before Ms. Coleman can manage to get back into the office." Mr. Stein's use of the word *manage* struck her as harsh and uncaring. Hailey was laying on an operating table, not playing hooky.

Mr. Stein sat back down. "I'll need an update first thing in the morning, Mr. O'Malley."

Ian confirmed with a nod. Sasha waited, uncertain where to proceed.

Like a gentleman, Ian gestured with his hand for her to exit Mr. Stein's room first. "My office is down the hall, Ms. Smirnova." He pointed the way with an outstretched arm. "It is off to the left."

She slowed her pace as Ian guided her to his office. Was that his hand on her back or had she imagined a phantom touch? He was close enough on her heels that he would crash into her if she stopped abruptly. That scenario had potential.

"The next office."

She cocked her head to the side like a dog directing their ear to the source of a sound, while exposing her neck.

"Go on in." The warmth of his breath caressed the sensitive skin beneath her ear.

Ian's office was considerably smaller than Mr. Stein's, but Ian's desk was much larger than her own. The warm woods, dark colors, and traditional style matched the theme throughout the firm. She hadn't yet had the opportunity to explore much of the firm's four floors in the Chicago high-rise. She envisioned the likely ostentatious appearance of the managing partners' offices up on the top floor.

She took a seat in one of the two visitor's chairs. Leaving his door conspicuously open, Ian sat in his desk chair with three feet of mahogany wood separating them. He sat up straight, obscuring his hands.

"Ian." She exhaled.

Ian stopped her. "I don't mean to be rude and cut you off but I think that while we are at work we should call each other by our last names, like everyone else does. Is that agreeable, Ms. Smirnova?" His professional and distant tone was a slap in the face. She had participated in discovery meetings where even attorneys on opposing sides were more cordial than Ian was acting.

"Of course, *Mr. O'Malley*." She made no effort to mask the disdain in her tone.

A pregnant pause ensued. They stared at one another. No questions. No proclamations. No accusations. He adjusted his pant leg a bit and scooted his chair closer to the desk. Was he purposefully hiding a growing reaction to her presence?

Ian cleared his throat and broke the silence. "Listen. I don't want any awkwardness between us while we have to work together. It probably won't be for long as I suspect Hailey will be back soon."

Did attorneys have no understanding of medical issues? "Her appendix burst! That's not a simple procedure and I'm sure the recovery is going to be painful."

"You don't know Hailey. She is very determined to stay on track to become partner. I'm certain she will return to work soon."

Was leaving a hospital against medical advice a requisite for becoming partner at the firm? She wasn't sure she wanted the answer. As well, his reference to Hailey by her first name rubbed Sasha the wrong way.

"I have all of the instructions of what needs to be done in terms of research and a brief inside the folder. If you have any questions, please ask. Assumptions usually don't work out well." He dismissed the topic of consideration for Hailey's health and reached for a manilla folder on the side of his desk.

"No problem, Mr. O'Malley." She glared as she grasped the envelope.

He didn't release his grip. She tugged lightly but still he clung onto the folder. They locked eyes. The office surroundings faded. The memory of him commanding her to look him in his light brown eyes shackled her in her place.

She blinked. "Mr. O'Malley?"

"Yes. Yes. Here you go." He finally relinquished the folder.

Although completely unnecessary, Ian stood to walk her out of his office. She turned right to head toward the elevators. "Ms. Smirnova. Wait." She turned her head and awaited further instruction. "Instead of going back to your office, why don't you work at Hailey's desk instead."

"Okay. Lead the way." She followed and avoided an unnecessary confrontation. She wanted to start on the work quickly to salvage the rest of her Sunday evening.

Hailey's office was only twenty feet away from Ian's. "In case you have any questions, I'll be close on hand to help." He smiled wryly. She turned away, keeping her flippant comments to herself.

Hailey's desk looked nearly identical to hers on the lower floor. She placed her computer down, paying careful attention to not disturb any of Hailey's personal items.

Ian loitered in the doorway. With the doorframe encircling him, he looked like a model in a photograph. "If you need anything, Ms. Smirnova, don't hesitate."

"Mr. O'Malley?" She leveled him with a look.

"Yes? What can I help you with?" His eyes brightened.

She clenched her jaw. "Would you mind closing the door on your way out? Thanks."

His closing the office door felt eerily similar to when he had closed the door on the potential of a relationship with her last summer.

Chapter 2

Ian

Ian plopped into his office chair and sighed deeply.

Damn, the smell of her perfume filled his office. He closed his eyes and appreciated the sweet combination of berries and vanilla. That scent had been plaguing him for months. It triggered his memory, of tasting her sweetness.

He swallowed hard.

The ability to work eluded him. Ian considered several excuses to go check on her while she was working. He attempted to justify the need. Instead, he tamped down his desire to see her by reminding himself of the benefits of becoming partner at the firm. His singularly focused drive had rewarded him in the past. He needed steadfast determination to hit this milestone in his career.

But was the sacrifice worth it? He slumped forward, catching his downturned head in his hands and closed his eyes.

Months had passed since *that* Fourth of July, but his memory had not waned. There had been no formalities that night. She didn't call him Mr. O'Malley and he didn't call her Ms. Smirnova. They'd been on an intimate first name basis.

It had all started when one of the partners had

invited him to the top floor of the firm's high rise, which sported a sensational view of the fireworks over Lake Michigan. Only a handful of other attorneys had been treated to such a perk. Those attorneys too, were on track to become partner. He'd maximized the opportunity to rub elbows with the other partners in a casual environment.

At the conclusion of the fireworks show, the older partners hopped in their cars with their families to return to their homes in the suburbs. He and the other younger attorneys bounced with energy. They'd all headed over to Lawson's Bar, a popular bar for attorneys in the Loop.

****

The Chicago heat and humidity assaulted him in the face as he exited the cool air conditioning of the law firm. Gridlock controlled the streets following the fireworks. Rather than waiting for a car, he chose to walk.

By the time he arrived, the perspiration coating his back acted like tacky glue affixing his shirt to his skin. He tugged at his polo shirt tucked into his khaki slacks and entered. The air conditioning was much preferred to the thick air outside. Everyone inside was dressed more casual than usual, like himself. The national holiday brought a levity to the bar. Laughter replaced the normal argumentative conversations.

Then there was her.

Her alluring red summer dress captured his attention. It was shorter than anything appropriate to be worn at a law firm, stopping a few inches above her knee. He estimated the number of inches between the hem and the apex of her thighs.

And those heels. They accentuated the definition in her legs. He wanted to run his fingers along those muscular lines. He wanted to indulge in kissing up every inch and drag his tongue from her knee to the upper most part of her thigh. He wanted to nudge her skirt higher until he had full access. It would be sexy as fuck if she were completely bare beneath.

Her soft brown waves danced below her bare shoulder blades as she talked animatedly. Her pale skin peeked between strands of shiny hair. The carefree look beguiled him as he was normally surrounded by women in conservative updos at work. He wanted to feel her silky locks slide between his splayed fingers.

The person sitting on the bar stool next to her vacated. She rose on her tip-toes and claimed the seat. The hem of her dress rose even higher in the process.

Ian's pulse increased.

She turned on the stool at the bar, faced him, and his dick came to attention. The low neckline of her dress revealed a perfect amount of cleavage. He needed an answer to the nagging questions: *What color were her nipples? Were they pink? Rose?*

Above and beyond all else, her warm brown eyes captured him. They were soul searing. He wanted to plunge his dick in her wet core and have her stare at him with those pools of chocolate.

She turned away from him and waved to one of the bartenders. He refused to allow that mere glimpse of her radiance be the last of their encounter. Ian maneuvered his way to her seat at the bar, skipping past some friendly faces as if he were blind to their existence.

He stood beside her and motioned for the bartender. The bartender came by, but rather than ask him for his order she addressed the gorgeous woman beside him. "Hey, Alex, need another?"

She held up her nearly full drink in answer.

"Okay, I'll check back soon." The bartender then turned to him, "What can I get you?"

He ordered himself a vodka on the rocks.

And then he took advantage of the opportunity. "Hi. I'm Ian and you're Alex, I presume?"

She laughed softly. She glanced at the bartender and shook her head back and forth before gracing him with a beautiful smile. "Hi Ian. I'm Alexandra." Her smile practically knocked him over. *She was simply beautiful.*

"Not Alex?" Had he heard the bartender incorrectly? Ian's brain wasn't functioning fully as his blood was rushing south.

She chuckled. "Kat is the only one that calls me Alex. She says that no name should have more syllables than the word tequila."

Ian laughed, but complimented her at the same time, "Well, I think Alexandra is a great name."

Kat returned and handed a glass to Ian. She wore a suspicious smile. Ian took a sip. His tongue danced in confusion. He narrowed his eyes at the bartender. Kat smirked. "You ordered a vodka on the rocks?"

"Yes." He challenged, as the glass was filled with water, not alcohol.

The bartender laughed. She gestured to Alexandra. "Well, here's Alex Smirnova. And, I would definitely say she's rocking that red dress tonight."

Ian's eyes widened and questioned Alexandra. "As in the vodka?"

"No. I have no relation to the vodka company, other than the fact that I do enjoy their products. Smirnova just happens to be an extremely common Russian name."

Funny, he hadn't detected any accent in her voice.

Addressing Kat, Ian commented, "Impressive bartending skills. I definitely like how you serve a vodka on the rocks." Ian turned toward Alexandra and looked in those beautiful eyes. "I whole heartedly agree that you are rocking that red dress. You look amazing."

He took another swig from his glass, allowing himself a second to think. He worried, "It seems like the two of you have this routine down to a science. Practice it often?"

Alexandra cringed and quickly corrected him, "No. Really, this is a first. Kat has a quirky sense of humor." She paled a little and covered her mouth. Ian believed her denial.

Kat set another drink in front of Ian. "This one is on the house. I hope I didn't overstep too far earlier."

Ian took a sip. Yup. This time it was vodka.

"Thank you for the drink, but I most appreciate the introduction. I'll be sure to add a good review online." He planned to tip her well too.

Kat smiled. "Excellent. Time to go spread my magic elsewhere." Then she split.

Ian eyed Alexandra's red, white, and blue drink. "So, what are you drinking, Alexandra?"

"It's a vodka-lemonade slushy." Sasha poked at her drink with her straw.

Ian raised an eyebrow.

Alexandra pushed out her chin and retorted, "Hey, don't knock it. It's the epitome of a good time in a bar. It's festive, tasty, and the drink acknowledges patriotism through its colors in a non-political kind of way."

Ian smiled. "My brother would probably agree with you about the benefits of the color in the drink."

She continued to share with him how she and Kat

got smashed the night Kat had masterminded the red, white, and blue drink concoction for the Fourth of July. Her enthusiasm for the drink almost had him wanting to order one for himself. Nonetheless, he had a reputation to uphold and wasn't going to be seen by his colleagues with that kind of drink in his hand.

She took another sip, smiling up at him. Her red lips called to him. He desperately wanted to kiss her.

She fixed her stare on his mouth and leaned toward him.

"Can I try your drink?" he toyed with her.

She raised and tilted it toward him.

Instead of sipping from her offered straw, he reached for the back of her neck and brought her closer to him. "I would rather taste it on your tongue." She exhaled and the sweet scent of lemonade tempted him.

She leaned in the rest of the way until her lips were on his. He claimed her mouth, swiping his tongue inside her before retreating.

His body hummed all over.

She gaped at him, her pupils dilating. Her cheeks flushed in a shade that neared the red in her dress. Then her gaze dropped again to his lips.

"You're right, the drink is very tasty. I could easily see myself getting drunk off of it." Ian stared at her lips. He wanted more. He wanted to kiss her more, with fewer judgmental eyes surrounding them. She finished off the rest her drink and her friend brought another round of drinks by without either of them needing to ask.

The conversation with Alexandra flowed effortlessly. She amused him with stories about arriving in America. She tried to teach him some Russian words, but he lacked any natural ability to pick up other languages. She nearly fell off the bar stool laughing at his terrible attempt. Unlike how some woman's laughter grated on his nerves, hers filled him with cheer.

Kat refilled their drinks three or four times. He hadn't concerned himself with keeping count.

Then Kat announced last calls for alcohol.

He didn't want the night to end. One-night stands weren't his thing, but his desire to go home with this vivacious woman had grown as the night progressed. He was hoping for what was happening between them to turn into more.

A flush seeped up her skin and her eyes dilated. He leaned in to whisper in her ear. The summer-time scent in her hair made him want to kiss her neck for hours. "Want to head out together?" he whispered.

She grasped his hand in answer and slipped off the bar seat.

Ian played with her hemline during the ride back to her apartment. He fought his desire to inch his fingers higher up her thigh and to ravish her in the car. The ten-minute jaunt was torture.

They entered her apartment and frantically ripped each other's clothes off. Her eagerness aroused him. His cock throbbed. He needed relief but at the same time didn't want the encounter to end quickly. He attempted to slow their pace and eased Alexandra back onto her bed. He stared into her brown eyes for a moment while he tried to figure out what he wanted to do first.

As if she read his mind, Alexandra reminded him, "We have all night. Don't over think our first time." The promise of repeated fun defused his stress.

He laid on top of Alexandra, his broad shoulders dwarfing her smaller figure. He loved the feel of her firm mauve nipples pushing into his skin. His dick was pressed up tight against her pelvis. She raised her hips to grind against him. A moan slipped past his lips as he lost the battle with control over his urges. She echoed the sentiment.

He leaned in for a punishing kiss, her lips already parted for him. Her taste mingled with his own and the vodka he had been drinking all night. Like slamming a shot of vodka, he wanted to pound into her. The way she caressed his tongue as he invaded her mouth sent a humming feeling straight to his balls. Pre-cum spilled from his cock.

She surprised him. Slowly easing back from the kiss, and with heavily lidded eyes, Alexandra urged, "Ian, I need that brilliant tongue of yours on me. *Now*."

He had never had a woman be so forward in bed, to outright direct him to go down on her. Her boldness made him trust the connection between them. She ran her fingers through his short brown hair in an appreciative manner. She encouraged him to savor each delightful inch of her body. He loved it.

He teased her nipple with his mouth and pinched it firmly between his teeth. She jolted and yanked his hair in response. She was willing to give as much as she got. He massaged her nipple with his fingers to ease the pain he had inflicted with his teeth. She started gasping and wiggled beneath him.

He was rewarded when he reached her silken opening. His wide shoulders spread her legs. Her honey tasted like heaven. He circled her clit with his tongue.

"Yes! Ian!" Alexandra wailed.

Again! Ian wanted to make her scream again. He plunged one finger, then two fingers into her. Her wet core greedily grasped his fingers. She groaned louder. He stroked her again and again. Her legs tightened around him. She fisted his hair again.

When he pinched her nipple, her channel squeezed his fingers. He immediately felt more wet warmth coat his digits. He sucked on her clit as she pulsed through another climax.

Her breaths came forcefully, one after another. Her breasts rose and fell in a hypnotic pattern that entranced him. As gratifying as it was to watch her state of bliss, his balls ached and screamed for relief.

She began to stir and managed to slither herself out of his reach. The lack of contact concerned him.

He grabbed at her leg, prepared to hinder a potential escape. To his delight, she extended her hand toward the drawer on her nightside table. The unwarranted tension in his muscles eased as she pulled out a box of condoms. The box of three was sealed. He was thankful that it wasn't a box of thirty-six condoms with only one left. Ian ground his teeth at the momentary thought of her being with another man.

She held up the condom and raised an eyebrow. "Yes?"

"Hell yes." He grabbed the foil package and quickly donned the condom.

He angled himself over her body and kissed her clit one more time before he crawled up her body.

She grabbed his sheathed cock and brought it towards her opening. "Please Ian," she begged.

"I need to see your eyes, Alexandra," Ian demanded. He waited until he had her full attention.

Her warm brown eyes stared deep into his lighter brown ones. Her gaze revealed an openness and trust that deepened their connection. He liked that she didn't hide from him.

He slowly inched his way in, loving the feel of forcing her channel to stretch.

Her eyes rolled back in her head. "Ian!" She began to pant.

"Alexandra. Look at me." He started moving inside her, also panting. Slowly. He savored those first few thrusts. "You feel so good, Alexandra." His voice came out raspy.

Her lips curled into a smile. She raised her hips as he pushed inside. They moved together as they sought mutual pleasure.

He picked up the pace and started forcefully pounding into her. "Oh, yes!" He tilted his pelvis, connecting with her clit every time he pressed into her.

"Yes, right there," she gasped, her voice raising.

Her eyes drooped closed every so often. "Eyes open, Alexandra." He craved the deeper connection.

Her fingers dug into his shoulders. "Yes, Yes, Yes." Her eyes widened. "Ian!" She shouted. Her back arched and her pussy squeezed his cock like a vice.

Fuck. So good. Ian threw her legs over his shoulder and drove into her deeper. Deep pounding thrusts. Tip to base, he luxuriated in her heat. His shoulders tensed. Her pussy massaged along his cock. And, with a final surge, his cock convulsed inside her.

Contentment ran through his body. If only it were possible to enjoy this connection forever. It sucked having to move himself away from Alexandra to rid himself of the condom. As soon as the seal of their sweat-covered bodies broke, Ian instantly felt chilled.

Alexandra seemed to sense Ian's unease and gave

him exactly what he needed. Before he had stood up to walk to the bathroom, she sat up behind him. Her breasts were pressed up against his back, warming him. Her breath caressed his neck. "Would you shower with me?"

Like she had wordlessly answered him in the bar, he pulled on her hand and they walked to the bathroom together. He discarded the condom as she turned on the shower. They waited outside while the water heated.

Damn, she was gorgeous. Her fine backside brushed against the front of his thighs while he stroked the back of his hand along the curve of her hip. He hummed while he continued fondling the sexy curve of her hour-glass shaped torso.

He wrapped his long arms around her perfect frame. He kissed the top of her head that barely reached the height of his shoulders. Spinning her around, he gently held her head between his hands like he was holding a precious piece of glass. Her eyes popped upward and looked at him. He smiled, feeling possessive, and kissed her full lips.

His brain was functioning more acutely after his orgasm. He appreciated the details of their connection. Kissing her while they were both naked felt right. She was shorter than him. Her breasts pressed into his lower ribs where his skin was more sensitive. Her nipples were hard and nudged him in the most enticing way.

He pushed his open fingers through her long hair and grabbed the back of her head. He brought her mouth to his. Again, she melted into his kiss. They continued without any concern for time, lost in the act of nibbling on each other.

He wanted to continue forever, but Alexandra pulled away. "Let's hop in the shower before my neighbor who just moved from California starts banging on my door and accusing me of wasting water."

Chuckling, he leaned over and gave one more peck to her smiling mouth before following her into the shower. The view from behind was as delicious as the front. He grabbed the body wash and lathered up his hands. He set out to explore her entire body but her nipples distracted him. Her responsive buds formed nice little tight peaks under his fingers. She moaned when he pinched tightly.

Alexandra spun around and pushed her breasts up against Ian's stomach. She kissed his chest and reached towards his head. Ian moaned as she massaged her fingers over his scalp.

He loved the way she touched him. His cock was impossibly hard between them. It twitched and flicked against her abdomen. She grabbed his cock with her soapy hand and stroked him base to tip. She gripped him firmly, unlike other women who were too gentle. It felt amazing.

For moments, Ian was overwhelmed in bliss. The only thing in his head was a sense of pleasure. Then Alexandra twisted her hand just a bit while she pumped his length. It was unbelievable. His balls began to tighten. His orgasm was approaching quickly. He wanted the release, but he didn't want to waste the opportunity with only her hand on him.

Ian's breathing ratcheted up and he struggled to speak. He was flummoxed. He wanted to let go. He wanted to hang on. He hovered on the brink. The pinnacle was paradise.

BANG! BANG! BANG!

Alexandra's hand stopped.

"What the hell?" Ian snarled.

"My neighbor," Alexandra clarified. She reached around Ian and immediately turned off the water.

Ian clenched his hand in a fist and rested it against the shower tile. He sighed deeply.

Alexandra grabbed his hand and pulled him from the shower and his disappointment. "Let's go finish in the bedroom and not let a little hiccup spoil our moment," she reassured him.

Ian remained a little irritated with the interruption. He appreciated Alexandra's ability to adapt quickly. However, Ian planned that next time Alexandra was coming to *his* place, and he wasn't going to have some other person breaking a great moment.

"Hey, you still with me?" She looked him in the eyes. Her warm gaze showed a great deal of compassion and concern.

Her sincerity caught him off guard. He wasn't used to a woman caring about his feelings. All the women he had been with since law school wanted him for his status as a lawyer. Nothing about tonight, about her felt like just a one-night stand.

Ian answered her with a searing kiss as they fell back onto her bed. He was most definitely with her. He wanted her. He wanted her to want him back.

Pulling back from the kiss, Ian confirmed, "I'm absolutely with you."

"Good, because I want you," she panted. The desperation in her voice sent a shiver through him.

Ian's cock hardened in response.

Rolling the condom down his length, Ian anticipated the feel of her tight sex. He peered directly into her eyes as he entered her. The look she returned touched his heart. The intimacy of the connection burned deep. And then, the grip of her sex sent electrifying shockwaves up his spine. The combination of her direct and indirect touch created an aura of sensual energy, surrounding him and incomparable to any previous involvement. She never looked away. When they orgasmed together, it felt like nothing he had ever experienced.

It felt…euphoric.

Chapter 3

Sasha

Sasha paused at Ian's open office door with the file in hand. She knocked as he didn't notice her presence. His eyes weren't focused on his computer. Was he dozing? Within a heartbeat, his dazed look turned warm. He smiled and in a friendly tone said, "Hi." His frosty demeanor seemed to have thawed from earlier. The switch confused Sasha.

He glanced at his computer and his previously relaxed body turned rigid. He sat up straighter in his chair. "Do you have a question, Ms. Smirnova?" Ian prompted.

Cold then warm, and back to cold. Ian was fickle.

Sasha gave what she got and stated in a matter-of-fact manner, "No, Mr. O'Malley. I completed the research and brief."

"I wasn't expecting you to complete the assignment so quickly." Ian's eyes drew together.

She was seriously offended by Ian's insinuation that she had rushed through the assignment and hadn't done a sufficient job. Although it was a typical mistake of beginning lawyers, she knew that the quality of her work product surpassed most other attorneys.

"I can assure you, Mr. O'Malley, that the assignment is not only complete and accurate, but also well-argued and documented." She did not appreciate the excellence of her work being questioned without a proper review of said work. And, she didn't intend to wait for Ian to review it. "If you don't need anything else tonight, I'm going to head home."

"That's fine. I'll see you in the morning." He opened the folder with the brief she had completed. She thought the conversation was over and turned to leave.

"One more thing. If you mix some canola oil or olive oil with dish soap, the paint will come off." She looked back at Ian in puzzlement. Those light brown eyes gazed back at her.

"Good night, *Mr. O'Malley*." Again, she infused his last name with a sarcastic tone.

She fought the desire to storm out the office like an angry teenager. Her list of aggravations ran through her head like the credits at the end of movie. The building had a revolving door in the lobby, which she added to her list. She would have preferred the satisfaction of slamming a door.

Sasha exited the law firm and headed purposefully towards Lawson's Bar. She walked with determination, but also with hopes that the brisk evening air would help cool her temper.

The place was nearly empty as it was a Sunday evening. She did not recognize any of the patrons as compared to a typical evening. She planted herself in her favorite seat at the end of the bar that offered her best friend the ideal location to talk to her while keeping an eye on the other customers.

Kat greeted her after finishing up an order. She put up a hand, halting Sasha from speaking. "Let me guess. Business suit with paint on your fingers." Kat pursed her mouth to the side and tapped a finger to her chin. "Hmm. I'm guessing, another Sunday night emergency at work interrupting time with the hot art teacher, which translates to white wine. Am I right?"

Sasha laughed. "Damn Kat! You are psychic. But I think I might need an entire bottle."

"I pour, you spill." Kat directed as she grabbed an empty wine glass.

"I need wine first, then I'll talk." Sasha corrected, pointing to her glass.

"Fuck, that sounds serious," Kat reached for a nearby bottle and poured.

After putting back half a glass of wine, Sasha exploded. "Not only did my boss ruin my Sunday-serenity and my hot-art-guy gaping, but I had to work *for* Ian." Sasha growled and finished off the glass of wine.

"*Ian,* Ian? As in Mr. Magnificent? As in mister I haven't fucked anyone since because he ruined me for all other men, *Ian*?" Kat refilled Sasha's glass.

"Yes, but stop calling him Mr. Magnificent. He fucking insisted that I refer to him as *Mr. O'Malley,*" Sasha ranted and drank from her glass.

Kat leaned forward, with both hands on the bar. "No fucking way! He expected you to call him Mr. O'Malley? What. The. Fuck?"

"No, he fucking *demanded* it. He said we needed to behave like professionals." She wiped at the perspiration forming on the back of her neck.

"Did he ask you to call him Master in bed too?" Kat waggled her eyebrows. "Did you hold out on the titillating details?" Kat joked.

"No, Kat! He didn't. Can you please listen?" Sasha took another sip and looked down in disappointment. "I think what bothered me even more was him calling me Ms. Smirnova. He knows that I prefer my first name to my last name. Refusing to call me Alexandra is plain rude." She pouted while her heart sunk.

"Fuck." Kat exclaimed apologetically, "Does it bother you when I call you Alex?" Kat stopped wiping down the bar.

Sasha nodded her head back and forth and explained, "You're my best friend. When you call me Alex, I hear it as an endearment. And, it's a cool nickname."

Kat returned to wiping down the bar and replied, "Good." She refilled Sasha's glass one more time. "You know that everyone only teased you about your name because they liked you. It was never meant in a mean or derogatory way." That was history. Sasha didn't care about that anymore.

"It was complete shit having to call Ian, *Mr. O'Malley*," Sasha spit it out like she had just eaten some awful tasting food. "And why must he be so damn good looking? Staring at his perfect jawline and broad strong shoulders makes it impossible to forget that night with him. The sex was more explosive than the fireworks over Lake Michigan. We went at it all night long. Neither of us wanted to stop. The next morning, we woke up in a tangle of bodies. There wasn't the usual feeling of awkwardness that generally follows a one-night stand. The only feeling I had was a profound ache deep inside to be with him one more time. In the light of day, completely sober, being with Ian was even better." Sasha sighed and her whole body drooped forward.

Despite having already shared this part of the story on a previous occasion with Kat, her exasperation over the current situation made the words jump out of her mouth. "But then Ian had written his number on the back of his business card. Why did we have to work at the same damn law firm! I mean, I realize it is a big place, encompassing a number of floors, and it was understandable that we had never crossed paths…"

Her irritation escalated, she sat up straighter, and she continued. "And then he had to go off on how awful an inner office fling would be for both of us to indulge in— no matter how great the sex. And yes, he admitted that the sex was great! Because it was off the charts, fucking fantastic. But no, he went on to say that he was vying for a partnership position and I needed to keep my nose to the grindstone. Neither of us needed an office scandal to mar either of our careers. I had no choice but to agree."

Sasha gulped down the rest of her wine. "And today, he hammered home his point that there is no hope with his Ms. Smirnova fucking attitude."

"I say Fuck. That. Shit." Kat's take no shit tone made Sasha smile. Kat poured her another glass because she definitely needed a little more to relax. "I totally understand that it is hard to get over someone that puts great sex on the table, or any other horizontal, vertical, or semi-vertical surface or non-surface. But as they say, the best way to get over a man is to get under another one. So maybe it's time to make a move and fuck the hot art teacher."

Sasha stared at Kat, twisted her mouth, and considered her suggestion. "I think…you're right. Now, pour me a few glasses of water so I can hydrate and hear about your day."

Amazingly, the next morning, Sasha's head wasn't throbbing from all the wine she had consumed. Those extra glasses of water saved Sasha from a nightmare of a hangover. New day. New week. New attitude. She was ready to prove her worth at the firm once again.

With paint-free hands, Sasha arrived at the law firm around 6:30 a.m. Ian's suggestion for removing the paint had worked like a charm. *Where had he picked up such a trick?*

She proceeded to her temporary office. Amidst the hallway illuminated solely in emergency lighting, a cascading glow emerged from a single office. She peered inside and found Ian busily working at his desk.

"Hey, early bird. I didn't expect to see you yet." Sasha smiled brightly, attempting to spread some good cheer.

"Good morning, Ms. Smirnova." She winced at the sound of Ian calling her by her last name. The cold tone of his voice didn't match his inviting smile. The dichotomy confounded her. "As you know, I'm very focused on becoming partner and part of that means being the first to arrive and last to leave. Why don't you take a moment to get settled and then come back here to discuss today's agenda."

"Sure, Ian." She slipped. *Oops.* All the memories of their time together had caused her to lapse. Realizing her error, she rallied and replied, "I'll be back in a minute, Mr. O'Malley."

She put down her coat and computer inside the small office. Setting down her items in an organized manner helped her feel more in control. She breathed deeply to steel herself before walking back into his office. She didn't want him to reprimand her, again, for using his first name. Rather than casually walking in, she knocked on the door. Damn, all the formalities bugged her.

She sat down, wishing to share in a regular conversation with Ian.

No such luck.

"Let's get to it." With steepled hands on his desk, Ian pressed forward. She wasn't sure she enjoyed this all-work, no-play Ian. "First of all, I was really impressed with the brief you wrote last evening. I admit I doubted that it would be based on how quickly you wrote it, but it was well structured and well-reasoned. It was extremely impressive for someone that's only been practicing law for a single year."

"Thank you, Mr. O'Malley. I take a lot of pride in my work." Ian nodded his head minimally in agreement. She probably would not have shared her thoughts on the matter with anyone else at work.

"I want you to know that I appreciate it." Sasha's eyes widened as Ian's acknowledgement surprised her. Like the previous evening, an uncomfortable silence sat between them.

Ian took a deep breath and murmured, "And Alexandra, I appreciate your professionalism." Ian rubbed at the back of his neck. He was articulate and didn't mince his words. She knew that he used her first name intentionally. Was his reciprocal use of her first name his way to acknowledge the elephant in the room, the ridiculous, mutually, awkward denial of their previous intimate encounter?

She suppressed her grin and avoided looking him in the eye. She didn't trust in her ability to shield her emotions. Instead, she cast her eyes downward on his desk as if she were staring at an imaginary line in the sand. She didn't dare to cross it.

He remained silent as well.

The quietness eventually became unnerving. Their awkward quiet was proof enough that he too was addled by the situation. Perhaps she was incorrect to assume that his professionalism was intended to be heartless.

Without regard to being in a subordinate position, Sasha took charge and brought the two of them back to reality. She cleared her throat, "Do you have another folder with instructions for me today?" He reached for the folder and handed it to her politely. She spared him an exasperated use of his last name. If he managed to be pleasant, she would work to do so as well.

The two of them continued to work together amicably throughout the day. They each ate lunch separately but that was more an issue of each working through lunch rather than taking a real break. But by the end of the evening, they engaged in some casual banter during their elevator ride down to the lobby of the building. Like a gentleman, Ian allowed her to exit first. They both went their opposite ways on the sidewalk.

The next day, they started similarly to the previous day with a quick hello and a folder of work passed from one to the other. Early in the afternoon, Sasha was working away at her desk when she gasped, startling at an unexpected opening of her office door. Her eyes widened at Hailey standing before her. She looked as pale as a ghost.

Hailey came forward and Sasha could see the sheen of sweat coating her face. "Hi, you must be Ms. Smirnova. I'm Ms. Coleman." Her thready voice matched her frail appearance. Hailey politely extended her hand to Sasha. "Mr. O'Malley informed me that you were helping out while I was out of the office."

"Yes. How are you feeling?" Sasha scanned Hailey

as if she were trying to decide if her presence was only a hologram. "I can't believe that you are out of the hospital. And at work!"

"Well, it isn't like I'm here to do physical labor. I can't look weak to the other partners. You know what I mean. We women have to be twice as tough and three times as good and four times as reliable to even be considered the equivalent to the men around here." Hailey didn't sound bitter, but more matter of fact. Sasha nodded at the validity of Hailey's belief. In fact, it was nice to hear another female state out loud what Sasha had sensed was true.

Hailey leaned against the extra chair in the room. Sasha's cheeks heated and she jumped out from behind the desk. "Oh my goodness, take a seat." She gestured for Hailey to sit. "You must be uncomfortable. Is there anything I can get you? Well, besides getting my stuff out of your office. I made sure that I didn't disturb any of your stuff."

"Thank you. That was considerate of you." She pinched her eyes closed and grabbed at her abdomen. Hailey took a few cleansing breaths. "Why don't you go check in with Mr. O'Malley to see how he wants to handle the shuffling of the workload."

Sasha wrinkled her brow. "Sure. Yes, of course. Can I get you some water or anything?"

With her eyes still closed, Hailey shook her head.

Sasha grabbed all of her belongings so as not to disturb Hailey any further.

She knocked gently on Ian's door and he waved her in. He was speaking on the phone and seemed to be finishing up the call. "Please," Ian mouthed and gestured to the chair. Respectfully, Ian hung up quickly. "I wanted to thank you so much for helping us out the past couple of days. I was very impressed with your work. I will certainly let your boss know."

Sasha grinned. She wanted to wryly respond, *I told you so*, but opted for a polite response. "Thank you for that. Positive feedback is always appreciated." Sasha bit her lip before continuing, "I have to say that I was extremely disappointed to see Hailey return to work so quickly."

"Were you hoping to work for me?" Ian teasingly half-smiled.

Sasha was taken back by Ian's tone and blushed a little. "Umm," Sasha faltered not knowing how to respond to Ian's insinuation. She recovered quickly. "I'm worried about Hailey's health. I think she came back too soon. She's trying too hard to prove she is tough."

Ian cocked his head to the side. "Being tough is part of the game. And, I wanted to thank you for being flexible and working productively despite the distractions. Your focus helped me. I am really grateful for your understanding and support for me to become partner." Ian's admission stunned Sasha. Maybe his cool exterior at work was something that he wore like his business suit.

After his disclosure, she felt more comfortable sharing. Sasha gazed at Ian. "I completely respect your ambition. Goals require sacrifice and I get that. Respect is very important to me."

Ian nodded his head in agreement.

Sasha exited his office but then turned around and greedily stole one last peek. He had his eyes closed and his nose was tilted in the air. She heard the rush of air as he inhaled deeply. She self-consciously checked to see if she smelled.

Without dealing with the added stress of working for Ian, she powered through her work much more efficiently the rest of the week. She even managed to leave the office at a reasonable hour on Friday. After the week she had with Ian, she deserved some time to relax and she enjoyed passing her time with her best friend at Lawson's.

Sasha observed Kat expertly mix a drink. She measured out portions of vodka, triple sec, brandy, apple cider, and lemon juice. She shook and poured the drink then placed it in front of Sasha. "Here, try this. I've been working on a few drinks for Thanksgiving. It's an apple pie martini."

Sasha held up the drink and examined it. "I like the job of being your taste tester." She took a sip, appreciating the mix of flavors. "Mmmmm. Absolutely my kind of drink. Sweet, but not tooth tingling sweet." She took a heartier sip. She held up her left thumb as she continued to drink. "Five yums out of five. So tell me how drunk did you get while you were coming up with this one?" Sasha wished she had been able to join in the fun, but her work always interfered.

"My cousins and I actually kept it under control. They're starting to get their feet wet behind the bar." Kat leaned on the bar and sighed.

"It would be good if they can get up to speed quickly and provide you some extra help that you can trust." Sasha felt bad that the entire burden of Lawson's fell on Kat's shoulders. Her father passed away shortly after Kat had passed the bar. She gave up a great law job to take over her father's business. She never complained, other than occasionally mentioning that she really missed her dad.

Kat pushed off the bar. "Hey, speaking of my cousins, the whole family is planning to go to mass on the Sunday after Thanksgiving and then come back here for a meal. Do you think you can make it?" Kat focused on wiping down the already clean bar. She avoided all eye contact.

"Of course I'll be there, Kat. You and your entire family have been so kind to me. I know it doesn't compare to the loss you feel, but he always felt like a dad to me as well. Thanks for giving me notice." Sasha felt a knot in her throat.

Kat smiled and wiped at her damp eyes. "Thank you," she choked out. Kat stepped away for minute and returned with another apple pie martini. Sasha watched as Kat bopped around helping other customers.

While Sasha nursed her drink, she noticed some of the other attorneys at her firm sitting at a table together. Marcus smiled broadly back at her. She scanned the rest of the table. Then her eyes landed on Ian. At the table.

Fuck! She spun back around and looked absently at the liquor bottles behind the bar. Her pulse raced. Her fingers tapped the bar top and her leg bounced frantically beneath the wooden top.

"Caught ya!" Kat startled her. Sasha glowered back at Kat. Unphased by her unapproving stare, Kat pressed. "Why are you staring at Ian again? Imagining him in bed or shooting daggers at him? Was it awful working for *Mr. O'Malley*?" She overemphasized his name as Sasha had shared her previous annoyance with the name issue.

"I was thinking about how fucked up the place is." Sasha didn't want to complain too much as Kat had been forced into giving up her law job. "It is so cut-throat that the woman that I was filling in for returned to work less than forty-eight hours after her appendix ruptured. I'm sorry but that is completely fucked up. I'm not sure the firm is the right place for me." Sasha shook her head.

Kat crumpled the bar rag in her hand. "I'm sure you will end up making the best decision for yourself, whatever that may end up being." Kat didn't say anything else and returned to serving other customers. She was a friend, not a crystal ball.

Sasha kept her view fixed on Kat, while she purposefully ignored the table filled with her coworkers as if she had blinders on like a horse in a race. A business card entered her peripheral view. The man holding the card popped out of nowhere. She flinched as he was uncomfortably invading her personal space.

He began to introduce himself.

Kat barked, "Get the hell out of here!" Kat's stern voice must have intimidated the thirty-year-old guy, as he held up his hands in surrender and slinked away.

"Damn, Kat." Sasha turned her palms up and plunked them back on the bar. "What just happened?" She was first caught off-guard by the guy and then shocked by Kat's reaction.

"That loser is always in here hitting on women." Kat grimaced, keeping an eye the man's departure. "What a fucking idiot."

"Thanks for coming to my rescue. You really are the best!" Sasha took the last pull on her drink and set it down. "I think I'm going to head out now. See ya, Kat." Sasha placed the cash, along with a hefty tip, on the bar top.

Kat threw her a quick wave as she was walking

away to serve someone else.

Despite Sasha's best efforts to tactfully avoid her colleagues, she begrudgingly put on a smile as she passed by their table. Marcus stopped her. "Hey, Smirnova. Are you on your way out?"

"Yeah. I have a lot to get done in the office tomorrow. If I stay out any later, I'll just work slower tomorrow." She needed to be at her best. There were no excuses for being tired and inefficient.

"Oh, come on. We just ordered the last round of shots. It's just a few minutes. Then we can all walk out together. Take O'Malley's seat. He left to go to another bar and meet his brother." Marcus pulled the seat out for her to sit.

With Ian gone, Sasha didn't mind stopping for a quick shot. She appreciated Marcus's suave and goodhearted attempt to ensure that she would safely exit the bar. Sasha conceded easily and joined the group.

"Hey, I saw Nichols from J and M approach you up at the bar. What did he want? You know he's pulled some sleazy shit that borders on getting his license yanked," Jonathon grilled.

Marcus shook his head disapprovingly. "Nichols pushes the limit of judicial ethics all the time."

"I know. I heard he almost got disbarred a few times. Kat had a little fun knocking him down a notch." Sasha smiled proudly, admiring Kat's tough attitude.

Cromwell piled on, "I love Kat. She's quick and has got a lot of hutzpah. She would have made a great attorney."

Sasha glanced at Kat and further boasted, "She's the type of woman that can do anything she wants."

Kat strode up to the table carrying a tray with shots

of whiskey. "Here's one to help keep you guys warm outside on the way home."

The group all threw back the shots and covered the bar bill. Kat gave Sasha a quick hug goodnight and spoke quietly enough that only Sasha could hear, "Maybe you should hit up the hot art teacher for a booty call tonight." Kat winked and headed off to finish out the rest of the bar tabs for the night.

In her bed, Sasha considered Kat's advice. She might not ever forget Ian, but she became resolved that nothing was going to happen again between the two of them. It hadn't happened in months. It was only one night. And after working with him this past week, she wasn't going to hold a torch any longer for a man that had made it clear that she wasn't ever going to be a priority in his life.

She needed a man that was open and interested. Time to move past challenging and difficult. Time to open herself to an opportunity with the hot, sexy art teacher that ignited a fire inside her.

Chapter 4

Ian

The next evening, Ian walked into Luxury Box. The bar provided the typical comforts of a sports bar with numerous televisions set to a variety of sports channels. Luxury Box was located near the ice arena and many hockey players frequented it. Loud cheering bombarded Ian as he entered, but the boisterous noise failed to distract him from yearning for Alexandra.

He needed a stiff drink to help vanquish the thoughts of Lawson's. He hit the bar straight-away. While he leaned on it, Ian looked to the corner where his brother and his friends typically sat.

Sure enough, his brother and a bunch of his teammates planted themselves in their usual corner. Well, JD's *former* teammates. His brother looked comfortable among all of the guys, although he was no longer one of the team. JD raised a glass in the air and his teammates repeated the action, which was followed by loud hooting and hollering that could be heard above the raucous bar crowd. Ian assumed that their team had won.

How did his brother maintain his jovialness on a night when his former team confronted the same team that caused his infamous career-ending game? In a single night, JD's hockey career died. His prospects for ever playing in the NHL were killed and even prevented him from continuing to play on the farm team. JD's entire prospects as a professional athlete had disappeared in a flash, yet he continued to kick back with the same guys. *Didn't hanging out with them constantly remind him of his loss?*

The thought of not having control of his livelihood unnerved Ian. Unlike JD, Ian had left hockey by choice and on *his* terms. He had been ready to leave the sport after playing hockey for a big ten school during college. He had used hockey to pay for college. He'd never wanted to play professionally like the guys sitting around JD. Instead, Ian favored more academic pursuits. Sure, he loved the game, but he preferred fighting in a courtroom to getting into fistfights on the ice. When he left hockey, he hadn't had any regrets.

Ian smiled at JD's resilience, and turned back to the bar. JD's desire to hang out with his old teammates worked in Ian's favor. Ian had preferred Luxury Box to Lawson's the past few months. During it, he and JD had grown much closer while spending time together with friends. But the absence of the temptress that threatened to derail his career was the essence of the appeal of the bar.

Ian held out his hand in an attempt to flag down someone to take his order. The bartender attended to several other people before lazily coming over to serve Ian. Maybe if he wasn't wearing a business suit and looking out of place, he would get served quicker. He needed alcohol to help dull the memory of Alexandra.

His previous fly-by at Lawson's was a lapse in prudence. His southern head defied the one resting on his shoulders. He proved powerless to a burning need. The cleaning crew at the law firm expunged Alexandra's scent from his office and he'd craved another hit of her fragrance. His desire dragged him to Lawson's Bar.

The sight of Alexandra sitting at the bar taunted him. Everything went red when he caught a glimpse of Nichols approaching her. Ian's fingers had curled into his palms; his fists were primed to connect with Nichols's face.

After Kat scared him away, Ian had known that he needed to leave before he did something stupid and ask Alexandra to go home with him. It had taken all his strength the past week not to beg Alexandra to forget everything he said about needing to maintain professionalism for the sake of his job and kiss her in his office. Hell, her scent in his office made his cock stiff. He didn't want a mere kiss. He wanted another night in her bed. Followed by many, many more nights.

Ian's patience with the slow bartender waned. He needed a drink. Now.

A hand on his shoulder and a recognizable voice startled him. "Hey bro." JD smiled. "Glad you made it."

The bartender finally asked to take Ian's order.

"Can I get a triple of whiskey?" Ian turned to JD. "Want anything?"

JD raised an eyebrow. "Nope, I'm good."

While the bartender filled Ian's glass, JD asked, "Bad day at the office, bro?"

"Rough fucking week," Ian grumbled, keeping an eye on the slow bartender.

Ian didn't elaborate and JD didn't push him to explain further. Sometimes, a guy just needed alcohol.

The crowd slowed JD and Ian's walk back to the table with the other players situated in the corner. A girl with long legs, a short skirt, bleach blond hair, and way too much make-up caught JD by the arm. She flirted like all the overly aggressive puck bunnies skating up to the players in the bar. She must have thought JD was on the hockey team. He still looked like a hockey player, as he continued to train hard and he still wore his hair long like most of the players.

The woman clung desperately to JD. He looked nonplussed at the attention, but failed to do much to dissuade her.

JD cordially introduced her to Ian. The puck bunny took one glance at Ian and looked down her nose. *Funny how a nice suit impressed some but not others.*

Samuel, one of the players and a long-time friend of JD and Ian, strode over and interrupted the awkward trio. "What's up Ian? I'm glad you stopped by tonight. I kind of needed to talk to you about something."

"Hey, Samuel. I heard you had a lot of great saves tonight." Ian patted Samuel on the back.

The eyes on the blonde lit up. She bounced on her heels and took a step away from JD and closer to Samuel.

"Thanks man. It was a good night. Winning is a good thing." Samuel shrugged his shoulders nonchalantly. He mumbled, "About the only good thing." Samuel spoke so softly that Ian wasn't certain if he had heard him correctly.

"You were unbelievable tonight." Blondie batted her fake eyelashes at Samuel. Her words were swaddled with more than just sporting admiration.

"Thanks, doll." Samuel smiled playfully.

"Jenny," she offered and extended her hand.

Ian looked to Samuel with questioning eyes. *What the fuck?* Samuel never flirted. He was happily married.

Ian didn't intend to be an asshole but wanted to offer a hand to a friend before he fell over a precarious edge. "Where's your wife?"

"Actually, that's why I came over to say hi. I was hoping that you could recommend a divorce attorney." Samuel scratched at the back of his neck.

Ian's stomach sank and JD's face looked crestfallen. Samuel's wife's absence was suddenly noticeable. They were such a cute, perfect couple. Why would he want a divorce?

"I can help you out if you need it. There's a great guy at my firm." Ian glanced around the surroundings. "Listen, this probably isn't the best time to talk about this. Why don't you give me a call tomorrow? I'll be in the office most of the day." Ian handed Samuel a business card.

"You're working on a Saturday?" Samuel scoffed.

"My brother never takes a day off." JD playfully punched his brother in the arm.

As soon as the word divorce was dropped, the blonde amped up her flirtation. "That's too bad about you and your wife," she offered, stroking a soothing hand over Samuel's biceps.

JD rolled his eyes as the blonde noticeably had switched her attentions toward Samuel.

Samuel gestured a small nod to JD, guy code for, "are we good?"

JD flicked his hand a little as if he were passing her off to Samuel.

Another group of guys from the team passed by JD and Samuel and beat them on the back as they said goodbye.

Ian put a hand on JD's shoulder. "I think I'm going

to head home too."

"Really?" JD questioned. "But you just got here."

"I'm tired and I have a lot of work to do tomorrow."

"You sure?" JD openly stared. Ian knew his brother could see through his bullshit excuse. "I know you are working your ass off to make partner, but you seem a lot more uptight lately. I get it if you are too tired to hang out. But, maybe what you need is to get laid."

Ian narrowed his eyes at JD and huffed, "Thanks for the advice. On that note, I'm out of here."

Ian managed to avoid JD's questions the other night, but his ability to hide expired. Per Ian and JD's usual Sunday morning routine, Ian offered JD a ride to his parent's house. Ian knew he couldn't avoid his brother's questions forever about his unsociably odd exit from Luxury Box, but he'd hoped JD would at least wait until after Ian got some oh-so-needed caffeine.

Not only did Ian feel guilty about how he behaved at the bar, but he was sure to face his mother's weekly guilt trip about not attending Sunday mass. Years ago, JD and Ian had negotiated a deal with his parents to join them every Sunday for brunch, at a reasonably late hour in the morning, rather than joining them at 7:30 a.m. mass on Sundays. Ian and JD had not agreed to the weekly guilty trip that was included in the brunch, but his mother never failed to include it. Ian perhaps should have opted to go to mass and confession as well.

Flurries swirled in the gusty breeze as they stood on their parents' stoop. His dad opened the door for Ian and JD.

JD stepped inside and embraced his dad in a solid hug. "Hey, Pops."

"Good to see you, Jameson." His dad was the only

one that called JD by his given name, Jameson.

His dad's usage always caught Ian's attention. The story behind the name was one that his dad liked to repeat often. His mom claimed that she outranked her dad via the act of carrying their child and she named their first born, Ian. Second time around, his dad claimed it was his turn to pick a name and he chose a twist on his very own name, James. His dad had fought hard with his mom to give Jameson that name. His mother worried that kids would tease JD and call him Whiskey instead of Jameson. Like most mothers, she was right. Well, at least partially.

As a toddler, the name Jameson was too much of mouthful for Ian. With a little influence from his mom, Ian and she started calling him JD. The name stuck for the past twenty-seven years.

Ian followed JD through the door, but his dad skipped a hello. "Ian, your mother said she had some legal question to ask you. Can you go in the kitchen to answer her?" His dad seemed more eager than usual to put their mother's concerns to bed which worried Ian.

"Hello to you too, dad," Ian offered sarcastically. Ian handled all their parents' legal and financial questions. JD, on the other hand, was in charge of all manual labor tasks. The rule of the house was duties first, food second.

"Thanks, Ian." His dad patted him on the back with a slight shove to the kitchen.

Ian snagged a cup of coffee while his mom told him about a small incident involving her sister, her sister's car, and an unsuspecting neighbor's mailbox. Ian would have laughed at the insignificance of the event, but he wasn't one to offend his mother by minimizing her concerns.

Afterwards, Ian joined his dad and brother in the living room.

"Everything okay?" His dad rubbed at his stubbled jaw.

"Sure. No worries. It was fairly minor."

JD's stomach rumbled loudly. The aroma of food wafting from the kitchen was making Ian's mouth water as well. His mom fortunately announced that brunch was ready.

"Thank God." JD sighed.

"JD! Don't you dare take the lord's name in vain!" His mom chastised JD.

"Sorry." JD kissed his mom on the cheek.

After saying grace at the table, his mom prompted, "Did you hear that little Sammy is getting divorced?"

Ian disagreed with the characterization. "Mom, Samuel is a grown man."

"Well, I still think of him as the little boy that used to come over and eat cookies here." His mom passed the bowl of cooked broccoli to JD. Ian clearly got his argumentative nature from his mother.

"That's terrible," his dad grumbled. "Kids today should respect the church's sanctity of marriage. They need to understand that marriage is something you need to work at constantly. It isn't easy and it takes a lot of compromise." He huffed in exasperation and pointed his fork at Ian and JD.

"Dad, a lot of marriages end in divorce," Ian noted. Probably half of his friends' parents were divorced.

"Exactly my point. Too many," his father emphasized and speared a potato with more force than necessary.

"Did Samuel come to your office for help?" JD asked, shoving a forkful of eggs in his mouth.

"You know I can't talk about that." JD rolled his eyes at Ian's response. Ian bit his tongue, knowing his brother didn't appreciate the seriousness of his duty of confidentiality.

"Honey, I wish you wouldn't get involved in divorce cases," his mother pleaded.

"Mom, I'm trying to make partner at the firm. I'll do whatever they ask of me." Ian looked at his plate, hating to disappoint his parents.

"I appreciate your work ethic, Ian," his dad conceded. Ian faced his dad, whose stern face could make the toughest man flinch. "But I don't want you or Jameson to ever think divorce is something that is acceptable. You two may not join us at church each week, but that is *not* how we raised you."

Their mother continued, "I hope that you both find someone that you find worthy of your love and affection. Someone that is your destiny. Someone that you love so much that you are willing to fight for her." His mom was the queen of standing on a soapbox. She had this speech on repeat. Ian had heard it more times than he could count.

JD's eye roll turned into a full-blown head roll.

His mom continued without pause, "And not one of your puck bunnies, JD." Ian laughed so hard at his mother's comment that his food shot out of his mouth and almost hit JD, sitting across the table.

"Mom!" Ian and JD shot back in unison.

"Oh please. You both think I'm old and don't understand anything. I know more than you can imagine." She looked across the table at her husband, the head of the house, and smiled.

"Please. We are trying to eat, Mom." The thought rolled Ian's stomach.

"Fine, but I can't wait to hear that my boys have met a real woman. Someone that they want to meet me and get to know the family." She looked upward and crossed herself.

"I met a woman." Everyone's head spun towards Ian, as if they were on a greased swivel. "Her name is Alexandra." His parent's stilled and Ian paused. Ian ignored JD sitting across from him.

"And?" His dad prompted.

"She's…amazing. She's brilliant and beautiful. She's warm and open, unlike all the bitch lawyers that I usually meet." Ian felt a warmth in his chest as he spoke about Alexandra.

"Language, Ian!" His mom didn't appreciate foul language in the house.

"But?" His dad pressed further. Ian had shared more than he wanted to. He looked down at the table, his calm and cool demeaner faltering.

His brother glared at him. JD didn't say anything but he was sure to offer his reaction later to Ian, away from his parents.

Ian turned to his father. "She works at my firm."

"So what?" JD continued to look at him suspiciously.

"So," Ian paused as if to say duh. "I'm trying to make partner. I can't have a fling with someone in the office."

His father nodded in understanding. "When you know, you know. If she is the one worth fighting for to make things work, you'll know."

"Maybe after you make partner," his mom suggested optimistically. Then she looked at JD. "And maybe one day you will think about settling down too."

In dramatic fashion, JD stopped eating, placed his silverware on his plate, and markedly set his hands on the table. "Just so you know, I passed on a puck bunny the other night."

Ian guffawed. "I think *she* dumped *you* for Samuel."

Ian's mom's head slumped into her hand.

"Whatever, Ian." JD scowled. "Just so you know I never had any intention of taking her home. I can't help it if girls like her flirt with me. In fact, I'm planning on asking out a student in my community art class tonight."

His mom perked up in her seat and asked curiously with an extra dose of motherly suspicion. "What's her name?"

"Her name's Sasha. She's cool. And smart. She's a newbie to art, but she has a great vibe." He quirked a smile and looked off to the left. "Speaking of, I need to prep for my class this afternoon." JD hopped out his chair and kissed his mom and dad goodbye, silencing his mother from further inquiry. Ian followed JD, intending to grill his brother.

When Ian and JD were on the sidewalk out of earshot of their parents, JD accused. "What the fuck, Ian? You never mentioned this *Alexandra* to me." JD shoved Ian's shoulder forcefully. JD may have been an inch shorter, but carried a lot more muscle than Ian. Ian fell back a step. "Since when do you not share details about your life with me? We were just joking about the fact that you needed to get laid the other night. What the fuck changed?"

"I did tell you about her. I *told you* about the girl

from the Fourth of July. *Her name is* Alexandra." Ian realized how pathetic that sounded after the words came out of his mouth.

"That was one night, dude. A long time ago." JD cringed.

Ian leaned forward, shaking his flexed hand out in front of him. He needed to explain himself. "I know. I know! But I haven't been able to get her out of my damn head. And, I had to work with her for a couple of days last week. I swear her perfume was making me fucking delirious. That's why I was late meeting you the other night. I stopped by Lawson's Bar where we originally met. I was hoping to run into her."

"And. Did you? What happened?"

"I did. I overheard her tell her friend that she is really unhappy at the firm where we work. I have to admit, I kind of hope she quits because I would ask her out immediately if she turned in her two-week notice." Ian nodded decisively. He would.

JD laughed. "Man, you really do have it bad for her. That explains your shit mood the other night."

Ian rubbed at his chin, "You have no idea. I really think she can be the one. I know it was only one night, but I think about her every fucking day."

JD looked at his watch.

"Shit, did my rant make you late for your class? I can give you a ride."

JD accepted Ian's offer to give him a ride to the university. When he and Ian neared the art building, he opened the car door. "Thanks for the ride, bro. I know it's out of your way and you have work to do."

"No problem. Didn't want you to work up a sweat walking from the train stop to class. You'll make a better impression on Sasha if you don't smell bad." Ian tilted his chin upward as a way of a sendoff.

"Appreciate it, bro." JD waved goodbye, wearing an overeager smile.

Chapter 5

JD

JD unlocked the art room and turned on the lights. Sunlight shone through the expansive windows and reflected off of the multitude of colorful pieces of artwork strewn about on shelves and on the walls. The mixed odorous smells emanating from the various art materials welcomed him. Like the stink in the ice arena's locker room, the odor represented the activities closest to his heart.

He checked the clock on the wall. Well over an hour before class began. Hopefully Sasha would show up for tonight's class.

The art supplies remained locked in a secure closet. College art students tended to be short on funds and weren't sufficiently trustworthy with access to art supplies. He retrieved all of the necessary materials for the day's class and placed them on a counter in the back of the room. The setup encouraged students to interact before they got locked into their individual art stations.

The clock continued to tick ahead.

He arranged all the easels and art stools. He sat on Sasha's stool and checked her vantage point. The view of his easel at the front of the class was terrible, but she never complained. However, every time he'd turned around to face the class, her gaze was always on him.

The tick of the clock echoed in the tiled room.

He retrieved Sasha's Matryoshka doll from a special locked cabinet in the storage room. The individually wrapped sized dolls were carefully separated by packing material in a waterproof box. He placed the entire box on the table next to Sasha's easel along with a printout of the arrangement of the dolls. He had snapped a photo for her during her hasty departure the previous week.

He checked the clock once more.

A couple of early bird students arrived. JD greeted them and encouraged them to gather their materials, but wait to get started until after he provided directions to the class. They meandered near the back of the room and examined all of their classmate's work. Unlike his college classes where students were critical of one another's works, the murmur of compliments flowed generously.

He peered at the clock and his heart fluttered in tempo with the audible ticking.

Then she was there.

Sasha walked into the classroom earlier than usual. Calm and relaxed features replaced last week's intensity and panic. He tracked her steps. The rays of light from the windows landed on her beautiful body. The golden hour lighting made her appear like an angel. None of his thoughts about the woman were pure. She fanned the flame of the devil inside of him.

He waited. Her ponytail swayed across her neck like a paintbrush on a canvass. He wanted to paint a streak of soft kisses across her neck. He conspicuously stared as she sauntered to her art station.

JD approached her at the same moment that her hand reached for the box on her table. "I told you I would take good care of your grandmother's doll."

"Oh." She startled. She opened the box that revealed her prized possession swaddled in protective wrap. "Wow. You really did take good care of her." Her eyes widened. She picked up the image of her dolls. "Oh my god. You even took a photo for me." She looked directly at JD. "Thank you so much for that. I owe you." The sweetness in her voice made him smile.

"No worries. Great to see you." He hoped that her work didn't fuck up his plans to ask her out after class.

"I'm glad to be here too." She crossed her fingers in the air. "Hoping that work doesn't rudely interrupt me this week." She reached for the side of her neck. "I apologize again for running out. Listen, I would love to repay you for dumping my art mess on you last week. I can stay afterwards and help you clean up the art room."

The extra time with Sasha enticed JD, but he preferred if the offer was more willful than repayment. "You don't owe me anything, Sasha."

"Well, how about I stay afterward to help you clean up so you can get out of here more quickly and then you join me for a cup of coffee?" She smiled brightly.

Yes! Exhilaration ripped through him. He had been asked out many, many times, but never by someone like Sasha. She carried herself in way that didn't over emphasize her body or flaunt her assets. Rather, her energy presented an alluring aura. "Yeah, that would be great." He attempted to hold back an exaggerated grin.

Throughout the class, and while JD assisted the other students, he stole glances at Sasha. The considerate way that she looked at her project intrigued him. He forced himself not to stare and pay attention to the other students. With something to look forward to after class, the time flew by.

After class Sasha helped clean up, unlike some people that dawdled and did nothing. With Sasha, cleaning up the room was amusing. She asked him lots of questions about how he got into art while he cleaned out brushes. By the end, JD reached for the light switch, he turned to Sasha expectantly. "I hope you still have time to go for coffee."

"Absolutely." Damn, her smile was beautiful.

There was only one empty table at the coffee shop. JD suggested that Sasha grab the table while he ordered the drinks. He joined her, handing her the coffee that she had requested. "Straight up coffee? I didn't realize that anyone ordered that anymore."

"Admittedly, I drink way too much coffee. I finally gave up all the cream and sugar because the calories simply added up too high after several cups." She looked away.

JD didn't think Sasha needed to watch her calories. He had spent a lot of time checking out her body and it was perfect.

She clarified, "Don't get me wrong, I simply prefer to save my high calorie experiences for more delectable treats." He wanted to taste *her delectable treats.* JD smiled because he didn't like women that were obsessed with dieting.

In quid quo pro fashion, Sasha asked, "What about you? What are you drinking?"

JD stumbled with an answer as he needed to refocus on the conversation at hand rather than his run-away thoughts of Sasha. "Hot chocolate. I'm not a coffee guy. I blame my dad. He got me addicted by buying me hot chocolate at the ice rink when I was a kid."

"Aw. That's really sweet. Are you close with your dad?" Her choice of follow-up questions charmed him.

"Oh yeah. My whole family is tight. We travelled a lot for hockey when I was a kid. We spent hours on the road together, weekend after weekend." JD laughed. "I don't know how my parents survived? My brother and I fought nonstop in the car." JD scanned up and down his arms. "I think I still have a scar somewhere."

Sasha's eyes widened and her jaw dropped open.

"I'm just kidding. My brother and I are best friends." JD smiled and nodded at the truth of his words. He felt the bond with his brother deep in his bones. "All that time together…either we loved each other or killed each other."

"You're lucky to have a sibling. As an only-child, my parents were attentive, but that's not like having a brother or sister." JD counted his blessings for his relationship with his brother.

"Unlike you, there was no hot chocolate around when I learned to skate. My dad taught me out on a lake near my home in Russia. The cold weather was too brutal to truly enjoy it." Her eyes moved from his face to his chest in an objectifiable way. He chuckled to himself, discreetly checking out her rack. "So, you played hockey? I heard you played professionally."

His smile slipped a little. Her question hit a nerve. Questions about playing hockey since his early retirement stung. "I played on a farm team, not in the NHL." He didn't over exaggerate like many other guys he knew when talking about his career.

"Played? As in past tense? You don't play anymore?" Sasha took another sip of coffee. Her nonchalance about the topic eased his tension.

He welcomed her frankness as compared to the recent pity that he often received when asked about his hockey career. "Injury last spring and now I can't play," he deadpanned.

"Do you like teaching art now?" The quick change of topic was an arresting twist. Other people usually pushed for more details.

"I like teaching your community class. But, yeah, the whole grading process ruins the experience in my regular classes. Art should be about freedom, not restriction." JD's muscles coiled inside in preparation to defend his choice of career.

She nodded emphatically. "I bet if you look, you will find the right opportunity to allow you the freedom for which you are looking."

The tension in his muscles released. *What a refreshing response without any judgment.* She didn't burden him with the stress of comparing him to the person he had been or who he could have been. She made feeling vulnerable feel safe. He admitted to the thing that he had been wrestling with. "It's been a tough transition for me."

"I can only imagine, JD. Take your time. Until then, I get to enjoy your class." He was happy to see her smile reflected back at him.

"Gonna take another art class?" he asked. Her presence in the class was a bonus. He looked forward to seeing her each week. "Hopefully you'll take one of mine."

Her cheeks flushed and she looked away coyly. Why did art cause her to blush? Maybe she had an interest in a nude drawing class? He would be willing to model for her. She blushed frequently. He controlled his curiosity so as not to embarrass her, but he itched to know what was going on in her head.

"I received an email about signing up for next semester, but I think I'll wait until they assign the teachers." She winked.

His stomach grumbled loudly, and Sasha laughed.

"Would you like to go get something to eat?" She didn't ask to go get something together, but he assumed that was the implication.

"Yeah, that would be great." His pulse raced. His phone buzzed. "Dammit." He scowled at his phone. He was having such a good time with Sasha that he had forgotten about his brother.

"Everything okay?" She asked, fussing with her coffee cup.

"It's my brother." He showed Sasha his phone. He didn't want her to think he was making up a phony excuse. He made it clear for her to see that the sender's name was Bro. The photo attached was a caricature of a man.

Bro—*Burger time! Going to an upscale place. Don't forget to put on some clothes that aren't covered in paint—*

"I'm sorry, I completely forgot that I made plans with my brother to go to dinner. He asked me a few days ago. Is there any way you would be willing to give me a rain check on dinner with you? Please?" JD flashed his best smile.

"Sure…" Doubt clung to her answer. She continued to play with her cup.

"How about next Saturday?" He reassured and hoped to get a committed answer.

She looked him the eye and smiled. "Yeah, that

would be great." Her enthusiastic answer encouraged him.

"Can I get your phone number so I can text you and we can work out the details later?" He handed his phone over to Sasha and she added her number.

He edited the photo for her contact info and changed it to an art palette.

"Do you always use non-photos for your contacts?" She laughed playfully.

He smiled and nodded. "Most of the time. For all my art friends I use a pic of one of their pieces of art. For my hockey friends, I use their jerseys."

"I like that. Very creative." Her giggle made him think of tickling her, which led to other ways of amusing her. He needed to stop those thoughts before he embarrassed himself standing up from the little table.

"I should get going. My brother doesn't like waiting. For anyone." Despite his words, he didn't make any move to get up and leave the table. He stared at Sasha an extra moment. He wanted to kiss her goodbye. It felt natural, like they already had a connection, but he wasn't about to the lean over the table and do it. He wanted their first kiss to be something special. Not a quick and hurried peck.

They both leaned in an inch closer. He stared at her beckoning lips. Her eyes were on his.

Instead, he took her hand in his. He refrained from kissing her hand, like he wanted to, instead reveling in her warm touch. "Thank you for the coffee. I'm sorry I need to run off so quickly."

"See you next week, JD." Sasha said as a goodbye. They kept their eyes on each as he slowly made his way to the door.

"Saturday!" He emphasized to make sure she knew he meant it. He threw her his best panty-dropping smile. *No way could she forget him.*

JD hustled back to his place to change his clothes. Even though he wasn't ready on time, he didn't keep Ian waiting. The man always came home late. Ian had called ahead when he was on his way and asked JD to be ready outside, rather than wasting his time trying to find a place to park on the street on a Sunday evening.

JD hopped in Ian's car. "Hey, I'm paint free and ready to eat."

"Hey," Ian replied but looked down rather than looking JD in the eyes.

"What's up?" JD worried.

"Glad to see you got all the paint off your hands. Paint and burgers don't mix well," Ian noted and drove away from the curb.

JD had worked with messy art materials his whole life. He didn't need reminding to wash his hands like a child. He disregarded Ian's weird comment and boasted, "I've got a date!"

"I like you too, as a brother, but I really wouldn't consider this a date," Ian teased.

"Ha. Ha. I got a date with *Sasha* for next Saturday." JD danced in his seat.

"Nice. What are you planning?" Ian pressed, keeping his eyes on the road.

"Shit, I don't know. I just asked her out. I haven't planned anything yet. We grabbed coffee after class and I got your message. I asked her out without any time to plan." JD's smile broadened, sharing the information made it feel more real.

"Fuck, I didn't cock block you?" Ian apologized.

"No man. I'm interested in getting to know her, not just screwing her," JD snapped. His defensiveness startled himself.

"Sorry. No offense intended." Ian bit at his lip. JD let the issue slide.

Tapping his fingers on the steering wheel, Ian added, "Truth be told, I'm really thankful that you are making time to grab dinner with me. You're not just a brother to me, but also a friend that I can trust. These days, I feel a bit skeptical of everyone around me."

"Isn't that your job as a lawyer? To second guess everyone?" JD preferred physical art to the art of deception, like his brother.

Ian quickly looked at JD and then focused on the road again. "You may be right. It makes cultivating and maintaining friendships rough when my time is extremely limited."

Since getting cut from the team, JD felt a strain on his relationships with his former teammates. They hadn't shunned him, but tamping down his jealousy of his buddies was challenging. Ian's recent habit of hanging out at Luxury Box with him helped ease the tension for JD.

JD avoided exceeding the acceptable time limit for discussing feelings with another guy and changed the subject. "So how far is this restaurant?"

"It's probably about a ten-minute drive." Ian checked the app on his phone.

"Dude, I'm starving." JD's stomach growled as if on cue. "Why the fuck are we going so far for a cheeseburger anyway?" He complained.

"I looked it up. It got great ratings." Ian quieted curiously.

"So? A burger's a burger." *What was wrong with his brother?*

Ian sighed loudly. "Okay. One of the partners at the firm was raving about it the other day. I thought I should give it a try." JD wasn't buying Ian's piss-poor explanation. "Okay, I know it sounds stupid, but with so little free time outside of the office, culinary experiences serve as the center of most water cooler talk. I need to work every angle to get one step closer to making partner."

"It's just a burger, dude." JD shook his head and rolled his eyes. "That's insane, bro."

Ian pushed back. "Hangry?"

"Sorry," JD grumbled and leaned his head against the cool window.

"Hopefully the food will be worth it. How's the teacher gig going? Besides hitting on your hot students."

Thoughts of Sasha, his hottest student, distracted JD. Thoughts of her made him feel energized.

Ian continued before JD had time to respond, "I don't think I ever mentioned this to you, but I was really impressed that you were able to find the job at a community college teaching art so quickly. I hope it is working out."

"It's not bad…" JD started. "The students aren't artistic geniuses. But, ya know, like hockey, gotta work on those foundational skills. Anyways, the school is just meant to be a stepping-stone. Though it makes it difficult to get very attached or interested in any one student in particular. It's not like I feel like I have a significant impact in anyone's art. The grading part kind of sucks. I didn't like the concept of grading art while *I* was in school, and I don't enjoy it as a teacher." JD tried to remain nonchalant about the situation. Moping wasn't productive.

"You know, if you wanted a different teaching position, you should start putting feelers out there now, in time for the start of the school year next fall. I just want to see you happy. I don't care what you choose to do for a living."

Ian's comment meant a lot to JD. He had felt like he had let down the entire family when his hockey career melted like ice on a pond on a sunny day. They fell into a comfortable silence, each lost in their own thoughts.

Ian managed to find a spot in the restaurant's dedicated parking lot. JD and Ian walked around to the entrance. A long line had already formed outside of the place.

"Seriously, Ian! A line?" JD raised his eyebrow and shook his head back and forth in disgust. "I'm hungry and it's cold outside," he whined.

The side of Ian's mouth turned down. JD glared at his brother, until Ian proposed, "We're already here. Hopefully it won't be that long of a wait."

JD crossed his arms in front of his chest.

Ian put a hand on JD's shoulder and offered, "Listen, I'm sorry about the wait. To make up for the inconvenience, dinner is on me."

"Fine," JD conceded, stuffing his chilly hands in his pockets. "You know, I really do want you to make partner at the firm. I guess I can do my little bit to help."

"*Thanks, JD.* I appreciate it." JD ignored the sarcasm, focusing on the line instead. Ian interrupted JD's moment of petulance. "Hey, you didn't mention the Sunday class you're teaching. How's that going? Clearly it has offered some nice side perks. Where do you think you will take her next Saturday? Sasha was her name?"

"Woah there, counselor. Do you always ask so many questions?" JD held up his hands as if to say slow down.

"Sorry, habit of the job." His brother acted like being an attorney excused intrusive questioning. JD preferred the softer manner in which Sasha inquired about things.

"Actually, that part of the gig is great. The school wanted to reach out to the community a bit more and bring in some extra money so they have classes on Sundays that anyone can take. Everyone seems to have a good time because there's no pressure."

JD blew warm air into his cold fisted hands, masking his broad smile as he considered options for his date. He quickly eliminated several ideas as he wanted to do something where they could talk and get to know one another. The idea hit him. "If the weather is decent, the pier could be cool."

Ian nodded in agreement. "That's a good idea. If things go well for you two, I hope to meet her. Eventually." Ian patted JD on the back. "Hey, maybe I should take your class. I need a break from the pressure of work."

"Bro, you hate art. Just go and get laid. Or ask *Alexandra* out," JD added pointedly.

Ian huffed and looked downward, shaking his head. "I think you will probably have a better shot of introducing Sasha to the family than I will have of introducing Alexandra. I'm not optimistic that my situation will sort itself out. And, unlike you, I don't still have puck bunnies falling at my feet like that chick last night."

JD narrowed his eyes at his brother. "I'm over the

puck bunny thing." JD began to frown. He didn't think badly of the puck bunnies that hung out at the bar. How could he? He screwed enough of them not to think badly of the women, but he had matured past them like childish pre-packaged lunch time desserts. The sweet, cream-filled cakes tasted great as a kid, but eventually kids realized that fresh baked éclairs tasted better.

Ian continued with the same line of questioning, "I take it that this Sasha woman isn't a puck bunny."

JD's eyes tightened. Did his brother not think he was capable of maturing? "No. She isn't," JD reiterated.

"You have my interest piqued about this girl. I really can't wait to meet her." Ian raised an eyebrow.

"Now, you're acting like mom. I think you got your pushiness and argumentative skills from her. Let me get past the first date." They both laughed.

The hostess at the door of the restaurant informed them that there were two open seats at the bar. "About time!" JD grumbled.

Ian placed an order for two double burgers with thick cut bacon before they sat down. JD hoped it wouldn't take long to get served. If he didn't feed the bear inside him, he thought he might turn feral.

The majority of the beers on the menu were microbrews that neither of them recognized by name. Rather than making a random decision, Ian asked for the bartender's recommendation. The bartender was quick with their beers, popping the tops and presenting the bottles with a cold glass.

They each took a tentative sip, followed by a longer gulp. "So, what do you think?" Ian asked.

"Not bad, but I wouldn't necessarily want another," JD shrugged.

"I agree." Ian frowned.

"I hope the burgers live up to the hype or this adventure will have been a bust." Ian scowled at JD. JD ordered another beer.

Fortunately for JD's stomach, they didn't have to wait long for the burgers to arrive. While they ordered double burgers, the sandwiches actually had three burgers on the bun. It was a weird gimmick for a restaurant. As soon as JD sunk his teeth into the sandwich he groaned. His head fell back as if he were having a food orgasm. JD closed his eyes in ecstasy.

With a mouthful of food, Ian agreed. "Oh my god, this is fantastic. The thick cut bacon, the gooey cheese, the sauce: It's sensational."

JD took a breath between bites and raised his burger in the air as if he were making a toast with a glass of wine. "Here's to eating burgers so you can become a partner."

Ian followed, "Here's to trying new things together."

Neither spoke until their burgers were gone. It was a testament to the quality of the food.

Chapter 6

Sasha

Sasha hurried down the blustery sidewalk. As the wind pelted her face, the dampness in the air sent chills through her entire body. November in Chicago meant all hope for a warm day was gone. The wind whipped around the buildings nearly blowing people down. She kept her head down in a protective stance against the abrasive frigid air. With her eyes cast downward and all her attention on getting in the warm lobby, she walked obliviously to those around her.

Relieved to be out of the cold and in the warm elevator, she raised her head and reached to press the button for her floor. Her hand collided with another, and a bolt of electricity travelled through her body. It wasn't a stranger's hand. *Ian* was by her side.

She looked up and found those light brown eyes gazing back at her. Damn. The eye contact brought back all the emotion again. An ache pulled in her core. They gaped at each other for the entirety of the elevator ride before it rudely dinged upon arriving at her floor.

"Good to see you," A slight grin appeared on Ian's manly jaw.

"Have a good day." She smiled back warmly, but would have preferred to offer him a warm kiss.

Ian's stare was permanently burned onto her retinas.

Would she ever be able to erase the memories?

She needed a distraction. Diving into work was the best temporary cure. She had a gift for focusing and being able to tune out everything else when she was researching and writing. She only stopped for coffee and food near lunch time.

Late in the afternoon, she received a text with an attachment. Opening it, she saw a cup of coffee with legs, arms, and a red superhero cape flying through the air. The image was captioned, *Captain Coffee is here to save the day.* Another message followed.

JD—*I enjoyed going for coffee with you yesterday*—

Smiling, she quickly texted back:

Sasha—*I had fun too. Taking a page from your playbook, I'm using Captain Coffee as the pic and name for your contact information*—

JD—*Happy to be a good influence (smiley face emoji)*—

If she had taken a photo of his ass, she would have gone with it instead. She certainly had a detailed recollection in her head, which led to thoughts of his *naked* ass.

Perhaps her mind had wandered too long as she got another message:

JD—*Looking forward to our date next Saturday*—

With all the dirty thoughts she was having about JD, she impulsively replied:

Sasha—*My turn to be a bad influence*—

She pressed return on her phone. *Regret! What the fuck had she just typed.* That was something Kat would say. Kat always said what was on her mind. Not Sasha.

Before embarrassment overwhelmed her, JD replied.

JD—*(smiling devil) GTG*—

The ominous tone of a gavel being pounded twice against a sound block caused her lighthearted spirit to plummet. Her boss's text came through, requesting for her to see him, immediately.

She rubbed nervously at her fingers on her way to his office.

"Have a seat, Ms. Smirnova." His tone was more serious than usual.

"Everything okay?" She clasped her hands and worried a thumb against the inside of her palm.

"Not really. I have to let you go," her boss grumbled.

"You're firing me?" Sasha screeched, leaning back quickly in the chair as if she were dodging a swinging fist.

"No. I'm sorry. I didn't mean it that way." He shook his hands like windshield wiper blades, scrubbing away his blunder.

She let out a huge breath. Her body collapsed slightly forward in relief.

"That came out wrong." Mr. Lane was unusually inept with his words. "As you may know, Mr. Stein, who you worked for last week, is the grandson of a named partner. He's decided that he wants you on his team. I guess Mr. O'Malley was raving about your work, and Mr. Stein's decided that he wants you. I wasn't given a choice in the matter."

"Oh." The news was very unexpected. She hadn't been trying to vie for the position, although it would be considered a step up. Crap! Would she be working *for* Ian? How should she respond? "I don't want you to think that I was looking to switch…"

"That's reassuring to know. I think it was more a

matter of timing. From what I heard, he fired his second year, Hailey Coleman, and is in need of another attorney. He probably doesn't want to waste his time training someone new."

Sasha's jaw dropped. She was astonished that he fired Hailey. Hailey had worked herself almost to death for Mr. Stein. She even checked herself out of the hospital early after surgery to get back to work. Why would he fire someone so dedicated?

"Mr. Stein is expecting to see you immediately. You probably shouldn't keep him waiting." Mr. Lane sounded resigned.

Sasha was diligent to a fault. "What about the paper I was working on this afternoon for you?"

"Leave what you have completed on your desk, and I'll get to it tomorrow." Mr. Lane added, "Thank you for all your hard work. I'm sorry if I didn't acknowledge it frequently enough."

Sasha grabbed her computer and went directly to Mr. Stein's office. "Hello, Ms. Smirnova. I'm pleased that you are going to be working for me now. Mr. O'Malley said that you did a great job and that's the kind of people I like working for me. Ms. Coleman clearly was lacking. There's no reason to waste more time discussing her. Why don't you go get started with Mr. O'Malley, as you had last week."

Fuck! She screamed in her head. Biting the inside of her cheek, she responded, "Of course. Thank you."

Sasha entered Ian's office, but this time she closed the door behind her. "What the hell, Ian? What did you do?" Sasha shot Ian a death stare.

"Can you please not raise your voice?" Ian hissed, resting his elbows on his desk. "I was simply giving credit where it was due, as you very much deserved. I had no idea what Mr. Stein was going to do with that information!" Ian took a deep breath.

"I can't believe he fired Hailey!" Sasha scoffed, shaking her head disapprovingly.

Ian motioned toward the empty chair and sat back in his own. "He didn't actually fire her. He told her today that she was no longer considered to be on a partner track. So, she quit."

Sasha saw the concern on Ian's face. "It's not going to happen to you. You *will* make partner," she reminded him.

"I hope so…" Ian trailed off. He broke eye contact with her and continued, "I'm sorry if working under me is terribly awkward."

She bit her lip at Ian's phrasing. His use of the word "under" amused her. Kat's words rang in her head, "The best way to get over a man is to get *under* another." Sasha bit a little harder and stopped her instinct to laugh like a schoolgirl.

"Listen. I will do everything I can to support you. I won't do anything to distract you. I have my career to protect, as well, you know," she promised. She leaned across his desk and extended her hand. "Deal?"

He reached across his desk, inclining his body and long arm closer than necessary to shake her hand. He audibly inhaled and his eyelids shut for a noticeable moment.

"Ian?" She pleaded.

Their eyes met. She felt a physical pull between them, she closed her eyes to break the connection.

"Deal," he conceded. His voice pried her eyes open.

The draw between them rivaled the natural force of

gravity. She didn't want to release his hand. If only she leaned forward a bit more. He was close enough to kiss. Besides the potential HR violation, her heart shuddered at the possibility of another round of rejection.

She pulled away from Ian and straightened her back. She needed to protect her heart, and stop hoping that he would reciprocate her feelings. "Do you have an assignment for me?"

Ian cleared his throat. "Here you go." Frowning, he handed a manilla folder to her. Without anything else to discuss, she walked out his door.

True to her efficient work capabilities, she finished the assignment much more quickly than the average first-year attorney. When she handed it to Ian around seven o'clock, he had told her to have a good evening.

She wasn't about to cut out of work at such an early time. At 10:20 p.m., Ian dropped by her office. "Hey, everything okay here? I thought you were going home earlier."

"Yeah, I was just finishing something up for my previous boss. I was in the middle of it when Mr. Stein brought me up here. I didn't want to leave Mr. Lane in a lurch." She turned her head back to her computer, signaling that she didn't have time to be disturbed.

When she was sure Ian was out of earshot, she muttered, "You're not the only one with a strong work ethic, *Mr. O'Malley*. I'm just as determined to make a strong impression as you."

Around 11:45 p.m., Sasha placed the brief on Mr. Lane's desk where he was sure to find it. She smiled when she received a thank you message from Mr. Lane the next morning. It was always good to part ways on a positive note, especially with someone so well-connected in the city.

The rest of her week continued like a never-ending trudge. She felt weighted down knocking herself out for Ian, wanting to do her best work and helping his career along. It wasn't like she worked less earnestly for her previous boss, but she'd been driven by the pure challenge of it. Whereas working for Ian, was personal. Maybe the extra effort she expended trying to deny her feelings exhausted her.

She looked forward to going out with JD Saturday night. He was exactly what she needed. As if her thoughts had conjured him, a text message came through.

JD—*It's Friday, shots of espresso or whiskey?*— Sasha—*Both!*—

Ian bound through her office door.

Surprised, her head popped up and she dropped her phone on the desk. The opportunity to turn off her phone fell right through her hands. Her messages to Captain Coffee glowed on her desk. If she reached for her phone again, it would only bring more attention to the fact that she had been caught texting while at work. The heat of embarrassment rose in her cheeks.

Ian looked down at her desk where the phone beamed brightly. The screen eventually went dark. She prayed he wouldn't comment on the phone. Instead, Ian boomed, "Great news. That big real estate company that I mentioned to you the other day had a disastrous meeting with our competitor today! They walked out and are now looking for new representation. They are on their way over here now. This is our big chance. Mr. Stein wants all hands on deck to make a strong impression. We are meeting in ten minutes in the large conference room upstairs." Ian radiated his excitement as he spoke quickly and swiftly strutted away.

Sasha had never been on the highest floor of the firm, let alone attended any meetings in the conference room. As a beginning attorney, she knew she didn't have any responsibilities at the meeting other than making an appearance, but she was looking forward to the experience.

She hurriedly freshened-up in the restroom and headed upstairs. The walls were covered in regal wood paneling, complete with ornate moldings. It felt like being in an old traditional library rather than a modern-day skyscraper.

Mr. Stein greeted the clients and introduced the members of his team. He made a pitch for the firm and the real estate group seemed to be receptive. They had lots of questions. Sasha watched from the side, impressed when Ian fielded a number of the questions. He was articulate and had a wonderfully charismatic presence. She formed a newfound respect for Ian. Or perhaps, it was a level of regard that seemed to grow over time.

As the conversation seemed to be reaching a lull, Mr. Stein suggested that they continue their meeting over dinner at his club. The clients agreed. Only a limited number of attorneys were included in the group to attend the dinner. She noticed that while Ian was included in that elite group, no female attorneys were invited to the dinner. Taking a breath, she could not ignore the pattern surrounding Mr. Stein. It didn't look optimistic for her career at the firm.

Without any further responsibilities associated with the real estate group, Sasha shut down her computer for the night. She needed one of Kat's mixology sensations.

Lawson's Bar was not the ideal place for Sasha to forget the tribulations of the week. All the lawyers at the bar reminded her of working at the law firm. Many of the attorneys continued their work discussions there. *Did these people ever think about anything besides their jobs?*

Sasha sat alongside a few of the other younger attorneys at the firm, biding time until she could politely excuse herself to sit at the bar, near Kat. An underlying level of competition existed between the group, but the need for mutual support over the past year superseded the former. Over time, the young attorneys she worked with had shunned a couple of people from the group of "friends" as they proved to be unreasonably competitive. One of those attorneys ended up getting fired and the other one was cast off to an island of his own making.

"What do you think the chances are of Stein landing that real estate company as a client?" Marcus asked because he always wanted to know the latest dish on what was going on at the firm.

Jonathon laughed. "For O'Malley's sake, I hope so. If not, Stein will probably blame him for something not going well. Stein never accepts blame, only compliments."

Marcus countered, "That's not true. He also accepts his partnership bonuses. He brags about all the crap he buys with the money." The whole table started laughing.

"Nepotism: great when it works in your favor, not so great when you end up working for a douche," Marcus quipped.

Sasha wanted to agree, but kept her mouth shut. Speaking her mind about how she felt about politics at the firm might bite her in the ass later. She excused herself from the table, having done her obligatory duty, and joined Kat at the bar.

Sitting at the bar distanced herself from the work conversations. Even better, she and Kat talked intermittently as Kat served drinks. She took a seat and Kat rejoiced. "Alex! Thank goodness you're here! I need a taste tester."

Yes! Now this was the kind of work she wanted to be in charge of tonight. "At your service. Ready, willing, and able to get blitzed."

"Perfect." Kat grabbed a high ball glass. She poured in some Irish whiskey and ginger ale, and topped it with a lime wedge.

Sasha took a sip. "I'm not sure. I think I might need a few more to be certain that I like it," she joked.

Kat beamed. "Excellent! You are my favorite guinea pig. You like all my drinks."

"What about that apple pie drink? What happened to that?" Sasha smiled, preferring sweeter drinks to other stronger liquor-based drinks. Of course, straight vodka was her one exception.

"I realized that I need to give a selection of non-sweet drinks as well as sweet drinks." Kat mixed a martini for another customer.

"I'm glad you don't call them girlie drinks and manly drinks," Sasha stated and added, "But I would have to admit that I do prefer the sweet ones like that apple pie martini." Sasha offered a cheeky grin.

"Finish that one and let me know which you prefer." Kat served up a martini to the customer at the other end of the bar.

Sasha was enjoying her drink when she heard a voice behind her, "Where are the shots of espresso and whiskey?" Sasha turned to face the familiar voice.

"JD!" Sasha exclaimed. "What are you doing here?" She corrected her less-than welcoming hello. "I mean, what a nice surprise to see you." *What luck!* The sight of him was better than the alcohol. His presence felt like a breeze sweeping in off of Lake Michigan as the sun peaks out above the horizon.

"Can I join you for a drink while I wait for my brother?" JD's smile woke up the butterflies in her belly.

"Absolutely."

"What are you drinking tonight?" JD gestured toward her glass.

"Not exactly sure, to be honest. My best friend, Kat," She pointed to Kat at the other end of the bar, "She put it in front of me and told me to drink it but ran off without telling me what it was. All I know is that she said it was supposed to have a fall or Thanksgiving feel. She's always trying to come up with drinks to match the season or holiday. Here comes the drink master now."

Kat shamelessly looked JD up and down. "Well, I was going to bring you a tall glass of water before the next round, but I see you already found yourself one on your own."

By all definitions he was gorgeous. JD stood out from all the other patrons. He was dressed in jeans and a thermal shirt. However, it wasn't the clothes that put to shame most. He differed because he didn't look like he had a pole up his ass like the other attorneys. Sasha casually hid her smile with her hand.

"Kat, let me introduce you to JD. He teaches the art class that you recommended to me."

"Oh, so *you* are the hot art teacher that I keep hearing about!" Kat wasn't shy about putting men on the spot and embarrassing them a little, but JD didn't seem offended in the slightest. Sasha wanted to gag her bestie.

"The hot art teacher, huh?" JD raised an eyebrow questioningly to Sasha.

Sasha squirmed.

Kat saved Sasha and corrected herself, "That's what all the other teachers call you over at the school."

JD looked toward Sasha. "Damn. I was hoping that you had given me the new nickname. I like the ring of hot art teacher."

Sasha's heart raced. "Well, I can't argue with that description. And I have *excellent* argumentative skills as an attorney." She smirked at JD. Her words were filled with bravado, but her cheeks flushed.

"Can I still call you hot art teacher?" Kat prodded.

"Kat," Sasha whined.

"JD would be fine. Unless you prefer Jameson, as my dad calls me. He stopped calling me hot art teacher a month ago. He said he didn't need two cocky sons," JD joked, easily winning over Kat.

"Ha! Jameson and Smirnova." Kat howled in laughter. "You two are perfect for each other. You're like an Irish martini."

The bar was crowded, and Kat needed to focus on orders, not jokes. "What can I get you guys?"

Sasha held up her glass. "Another would be great."

"Can you make that two? Please," JD added.

Sasha liked his go with the flow easy nature as it made her feel more relaxed. They chatted while waiting on the drinks, before they were interrupted by JD's phone buzzing with a message.

"Everything okay?" Sasha asked, hoping that JD didn't need to run off again to meet his brother. Kat came by dropping off their drinks before disappearing again.

"Well, that depends. My brother just blew me off for the night because of something at work. But if you have time to hang out, then everything is aces." JD looked at her expectantly.

"Aces it is." Sasha grinned.

JD reached out and took his glass, taking a quick sip. Recognition washed over his face. "Is Kat mocking me with the whiskey in the drink?"

"No, the drink is the same as the original one she made for me earlier. And Kat isn't one to make sly jokes. She's much more upfront."

"I like people that are upfront. In hockey, players put it out all on the ice. It's all about acting and reacting to what is in front of you." JD took a swig of the drink.

"What about art?" Sasha flirtatiously brushed her hand against JD's arm. "Isn't the best art considered what has more depth and meaning. Not just superficial beauty?" *Was JD more than just a hot muscular man?*

"Art is thought. Lawyers use words, but an artist can use paint, wood, fabric, or any kind of medium. They say a picture is worth a thousand words." JD's gesticulations while he spoke animatedly about art resembled his arm movement when he painted. Sasha became easily captivated.

"Do you have a stronger connection to hockey or art?" she asked. The range of his interests were unusual as art and hockey were at opposite ends of the spectrum. At least to her they were.

"Why should I choose? I like both. Not everything has to be compared like a hockey team's standings." JD used his finger to draw circles on the back of her hand that rested on the bar, sending goosebumps up her arm.

"Like ice cream. My favorite combination is a scoop of blackberry and a scoop of chocolate hazelnut together. I can't ever choose between either." The thought of her favorite ice cream had her salivating. Or was it the sight of JD?

"Throw both scoops in a blender and make a milkshake and I'm all over it." JD's eyes flashed.

She mocked his suggestion, "But then you can't appreciate each flavor. Slowly licking it off a spoon so that you can taste the nuance of each morsel. Mmmm. Fruity, rich chocolate, and the nuts. Oh, so good." Her head fell back and she moaned with half lidded eyes. When she opened her eyes, JD's gaze was directed on her lips.

"I'm all about the licking and savoring." His gravelly voice sent chills down her spine. She downed the last of her drink in a long gulp.

"Are you ready for another, or how about we go for ice cream?" He winked.

She didn't want any more alcohol and she didn't want to say goodnight to JD. "How about next round at my place?"

Stealing Sasha's phrase from earlier, JD smiled broadly, "Absolutely."

Chapter 7

JD

He held Sasha's hand as they entered her apartment building. She returned her doorman's greeting in a friendly and personable manner. He stroked his thumb over her hand, approving of her behavior. He really disliked women that treated people in service as if they were better than them.

The elevator took a long time to reach the thirty-first floor, which made JD grateful for the fact that his apartment was on the first floor of a two-flat. He preferred running up steps to waiting for elevators, but he appreciated the fact that Sasha's building was probably safer for a single female.

He eagerly followed her into her apartment. It was exceptionally tidy and didn't appear completely lived in. The gray couch was fairly basic with simple clean lines. The bright colored blankets draped over the side of the couch stood out. A book rested on the end table with a bookmark peeking out. He pictured Sasha curling up in the striped blanket and reading, wrapping herself in a rainbow.

Sasha's voice broke into his illusion. "Want a beer?"

He turned to see her bending over as she looked in the refrigerator. Damn. He banked that position in his head for later. He gravitated closer to her and grabbed her around the waist. He placed his head next to hers and pretended to care about checking out the type of beer. Whatever she was serving, he wanted. "Sure."

Tilting the bottle back and swallowing, he noticed the hoard of bottles of vodka on top of her refrigerator. "What's up with the all the vodka?"

She rolled her eyes. "That was a graduation surprise. In law school the professors always called us by our last names. On the first day, one of the professors mispronounced my last name and changed it to the masculine form. My classmates thought it was hysterical. For whatever reason, the old crank couldn't manage to correct his pronunciation the entire semester, so the nickname stuck."

"Looks like you had a lot of friends in law school." He approximated a dozen bottles on top of her fridge.

She looked like she was going to argue, but then stopped. She cautioned, "I apologize, my mixology skills don't compare to Kat."

"No worries, a beer is fine. I'm not a picky drinker." He sat on a bar stool at her kitchen counter and took another pull from the beer bottle. "Come sit with me." He wanted her close enough that he could touch her.

"Would you mind if I went ahead and threw on some casual clothes? Wearing a suit is not conducive for relaxing." She wiggled out of her suit jacket, revealing a silk button blouse that called to him to reach out and touch.

"Please, go ahead." JD enjoyed the view as she walked away. Her ass looked great. She wore her hair up in some kind of bun thingy. He wanted to skate his nose along the sexy curve of her neck.

She returned quickly in yoga pants and a tank top.

JD thought she looked great in her suit, but he preferred her in her casual clothes that she wore to his class. "Feel better?" As she neared him, he realized a very sexy difference than how she dressed for art class. She wasn't wearing a bra.

"Much." She sighed deeply and his cock thickened.

"Good. Now please come sit with me." JD would have liked if she had chosen to sit on his lap, but she stood by him instead.

She smiled. "You know, you are the only one that calls me Sasha."

Confused, JD asked, "I thought you said your mom and dad call you Sasha."

"True. Let me correct myself, you are the only one in America that calls me Sasha. I really like it. It reminds me of a carefree childhood. Once I came to school here in America, everything became very serious. I feel more at ease when you call me Sasha." She drifted closer to him.

"I like that I get to call you by a special nickname." JD held up his beer, "Cheers to being wild and carefree." He took her hand in his and pulled her closer. He spread his legs. She stepped between his thighs. "Come here, Sasha. Damn, you are beautiful." He brushed his thumb along the curve of her neck. JD looked into Sasha's chestnut eyes. "And during class, when you are painting, your beauty shines. It attracted me to you from the very beginning." Her lips parted.

Sasha's cheeks turned pink, again. "What's got you blushing?" He ran a finger over her cheek. A faint heat emanated from the glow.

As the flush spread, Sasha replied, "I was thinking how I find absolutely everything about you to be attractive. And…I was thinking particularly about your ass."

"I think I may like seeing you blush almost as much as I like watching you paint." JD's eyes moved from focusing on her cheeks to her matching, pink-stained lips. He wanted to kiss her full lips. Her nipples hardened beneath her top and he wanted to see how she reacted to his pinches. His jeans felt much tighter.

JD set down his beer and focused his gaze. "I have wanted to kiss those lips for a while now." He gently rubbed his thumb over her bottom one. "I almost kissed you at the coffee shop last week." He languidly pulled on her plump skin until a relaxed sigh escaped her mouth. "And I really wanted to kiss you at the bar tonight."

"I wanted you to," Sasha muttered, leaning even closer to JD.

"I don't like quick kisses, Sasha. When I kiss you, I'm not going to want to stop. I want to savor you. I want to be able to hold you and not let go."

"Yes, JD," Sasha panted.

JD moved his hand and palmed her cheek. He slowly moved off the bar stool, closing the slim gap between them. He towered over her and claimed control. He snaked his other hand around her back, holding her in place as he bent down until his lips reached hers. She melded her lips with his. *Oh fuck, yes!*

Her head pressed into his hand, begging for his touch. And then she opened for him, escalating the kiss into something more. More tension. More heat. More fever-pitched desire. The warmth spread across his body. Her hand moved to his face. He loved feeling her need to touch him as well. The mutual connection hummed in the air. Their kiss intensified as they explored each other's mouths.

Damn. She tasted amazing! She kissed like she enjoyed it. She didn't rush.

He lifted her onto the stool and wrapped her legs around his waist. He wanted every bit of her touching him. "Sasha, you feel so fucking good."

"JD. Oh god," Sasha moaned between kisses.

"I need to feel all of you." He paused to give her the opportunity to change her mind. God, he hoped she didn't.

"Yes, JD," Sasha breathed.

Oh hell, yes! JD didn't hesitate and ripped off his shirt. Unlike how he removed his shirt, JD slowly drew Sasha's tank top up her torso allowing his hands to skim along her soft skin. His cock grew even harder as he revealed her perfectly full breasts. He unceremoniously dropped her top on the floor while continuing the kiss. He loved the feel of her smooth skin against his own.

But then she backed away. He hated the chill of the air that blew between them.

She gaped at him. "Damn!" Sasha rubbed her fingers over his pectorals and the muscles flexed. She trailed a finger between all the divots separating each section of his abs, making him shiver in response. "Michelangelo should have used you as a model rather than that David guy."

Her compliment touched him in a way that no woman had ever affected him. He was used to being ogled, but Sasha's words struck a chord. His restraint hung by a thread. "Thank you," he said through gritted teeth, straining not to rush. He lifted her chin and pressed his lips to hers one more time.

A fire ignited and his control was incinerated. The intensity between them exploded. Sasha yanked his long hair. Her roughness turned him on. With her legs wrapped around him she ground herself against his length. She repeated the action again and again. He became impossibly hard.

"Oh, yes," Sasha begged. "JD, please," she strained as she rubbed her entire body against him.

"Oh hell, yes." JD agreed. His body vibrated with need. His cock throbbed. "Lose the yoga pants," he demanded.

She reacted immediately, dropping her legs from around him and hopped off the chair. She growled as she tore at her pants.

JD grabbed a condom from his jeans before stripping them off as well. He quickly rolled it on and threw Sasha on the kitchen counter. "Wrap your legs around me again, Sasha. I want to feel more of you."

She squeezed tightly with her legs drawing him inside her. Her warm wet core felt amazing around him as he slid inside. He buried himself to the hilt. Every inch sensitized. He needed a moment to appreciate the sensations, the tightness, the heat. But then Sasha bit his lip and lit a savage need to drive into her.

"Fuck, Sasha. You feel fucking amazing." He grunted. She held on tight with her arms and legs as he thrusted into her over and over again.

"Oh god, JD, yes." Her screams grew louder. Her legs tightened around him. He wanted to hear and feel her come apart. He fucked her deeper, his pelvis connecting forcefully with her clit. "Oh fuck, JD, I'm about to come."

"Beautiful, come! I want to feel your sweet cunt grip

my cock." JD drove in as deep as possible. When she started to fall apart, he refused to slow down. He wanted to make her come again, and again. He reached his hand between them and found her clit. He caressed the sensitive flesh around the firm little bud. Another ripple tore through her as her body flushed with the oncoming orgasm.

"JD! Fuck!" Sasha screamed out uncontrollably.

JD wasn't going to let up now. "Hang on tight." JD lifted Sasha up and pressed her back against the wall. Her grip tightened around him. It turned him on. When her cum started dripping down his balls, he pumped harder and harder until he exploded inside her.

He still had her pinned against the wall.

"Damn. I didn't really think that it was possible to be fucked against a wall," Sasha breathed heavily.

JD laughed. "Put your legs down before they cramp up," he warned her. When she let go and put her feet back on the floor, she wobbled.

JD rested his forehead against hers. "Don't move. I don't want to let you go." He kissed the top of head.

Her breathing slowed.

He made no motion to move.

"JD, I'm exhausted, can we please go lay down?" Sasha asked tentatively.

"Sure. But let me finish this beer. I'm thirsty." He tossed the condom in the trash and then chugged the rest of his drink before placing it in the recycling. He snatched a permanent marker next to a grocery list on the kitchen counter and followed Sasha to her bedroom.

They both laid down in her bed. She wasn't fussy and didn't demand to take a shower. He liked having remnants of her perspiration clinging to his body. Her breathing evened out and she appeared to be drifting off to sleep, as she rolled onto her side.

He started tracing his finger along her shoulder. "You would look good with a tattoo right here." He continued using his finger to draw on her. "Have you ever thought about getting a tattoo?"

Mumbling sleepily, she replied, "I never settled on a single one that I would want permanently. One day I want something, and then I find some other image the next day that I think would look better."

JD reached for the marker that he had brought from the kitchen. He uncapped it and started drawing on Sasha's shoulder. She didn't react to the touch of the marker on her skin. By the time he finished she was lightly snoring.

In the morning, JD woke early, a habit with which his body was accustomed. Sasha hadn't stirred out of his embrace the entire night. He remained comfortably snuggled up to her warm length. The bond of their skin touching extended from his chest down to his feet. They were completely connected. He shifted his head and nuzzled her long brown hair.

The shriek of Sasha's alarm killed the nirvana. She jolted and shut it off.

"Why the hell do you have an alarm set so early on a Saturday?" JD grumbled.

Sasha sat up. "Because I have a hot date tonight and I wanted to get into the office early enough so I wouldn't be late." She quickly kissed JD and then hopped out of bed.

He wanted to pull her back into the bed and snuggle. And more. But he liked that she was thinking ahead to spend time with him. "A hot date, huh? You should definitely plan accordingly."

With her naked back to JD, he got a full view of the snow leopard on her shoulder. This was a view he would like to draw. He imagined being able to stare at her for hours while she posed naked for him.

Sasha presented a steamy opportunity, equally as appealing as his fantasy. "I should get into the shower. Care to join me?"

JD preferred to stay in bed with Sasha, but hopped at the chance of spending time with her, wet and naked.

Sasha stopped abruptly in the middle of the bathroom. She twisted her back and looked in the mirror. She shifted and turned and attempted to spin her head like an owl, before grabbing a smaller mirror. She angled her back completely to the mirror on the wall, and used the smaller mirror to see the ink better. He watched as she studied the image of the snow leopard on her shoulder.

"When did you do this?" Sasha asked.

JD couldn't read the expression on her face. *Was she upset?*

"As you were falling asleep. What do you think?" JD hoped she wouldn't be angry. He thought she looked fucking hot with it. But she wasn't smiling.

"It is rather…shocking. I'm not sure how I feel about it. You did a great job, of course." Sasha wavered. Her eyes drew together as she tilted her head.

"It's only a marker, it will eventually wash off. And I'm happy to help with that if you want." He winked. Her lips didn't even twitch and JD worried that he had really done something wrong. "I'm sorry if you hate it—"

Sasha cut him off, "No, it's not that. I like it. I guess, I'm most surprised by how much I *do* like it."

"You sure? Your reaction is actually making me a little nervous." She was staring a little too hard in the mirror with a strong contemplative look on her face.

"No, I'm sorry JD. It takes me time to warm up to changes in my life. Even when I like something, I spend a lot of time second guessing things and trying to look at things from lots of different perspectives." She continued to look in the mirror.

"Why a leopard?" Her expression softened. "I like it, but I never would have considered it." She finally looked at him and he sighed in relief.

"It's actually a snow leopard, which lives in Russia. Ya know, a little pride in Mother Russia." His parents had shared countless stories with him about Ireland. "And they're fierce, like you." He couldn't wait to bring out her animalistic side again. Sasha blushed.

She looked in the mirror a final time, and smiled. She turned and kissed him. "Thank you."

JD smiled tentatively. "You like it?" He needed a little reassurance.

"Yes, but let's get moving."

JD followed her into the shower. He grabbed the soap and started washing at her the ink. She quickly pulled her shoulder out of his reach. "No. I like it. Don't wash it off. I like the idea of a temporary tattoo as a way to get used to the whole idea. Maybe I'll even consider getting a permanent one someday. This is like a trial tat." She kissed him. "Thank you, JD. I really like it." She kissed him again. Her kisses reassured him.

He grabbed her and gave her a firm kiss on the lips. Then he held her head in place as he kissed a line up her neck. He nibbled the shell of her ear and a shiver snaked through her body. "Cold?" He placed her chest directly in the flow of the warm water, while he pressed his chest up against her back. "Does this help?"

"Mmm, yes," she mumbled.

JD cupped her left breast in his hand. Massaging. Kneading. Her breathing was louder than the rushing water. He countered the leisurely movement with a firm pinch of her nipple on her right breast. A guttural moan echoed against the tile.

Her throaty tone awoke JD's primal needs. "JD," she whimpered.

His erection was pressed up against her ass. He pulled on her hips. He wanted her to feel ever inch. She wiggled her hand between them and cupped his balls. He reflexively bit down on her shoulder.

"Ahhh," she wailed. She lightly scraped her fingernail along his sac. The tantalizing sensation spurred his desire.

One hand on her breast and another grabbing her sex, JD pulled her tightly against himself. Her hand was trapped between their bodies. Her fingers were driving him mad. He wanted to be in her, but he didn't have any other condoms with him. He tightened his grip on her.

"JD! I need you in me." Sasha pleaded.

"Condom? Where?"

"Under the bathroom sink. In the bag, I hadn't had time to unpack after I went shopping." JD released Sasha in search of the bag. "I told you, I have a hot date tonight, I needed to pick up some things," she yelled, her voice muffled.

JD hurried back into the shower. He kissed her hungrily and backed her up against the wall. "Turn around," he ordered. He saw the snow leopard on her shoulder. Before it wasn't much more than a doodle on her. Now, seeing her naked with his artwork on her body, he felt possessive of her. And fuck did it turn him on. He positioned his cock at her entrance. Her heat beckoned him.

She screamed, "Fuck me. Now!"

He thrust his cock deep inside her. Pounding her over and over again. The sight of the snow leopard heightening the experience, an added connection between the two of them. He was breathing hard. Lost in the sensations.

"JD, I'm about to come," she whimpered, as she panted, pushing back against him.

"Yes. Fuck yes!" JD fucked her hard, relentlessly. Her screams of ecstasy pushed him over the edge. He buried himself deep inside her as he came.

With her back against his chest, JD held her as their breathing slowed together. No cold air chills ruined the moment as the spray of water kept them warm. Fuck, he loved shower sex.

"Damn JD. That felt so good." Sasha rested the back of her head against his chest.

"Yes, it absolutely did," JD whispered in her ear. "By the way, seeing the snow leopard on your shoulder fucking turned me on." He smiled proudly.

"Really? I think I truly like the idea of your art on me." She turned and kissed him.

That was probably the highest compliment for an artist to receive.

Later, as they got dressed, JD teased, "Did you really think a package of three condoms would be enough for your hot date tonight?"

Sasha blushed.

"Let me tell you: No." JD went over to Sasha as she

wore only her bra and panties. He kissed her lightly and continued, "I am going to be in you. All. Night. Long. And I am going to make you come over and over again."

"Now that sounds like an excellent incentive for me to hurry up at work." Sasha smiled broadly before turning back to her closet. She picked out a sleeveless dress to wear. She admired how the snow leopard peeked out from underneath.

"Aren't you going to be cold in that dress? Don't get me wrong, you look beautiful." JD worried for her comfort.

She pouted. "You're right, but it is a shame to hide your artwork." She threw on a wrap-around sweater. It may have covered her more, but it also accentuated her curves rather than obscuring her body.

JD reiterated, "You really look beautiful in that dress. It is much more feminine than the suit you wore yesterday."

"Thank you. I wish I could dress more like this to work than the boring business suits that I wear Monday through Friday." Sasha's smiled diminished.

"Even in the business suit, you convinced me to come home with you last night." JD joked, trying to bring her smile back.

Sasha walked over to him and spoke in a slow sultry drawl, "Do you think I might be able to convince you to come home with me tonight?"

JD kissed her before answering, "My bet's on yes." He kissed her one more time.

"Your kisses are too tempting." She pushed on JD's chest as if to push him away, but years of hockey made him impenetrable. "I need to get to work."

"Okay, okay, okay." He gave her a final quick peck.

He didn't want to push her too far and frustrate her. Stepping away from Sasha, he threw on his jacket to leave.

"JD, wait. If you have a minute, I can walk out with you." She moved around quickly, putting on her shoes and grabbing her coat.

"If that means I can snag an extra kiss, then sure." JD shot her his most irresistible smile.

She smiled in return, which boosted his confidence.

After she locked her apartment door, she reached for his hand and entwined her fingers with his. He squeezed back. He liked that she initiated the contact. With her hand in his, he enjoyed the fact that her elevator was as slow as a puppy walking down stairs for the first time.

Outside on the sidewalk, as promised, she kissed him one last time. She didn't dash off, but rather gifted him an emphatic, but not obnoxious public display of affection. With an extra pep in his step, he headed home. He hadn't felt this optimistic in months.

Chapter 8

Sasha

Sasha sat in her office and sipped at her coffee. Her mind drifted off to thoughts of her amazing night with JD. She needed an extra fix of caffeine to help her focus on her work. She promised herself one last sip before getting started.

The door of her office suddenly flung open, and Ian burst inside. Sasha startled and jolted in her seat. Her coffee jostled out of the mug and all over her sweater as Ian exclaimed, "We did it! We signed the real estate company as a client!"

Sasha swore under her breath and scowled at him.

"Oh, shit, I'm so sorry. I didn't mean to scare you. Let me go get some towels to help clean up." Ian stepped out of the office.

She hurriedly removed the sweater before the coffee seeped through and soiled the dress beneath it. Without the sweater, she shivered. She opened the small closet at the back of her office and grabbed her spare blazer. Sasha frowned. The blazer didn't enhance her outfit as well the sweater. She considered forgoing the blazer, but remembered the tattoo on her shoulder.

Ian announced, "Here I have both wet and dry paper towels for your sweater."

Decision made, she quickly donned the blazer.

Ian mumbled, "Was that a…" He stopped short of completing the sentence.

Sasha turned around to face him. He didn't look her in the eye, but rather seemed to be looking at her shoulder. Had he seen the tattoo? She ignored his utterance, reaching out and grabbing the towels in his hand. "Thank you." She blotted at her sweater.

"Again, I'm sorry. I'm happy to pay for the dry cleaning."

"Don't worry about it. More importantly, congratulations! That's great. I was really impressed how you handled yourself and fielded questions in the meeting last night," she praised him as she continued to blot. "I heard that you were integral at the dinner afterwards as well."

"Thank you. That's really thoughtful of you to say. Hopefully the other partners heard the same thing." Ian swallowed loudly.

Sasha paused from blotting and looked up at him. The tall dark-haired man looked less confident than usual as he cracked his knuckles. Did Ian not understand that he was doing more positive things for the firm than his boss, a partner at the firm? His insecurity surprised her, but his willingness to admit to it stunned her even more.

"Everyone can see what a great job you are doing," she reassured. "I would think that helping bring in a big client will help secure the next step in your career."

Ian looked at his phone suddenly. "One of the partners announced that we are going out to get drinks and celebrate at Lawson's Bar. You should come too," he encouraged.

Getting an opportunity to rub elbows with some of the partners had potential for helping her career. She appreciated Ian extending the offer, but weighed her priorities for the day. "Thanks, but I still have more work to get done here. I have a reputation to uphold too," she emphasized.

"Your work is regarded highly. When you finish, you should stop by," Ian pushed again.

"I have plans later," Sasha replied. She offered a vague answer on purpose. She didn't want to admit that she chose a personal commitment over furthering her career.

"Oh." Ian hesitated and stared at her in a confused manner. "Okay, have a good evening."

"You too. And congrats again." Sasha smiled brightly.

After Ian's drop by, she found it much easier to concentrate on work. She found Ian's consistent work ethic admirable. He motivated her to work even harder.

She remained in the zone, working all afternoon. The rattle of her alarm broke her concentration. She excitedly grabbed her phone and shut off the alarm. Where had the time gone? She took stock of all she had completed in the day, and she smiled, pleased with herself. She hummed as she started shutting down her computer for the day. She was looking forward to her date. Her phone buzzed with an incoming text.

JD—*Hey Sasha. Are we still on for tonight?*—

Seeing his message sent a feeling of calmness through her. He wasn't pushy or demanding. She replied instantly.

Sasha—*Absolutely! Heading home to get ready*—
JD—*Great! Dress to be comfortable outside*—
Sasha—*Sure thing (smiley face)*—

When she got home, she hurried to get ready. She

soaked her sweater in some light detergent, hoping that the coffee stain wouldn't set permanently. The process of washing the sweater was like rinsing Ian out of her life. She focused instead on her soon-to-start, great date with an incredible, hot guy.

With JD in mind, she tried to pick out an outfit. The weather app predicted a typically chilly November evening in Chicago. Sasha threw on a pair of slim fitting jeans. She checked in the mirror to make sure that the jeans made her ass look good. Check! She complimented them with a pair of stylish boots. The temperature was expected to be around thirty degrees Fahrenheit, so she layered a sweater over a long sleeve top. She took her hair out of the bun and let it down. She flat wrapped her hair around the hot iron, creating lazy curls. She topped off the look with some fresh and fun make-up, with a wing tip eyeliner, as opposed to her conservative look at work. A spritz of perfume and she was ready to go.

The butterflies in her belly fluttered when the doorman called up announcing she had a visitor. The elevator ride to the thirty-first floor wasn't the speedy kind like in the other massive skyscrapers in Chicago, but it allowed the anticipation of seeing JD to build.

She yanked the door open. He greeted her with a sexy ass smile, highlighted with his frosty pink cheeks. He stepped through the doorway and took her face in both hands and kissed her passionately. The chill of his fingers faded and the butterflies yielded as a warmth spread throughout Sasha's body. Damn. JD was an *excellent* kisser.

"Hi," Sasha said dizzily.

"Damn. You look good." Sasha blushed at the compliment. He hadn't even gotten a view of her bottom yet. "Are you ready to go?"

"I just need to grab a jacket and I'm all set." Sasha was a little leery if she was dressed appropriately. "Where are we headed?"

"I was thinking if it's all good with you that we would go and get pizza. Then, I thought we could walk off the pizza and head over to the pier. I got us tickets for the Ferris wheel. What do you think?" he called out from the door as she slipped into her room quickly before returning to his side, jacket in hand.

"Yay! I've never been on the Ferris wheel. That sounds like so much fun. And I'm starving so food first is great." Her head still felt dizzy. Either it was from hunger or JD's kisses.

"Passing out from hunger, not so good. On the other hand, passing out from multiple orgasms is the plan for later." JD punctuated his thought with a kiss. Sasha reconsidered her need for food. Skipping the pizza and fast forwarding to his other plans might be a better option. Unfortunately, her stomach disagreed, growling at her.

She shoved a warm hat and gloves into her jacket before heading out the door.

They agreed on a pizza place before leaving her building and enduring the cold. JD apparently had strong opinions on pizza. Fortunately, they both agreed that stuffed pizza was the best and they chose the restaurant based on proximity to her apartment.

While they were waiting for their pizza, which took almost forty-five minutes to cook, they each had a drink. Chicago-style, stuffed pizza was always worth the wait. The tempting aroma inside the restaurant heightened her hunger. Though looking at the man beside her made her crave something else.

"So, what were you up to today?" she wondered out loud. If she didn't have to work every weekend to hit her billable hours for the year, she wasn't sure what she would be doing. Maybe more painting for herself?

JD bit at his lip and cleared his throat. "I started updating my resume. I gave some thought about what you had said about finding the right fit, and my brother encouraged me to start looking sooner than later."

"I'm sorry, if you don't want to talk about it." *Had she unintentionally hit a nerve?* "Hey, I might not be able to hit a hockey puck in a goal or paint like Picasso, or anything that requires physical talent, but I'm great at coming up with ideas."

He shook his head back and forth. "Nah, your ability to wrap your legs around me, while I fucked you up against the wall last night, was the best talent." He brushed his fingertips across his smug smile.

She looked away, bringing her hand in front of her face to shield her embarrassment.

"You turn all different shades of pink when you get embarrassed. It's adorable," JD teased. She hung her head down, covering her face with both hands.

Shaking off her embarrassment, she teased him right back, "You were pretty good last night."

"I'll aim for better than pretty good, later." His cocky smile made her ache for his touch.

"I'm sure you are good at a lot of things," she pressed as he dropped his shield. "I assume you have already considered coaching hockey."

JD appeared unimpressed with her suggestion. "Yeah. I know a lot of players who made that transition from player to coach as their playing career came to an end. I've seen too many of them turn into horrible coaches. I just don't see that for myself."

She didn't allow the dismissal of her first idea to dissuade her from continuing the discussion. "Duly noted. What if you could do something to change coaching?" Sasha tried to think of something more top down. "What if you ran an entire hockey program or worked for a hockey association?"

When he didn't respond either way, Sasha assumed that her ideas weren't hitting the mark. She asked, "Or is art more the direction you want to go in?" JD remained quiet. "JD?" *Had she completely put her foot in her mouth and offended him?*

"Sorry, I was just thinking. I guess there are a lot of options out there. Last summer, when I finally had to admit that I wouldn't be playing, I tried to find a job as quickly as possible. I just wanted to work." JD took Sasha's hand. She clutched his hand in return, relieved that she hadn't irritated him.

"Thank you for suggesting I take a beat to think. I guess there really isn't any rush. I need to figure out what I really want. It's just that—my brother has always known what he wanted to do and is very driven. I sometimes feel like I need to be like him in the sense of moving full steam ahead." JD started drawing on the back of her hand with his finger. She was unable to discern if the pattern was random or not.

"Maybe you should take a moment to refuel at the train station before setting out on the tracks *and,* continuing with the silly metaphor, you are in charge of the railroad switch." Sasha understood wanting to take time to evaluate a situation. Sometimes life presented situations that pushed a person to choose without sufficient time to think.

JD squeezed Sasha's hand. "Thank you. I really like that you ask and don't push." He moved over and gave her an appreciative kiss.

The waitress placed the piping hot pizza on a stand on the table. The cheese pulled and stretched as the waitress used a pie cutter to lower a slice to each of their plates, serving each of them a cheesy slice of heaven. They both picked up a fork and knife and dug in.

"Fuck. This is so good," JD said between bites.

Sasha finished chewing the bite in her mouth. "You were right. This place does have the best pepperoni." She struggled to talk and eat without being rude. After the first slice, and the hunger pains subsiding, it was easier to hold a conversation.

"When I first came to Chicago and tried stuffed pizza, I had no clue how to eat it. I never had pizza that required a fork and knife, but it was love at first bite."

"Thank god you like pizza. I'll introduce you to all my favorite places." He winked. Damn. He was cute, not just hot.

They continued eating. "So how about you? Do you enjoy your job?" He stopped eating and waited for her answer.

That had been a hot topic on her mind for a while. "I really like working as an attorney, but...I'm not sure I fit in well at the firm where I work. I think...I might be happier at a smaller practice."

Sasha really didn't want to discuss her work. Attempting to change the topic, she continued in a different direction, "With all the time you spent playing and traveling for hockey, did you ever have time to visit art museums?"

"I was lucky to see a lot of different museums across the States. My mom forced my dad to take me whenever possible while we were on the road." His heartfelt smile tickled her.

"Have you ever travelled out of the United States?" Sasha had travelled every summer with her parents and seen much of Europe. She wondered if she and JD shared similar experiences.

"Nah. Maybe someday. What's on your bucket list?" JD shifted in his seat, leaning backward awaiting her response.

Bucket lists tended to reveal a lot about a person. Her cheeks burned as a few dirty sex things crossed her mind. Maybe they didn't share travel experiences, but she would definitely be into crossing off *other* things with JD. Rather than sharing her thoughts, she answered, "Kissing you at the top of the Ferris wheel tonight." She stuffed another bite in her mouth, preventing the naughtier ideas from slipping out.

"Blushing again. Hmm? I'm not so sure that's what you were really thinking." He didn't push her to elaborate. "I'm certain we can cross that one off tonight."

They finished up the pizza and started walking towards the pier. It felt good to walk off the pizza. Sasha kept her gloves tucked in her pockets and intertwined her fingers with JD for warmth instead. They walked hand-in-hand and chatted about all the sights in Chicago. She enjoyed the window shopping along the way, and the conversation of the array of fun summertime activities to do in the park.

In the distance she saw the enormous, illuminated Ferris wheel. They walked down the pier, the length of the line out front dauntingly long. Walking in the cool air was invigorating but standing still without the tall buildings to block the wind would be frigid.

JD tugged on her hand when they neared the back of the line. "I bought fast passes for the ride ahead of time. We get to skip the line. Who wants to stand in the cold, if you don't need to?" JD winked.

She kissed him. "I like a man that thinks ahead."

"Don't think that quick peck excuses you from kissing me at the top of the ride." He smiled playfully.

"More the better." His fun-loving attitude warmed her so much that she forgot about the Chicago chill.

The gigantic Ferris wheel moved slower than Sasha was expecting. The skyline looked amazing. The city lights twinkled against the snow flurries that started to fall. And as promised, when they reached the top of the Ferris wheel, JD pulled her close and laid one on her. Kissing on top of the Ferris wheel, with the snowflakes glinting in the lights, was the epitome of romance.

They stepped off the ride still holding hands. She loved that JD always reached to hold her hand. Her much smaller hand tucked perfectly into his strong grip. All his little touches, kisses, and the hand holding accumulated into warm fuzzies. While in JD's company, her work stress evaporated. The fact that JD was sexy as sin was an added delight that left her aching.

"Would you like to go get drinks?" He cocked his head in the direction of the nearby bars on the pier.

What Sasha wanted was JD. "I'm happy to grab a drink if you want, but I was hoping that you would prefer to head back to my place." She fought back the urge to jump his bones in public.

"Objection sustained, counselor," He teased and eagerly took his phone out to schedule a ride.

They hopped in the car together. While she enjoyed the walk to the pier after satisfying her appetite for pizza, she desired a faster mode of transportation to satisfy her sexual appetite.

Though, JD's refusal to hold her hand when they got into the car concerned her. Had something changed between them? She worried that he would rebuff her advances. But then, he moved closer to her. He plucked off her winter hat and tossed it in her lap. The weight of his arm around her shoulders soothed her momentary alarm. She nestled into his side and the feeling of contentment blanketed her. His fingers crawled up her neck and snaked through her hair. The sensual massage of his fingers against her scalp was blessedly delightful. She turned into a puddle of relaxation.

Sasha rested her hand on JD's leg as he continued his unhurried movements. She mirrored his languid touch and gently ran her fingers along his thigh.

Evidence of his arousal extended down the leg of his jeans. In the darkness of the car, without thinking, she reached out and touched him. She used her finger to trace the outline of his manliness. The more she concentrated on his shape, the more she wanted to repeat such motion on his bare cock. She wanted to use her tongue to feel every ridge of his shaft. Her arousal drenched her panties.

The light touches in her hair intensified and transformed into playful tugging. Her need for him heightened. She would have liked to yank his jeans open and straddle him right there in the car. But getting arrested for public indecency in a rideshare car was decidedly *not* on her bucket list.

The car stopped. She peered out the window of the

backseat. They had arrived at the front of her building. *Thank fuck!*

Sasha eagerly jumped out of the car, but JD struggled as he adjusted himself in his jeans. She watched him, seeing how his winter jacket was just long enough to conceal his hard-on. Smiling to herself, Sasha walked quickly toward the elevator, hardly slowing to shoot a hurried greeting to the door man.

They stepped onto the elevator and Sasha pressed into JD, unzipping his jacket as well as her own. She pressed her body firmly up against his, feeling his hard cock jut into her abs. He kissed her lips.

"Are there cameras in the elevator?" JD hesitated, looking up and around the ceiling of the elevator.

"Um, not sure," she murmured, continuing to kiss him.

"Let's wait." JD turned her around so that her back was to his chest. "I don't ever want to put you in an awkward position." Sasha continued to breathe heavily as JD's arms caged her in.

As soon as they crossed the threshold of her apartment, Sasha pushed the door closed more firmly than necessary. She kissed JD emphatically. Their lips mashed together. Tongues dueled. She pulled at his long hair. She attempted to remove her winter jacket but failed. Her arm caught in the sleeve, and the jacket got turned inside out. "Damn coat," she growled, throwing it to the ground.

JD removed his jacket with much more grace. She glared at his sweater. There were too many layers of clothes between them to turn the moment into a sexy strip tease. The laborious act of removing her clothes tested her patience.

"I want you naked. Now. And I want to go down on you." She didn't blush. Her arousal pushed her past her shyness. She owned her desires and didn't fear letting JD know what she wanted.

"Aw, hell, yes!" JD's eyes darkened with desire.

Removing her boots and jeans took more time than she cared for. The lace-up boots looked great on, but took way too long to remove. And her skinny jeans needed to be peeled off her body. Slowly. She grunted in frustration, hurling her jeans to the floor when she finally removed them.

"Don't hate the boots and jeans. They made your ass look great tonight." JD cocked an eyebrow.

Sasha laughed and looked away. JD knew how to lighten the mood.

"Okay, you tell me a second ago that you want to give me a blow job and you don't blush. But now, your cheeks are a bright pink. You have to tell me what you are thinking! Please. I'm dying to know." He reached for her chin and made her look up at him.

"Your comment about my ass," Sasha started, glancing downward.

"Did I embarrass you by flattering you? If so, you are going to have to get used to it, because you are gorgeous, and I plan on telling you frequently." He punctuated his point with a searing kiss.

Sasha laughed again. "Not exactly, but thank you." The heat in her cheeks spread to the tips of her ears. "I can't tell you how many times during class I stared at *your* ass. I was concerned that the other students noticed me." She struggled to maintain eye contact while making such an embarrassing admission.

JD grinned. "I'll take that as a compliment. Thank

you." He kissed each of her flushed cheeks. "While we are admitting things, I have thought of your ass many times since I met you. Like grabbing it." He pulled her closer, both hands grabbing her rear cheeks, and kissed her firmly. "And feeling your entire body up against mine."

"Fuck, you feel good up against *my* body." Sasha temporarily got lost in the blissfulness of the contact.

JD prompted them to shuffle closer to the bedroom area of her studio apartment.

Mentally returning to the here and now, Sasha shoved JD toward the bed. "Lay down. I want to taste you JD." He didn't resist being shoved this time.

He moved into the middle of the bed with his legs slightly apart. He lifted his head off the bed, contracting all his abdominal muscles. All eight sections were a delicious background for his thick length, but his eyes, devouring her, captivated her attention. The intensity of the look was like gravity pulling her to him.

Every extraneous thought flew from her mind as she crawled onto the bed and between his legs, extending her tongue out and around the bulging tip. She looked up through her eyelashes and saw him gazing back down at her. She tossed her hair to the side and granted him an unobstructive view of the show.

"Oh hell, yes." JD praised and encouraged. He continued to watch.

She grabbed him around the shaft and pumped his length a couple of times as her mouth descended closer. She licked her lips and opened wide. Closer and closer until his warm length was inside her mouth. She wrapped her lips tightly around him and swallowed every inch she was able to muster.

His head fell back and thumped on the bed. "Fuck," he exhaled.

She swiped around the head of his cock. Trailed her tongue under the ridge. Around and around, until she slowly dragged the flat of her tongue across the tip. Slowly she took more of him into her mouth. She retreated after each inch, incrementally moistening his length. Then took him as far back into her mouth without gagging. The sensual movements were making her hot and wet.

"Sasha, that feels so good," JD groaned. "Come here. I need to touch you." He shifted their naked bodies on her bed, until her naked sex was within his reach.

JD found her core and inserted a finger. She groaned at the connection. "Jesus, Sasha. You're so wet...so fucking hot." His consistent approval heightened her arousal.

She rocked against his hand. Her pleasure continued to build. She tried to concentrate on making him feel good, but was overwhelmed by the ache between her legs. JD's touch sent a flick of shivers through her.

"Hmmm," Sasha hummed around his cock in her mouth and felt the vibration in his balls cupped in her hand. She hummed again and massaged his balls with a firm grip.

"Sasha," he warned considerately but she didn't care.

Rather than backing off, she sucked harder.

"Sasha!" He cried out.

She wanted him. She wanted his orgasm. All his muscles flexed beneath her, before he exploded in her mouth. Triumph. She swallowed his release, pleased with her ability to make JD lose control.

She didn't take offense to JD's heart rate returning to normal quickly. He was an athlete after all. Instead, she took advantage of it. "I want your mouth on me."

JD answered her demand by sitting up and pushing her down on the bed. His powerful muscles turned her on. Everything about him turned her on.

Then he kissed his way down her chest and abs until he reached her clit. She was extremely sensitive after coming while she had been sucking him off.

"I need your fingers in me, JD." Sasha wiggled her hips.

"I aim to please." JD plunged two fingers into her core.

"Yes! *JD*. Like. That." Sasha panted between each word, but was determined to offer him positive feedback. She knew what she wanted and knew what she needed. With her guidance and his attention, she climaxed intensely within seconds.

One minute he was between her legs and the next he was kissing her mouth tenderly. "You are so beautiful when you come apart like that," he whispered. Unlike him, her breathing took much longer to slow to a normal pace. "It was hot as hell having you be clear about what you want in bed."

He pulled her in for a deeper kiss, his tongue demanding entrance, while he pulled her body on top of him. As they laid there, kissing, his cock stirred to attention. Teasing him, Sasha ground her pelvis against his length.

"Sasha, I want you. Ride me, beautiful," he said on a groan.

She grabbed a condom from her nightstand and admired his length as she rolled it down. With her hands on JD's chest and his hands on her hips, she sank down on top of him. She loved the feel of every inch going deeper and deeper inside her. She bent over and kissed him, feeling the twitch of his cock inside her.

They moved together. She rocked her hips, her head thrown back in ecstasy. JD pulled her down over him, so she was completely filled by his length. He grabbed her ass tightly. "Oh yeah, your ass is amazing. You feel so good Sasha." Sasha's tongue failed her. She couldn't articulate any thoughts.

She muttered, "JD, yes." She started moving faster. As she felt the beginnings of another orgasm building, she moved her hips more forcefully.

"Oh hell, yeah. Like that Sasha. Don't stop." JD spurred her movements by pulling on her hips.

She wanted to come with him. "I'm close JD," she gasped out.

JD thrust from beneath her. He pulled her tight to him. They worked together in sync to reach the height of their release. They both shouted at the same time. Until, finally, Sasha collapsed on top of him. She would have stayed there and fallen asleep if he hadn't gently pulled out of her to take care of the condom.

Sasha briefly considered a time where they would not need to worry about using condoms. She was on the pill and didn't need to worry about getting pregnant. But she refused to consider the fantasy further as she didn't want to think about JD with any other women.

Chapter 9

Ian

While waiting for JD to arrive for Sunday brunch, Ian asked his mom how his aunt was faring following her mailbox incident. His mom confirmed that his idea for a check, a new mailbox, and a plate of his aunt's famous cookies resolved the matter without a trip to a courtroom.

JD finally showed up about forty-five minutes late to brunch. He kissed his mother's cheek. "Sorry I'm late mom, I missed the L and had to wait for another."

Ian looked at him and rolled his eyes. Did JD think that excuse was going to fly? His mother had lived in Chicago her entire life and was familiar with the elevated train system and knew that they ran every ten minutes. Ian leaned back in his seat waiting for his mom's grilling to commence.

His mom tilted her head on an angle and glared at JD. "A late train, huh? There isn't a train that runs between your apartment and our home, so I assume that you weren't coming from your place. And, I assume that since you were somewhere besides your apartment early on a Sunday morning that you were with a woman. And, I assume that since you were with a woman that it wasn't one of your puck bunnies because I know you never spend the night. And—"

JD stood his ground. He didn't cower to his mom's

harassment. JD cut her off, "Stop with all the assuming." JD scoffed, flattening his normally smiling lips.

JD looked at Ian and gestured to his mom. "So this is where you got your lawyerly skills from? Mom?"

"Appears so." Ian laughed at JD's discomfort, like they were teenagers. His mom smiled broadly, which amused Ian.

"So can I assume that you were with the girl that you had talked about last week?" His mom pried, stopping her process of tidying up the room.

"You know mom, maybe you should have gone into law. You would be great at deposing witnesses." Ian fanned the flames of JD's irritation. JD scowled at him.

Ian's dad decided to get in on the making-JD-suffer fun. "Is that a new shampoo you are using? A little more feminine than I would care to use." JD crossed his arms across his chest and his smile disappeared.

Ian caught a whiff of JD. The scent smelled slightly like Alexandra's shampoo. If Ian knew the brand of shampoo, he would buy some. Ian covered his mouth with his hand, hiding the smile the scent triggered. That damn scent made him stupid.

"Ok, enough with the third degree," JD begged and looked at Ian with pleading eyes.

Ian shook his head at his brother. He wasn't about to help him. This was better than watching a cop show; Ian wanted to grab a bowl of popcorn, kick up his feet, and watch his parents interrogate JD.

"Were you with the girl from your art class?" His mom inquired while she returned to straightening up things. Ian was in awe of his mom's manipulative trick to act less interested in order to extract information.

Ian listened intently to JD's answer. Why hadn't JD

filled *him* in earlier?

His mom successfully broke JD. "Yes. I was with Sasha. We went for coffee last week. And Friday night, after my dumbass brother..." JD sneered at Ian, "Blew me off, we hung out at Lawson's Bar."

Ian's head popped up and interrupted. "Is she an attorney? Almost everyone at that bar works at a law firm."

"Don't be rude, Ian, your brother was talking." His mother chastised and shushed him.

JD faced him with a bored look on his face, "Answer to your question, yes, she is an attorney." JD returned to face his mom. "Anyways, we had a great time talking and had a few drinks at the bar."

Did they hook up after the bar? Ian wanted the details on the part of the story that JD conveniently skipped.

Ian's mom cleared her throat. "That was Friday night. Care to explain this morning?" She raised her eyebrows.

JD relaxed his arms and smiled. *Oh yeah, his brother totally got laid.* "Last night we went out for pizza and to the pier." JD glossed over the rest.

Three times in one week. That was a lot of time with one girl, particularly someone new. "Do you like her?" His mom had been able to read JD and Ian like a book their entire life. They were both incapable of hiding anything or lying to her.

"It's early days, but yeah." JD was short on words, but the fact that he spent so much time with her spoke loudly.

"Which is why you were late?" Ian snickered.

"Ian!" His mom scolded. Ian looked down

sheepishly, knowing his mom didn't appreciate distasteful insinuation. JD maintained his Cheshire cat grin.

JD's dad asked, "She knows that you aren't going to play hockey again?" The question was posed as an accusation. JD sunk back in his chair as if he had been shot by an arrow. Ian narrowed his eyes on his dad. He was shocked that his father would say something so abrasive to JD.

"James!" His mom shouted. "Hockey isn't everything." Ian appreciated his mom's protectiveness. JD didn't deserve his dad's impertinence.

"Ian left the sport and you didn't have a problem," JD spit out. His fists were clenched tight.

Ian tried to defend his brother, "If she is hanging out at Lawson's my guess is she doesn't care about hockey, dad." Ian didn't think his words penetrated either man.

"Actually, she's been supportive and helping me figure out what I want to do next," JD stared at his dad and passive aggressively accused him.

His mom stepped behind his dad and placed a hand on his dad's shoulder. "What does she want you to do?" His mom asked with suspicion.

"Nothing. She's been trying to help me figure out something that would make *me* happy. You know, look outside the box." JD looked expectantly towards his parents.

His mom smacked a hand on her thigh. "I think I like this girl." His mom said dramatically. "I want both of you to find someone that has your best interests at heart." His mom headed toward the dining room, calling out, "Why don't we all go sit down and eat."

After leading the family in grace at the table, Ian's

dad focused on him. "So, Ian, what about that Alexandra girl you mentioned?"

Now, his parents were turning the interrogation on him. *Great.* "Hah!" Ian guffawed, shaking his head.

JD's head spun towards Ian, "What's so funny?"

"She got moved in the firm. My boss fired someone and decided to bring in Alexandra to replace the person. Essentially, Alexandra directly reports to me. There is no chance I can pursue something now." Ian sunk back in his chair and sighed.

"That is a tricky pickle," his dad admitted, sitting forward in his chair with his forearms on his legs.

"It's a human resources stalemate is what it is." Ian raised his hand to his aching head.

"Wow, that really sucks, bro."

"Language, JD!" His mom scolded and narrowed her eyes at JD.

"But on a good note, I was able to convince a huge new client to sign with the firm. It was a really big deal and many of the partners congratulated me." Ian tried to smile, but his frustrating thoughts of Alexandra tarnished his enthusiasm.

"Congratulations!" His mom jumped up and gave Ian a hug.

"Bro, way to go!" JD knuckle-bumped his brother from across the table.

"Nice job son." His dad beamed with pride. The look on his dad's face meant the world to Ian. Winning his dad's approval meant nearly as much to him as winning on the ice or in court.

His mother smiled too, but there was a sadness in her eyes as well. When she offered her repeated comments about finding a woman, she wasn't selfishly vying for grandkids. She and his dad had an amazingly supportive marriage. She wanted him and JD to experience the same in life. He regarded the look on his mother's face and realized that it mirrored the sadness in his own heart.

Ian left his parents' house in an introspective state. He was happy for his brother's budding relationship and positive outlook on defining his next career move. In comparison, where was he? His career had momentum, but it always seemed like he was chasing a moving carrot. Would he ever actually manage to make that leap to becoming partner? Maybe he was too greedy to want both career satisfaction and an affectionate relationship. Ian fell back on what he did best and focused on work.

His office phone rang, which was unusual on a Sunday. One of the senior partners called to compliment him on the acquisition of the firm's newest client. He also asked numerous questions about how Stein aggravated the negotiation process. Ian refused to outright speak negatively about Mr. Stein. Speaking ill of his current boss could get him a lot of trouble, but not accepting his well-deserved credit for the client win could defeat his opportunity for making partner. *Office politics sucked.*

He returned to the work at hand, until he was interrupted once again. A soft knock on his door broke his stream of thought. He smelled her sweet scent before the opening door revealed her lovely face. His smile faded when he saw her swollen eyes. "Everything okay, Alexandra?" Ian worried.

"Everything's fine." She wore a forced smile on her face that looked terribly wrong on her.

Ian stood up and pulled his door shut. "I can tell that

everything is *not* fine Alexandra. What's going on?" He returned to his chair, keeping a desk's distance between them.

"Um, Mr. Stein just came into my office ranting about the fact that I failed to support him and his win last night by not showing up at Lawson's. He claimed that it was my duty. He didn't even let me know about an event at Lawson's, let alone invite me to join. If you hadn't mentioned it to me, I wouldn't have had any clue about what he was even talking about." She started breathing more quickly.

"I explained that I stayed late at the office, working on a brief. Then he sternly reminded me that I report to him and not to you. Then, in a semi-threatening manner, he noted that he had higher hopes for me than Hailey Coleman who didn't last long at the firm."

She swallowed and took a shallow breath. "Ian—I mean Mr. O'Malley, I don't know what I did wrong or how to go about fixing the situation." Her eyes were glassy by the time she finished.

Ian wanted to reach out with his arm and console her in a hug. "Alexandra, it will be okay. I don't think that Mr. Stein was in fact angry at you at all. You didn't do anything wrong and certainly didn't fail anyone." Damn, he preferred calling her Alexandra. Hearing her refer to him by his first name made his cock hard. He wanted to hear her screaming his name in ecstasy.

"I'm probably a fool to be telling you any of this. I don't want to put you in an awkward position. I know how much it means to you to make partner. I wouldn't do anything to screw that up for you. I promise." She hung her head in defeat. Ian felt a pull in his chest.

"Alexandra, it's okay. I want to help if I can.

Perhaps I didn't give Hailey enough help." Ian averted his eyes.

"Thank you for your concern, but this isn't your problem." Her eyes dropped to the desk. "I'm not good at this type of office politics." She breathed in deeply a few times. He wanted to walk around his desk and offer her a sympathetic hug.

A hug that led to more, which wouldn't have been bad, either. Well, it would have amounted to a total HR shit storm. Otherwise, it could have been spectacular like on the Fourth of July.

Ian remained on his side of the wooden desk. "Hey, I can understand your frustration. I'm not the best at office politics, either and I have only been here a handful or so more years than you. I'm probably not the best one to give advice as my singular focus on making partner might not offer you the best perspective. Maybe you should consider finding a mentor here. I think HR might have a program to help out." Ian wanted to help. He didn't want to accidentally enflame her situation unknowingly.

Alexandra swiped at her eye. "That's a good idea. Thank you, Ian, and thanks for caring enough to take the time to talk." Alexandra looked him directly in the eyes. Again, his heart felt a strong tug. "And Ian, be careful about Mr. Stein. I think he is trying to take all the credit for landing the new client. When he spoke with me, he referred to it as *his* win, not the team's win. He took complete ownership of signing the client."

Ian wasn't surprised by Mr. Stein speaking in such a manner. "Thanks Alexandra. I appreciate your concern." Ian couldn't speak out of turn about Mr. Stein, even in front of Alexandra. *Office politics sucked.*

Alexandra lingered in the doorway. Ian stared wordlessly. *Did she want something more?*

"I'll let you get back to work." Alexandra turned and walked out.

Ian did as Alexandra suggested and got back to work.

His uncertainty about dealing with office politics intensified as the week continued. Several senior partners reached out to him, asking him details about the negotiations with the real estate group. They asked very pointed questions about Mr. Stein. Ian never resolved to find an ideal answer that didn't outright highlight Mr. Stein's incompetence. He only hoped that he didn't jeopardize his job by answering poorly.

By Friday, he hoped not to be cornered again with questions in regard to Mr. Stein. But then he received a message from a senior partner to meet upstairs immediately. *Shit.* Ian's heart started to race, and his hands became damp.

During the elevator ride up to the fourth floor of the firm, he straightened his tie. He tapped his toes inside his shoes. He blew out slowly and stretched his fingers at his side. The elevator doors opened. He stood up straight, bit the inside of his mouth, and smoothed all expression on his face. He reminded himself to think positively.

A desk faced the elevators like a blockade. The receptionist served as the gatekeeper for the floor. The woman stood and walked toward him, greeting him but not offering a hand to shake.

"Mr. O'Malley? Follow me, please." She smiled politely.

He did as she asked, placing each foot methodically in front of the other. After passing several offices, they neared the large conference room. His view of the room was blocked by the blinds on the windows. His fingers began to tingle.

She opened the door and gestured for him to step inside. He was greeted by a couple of dozen people standing and staring at him.

His eyes went bright. He locked his wobbling knees.

One of the founding partners emerged from the group and acknowledged him. "Welcome, Mr. O'Malley. On behalf of all of us here, and those partners that weren't able to join us here today, we would like to ask you to be our newest partner at the firm."

His mouth went dry. He stared into all of their eyes.

"So, what do you say, Mr. O'Malley?" Everyone stared at him, waiting for his response.

He lost his ability to camouflage his emotions that he often utilized in a court room. He smiled like a hockey player skating around a rink carrying the Stanley Cup.

"Absolutely. There's nothing I want more." He rejoiced. His chest heaved as the restriction had finally been lifted. He beamed with pride as he shook all of their hands. The event spiraled into a mob of thank-yous and congratulations.

He returned to his office to read and sign the paperwork for the partnership agreement. As soon as it was signed, he reached to call his parents, but it was time for Mr. Stein's lunch and the announcement of Ian's partnership. The good news needed to wait.

With everyone in his section of the firm standing around, Mr. Stein quietly asked Ian to come forward and stand with him. Then, Mr. Stein addressed the entire group, "I would like to personally congratulate you, Mr. O'Malley, on a job well done. It seems as though my mentorship has paid off for Mr. O'Malley as I would like to introduce all of you to the newest partner at our firm. Congratulations Mr. O'Malley." Ian shook Mr. Stein's hand, who attempted to grasp Ian's hand unnecessarily tightly. With all of his years of playing hockey, Ian knew that he had the strength in his grip to crush Mr. Stein's fingers. While part of him would have enjoyed that, he refrained.

The entire room clapped in support of Ian. Pride exuded from him like sun rays. One by one, people congratulated Ian. Everyone was in good spirits, or at least pretending to be.

Ian looked around but didn't see Alexandra anywhere. He had seen her at the beginning of the lunch as he was always acutely aware of her presence. He assumed that she had heard the news about him becoming partner. *Why hadn't she taken the time to congratulate him?* Her absence was a black spot on his mood.

Immediately, after he returned to his office, Alexandra followed behind on his heels. Her timing was conspicuously opportune. It was too perfect to have been happenstance. She must have been attuned to his presence as he was to hers.

She carried a sizable, rectangular gold box with a white bow. She bounced on her toes with a giddy smile on her face and handed him the gift. "Many congratulations Ian. I couldn't be happier for you. I have been holding on to this bottle for a bit waiting for the big announcement. I always knew it would happen." She excitedly handed the gift to him.

"Thank you so much, Alexandra." He was more thrilled by her presence than receiving her present. He wanted to share this great moment with her. He wanted to hug her and kiss her. Instead, he looked down and looked at the label on the box. Holy Crap. Ian guessed that the bottle of champagne probably cost over five-hundred dollars.

"This is a very generous gift…" Ian shook his head in disbelief.

"I'm thrilled for you Ian. Now, you have everything that you wanted." Alexandra's grin reached her eyes. There was no sarcasm in her tone. No jealousy. No rancor. She stood in his office smiling, looking gorgeous.

Ian peered into her warm brown eyes. The same eyes he'd stared into as they joined intimately. The eyes that bore into him as she exploded in ecstasy around him. His heart clenched. There was a stabbing pain in the middle of his chest. His dad's voice reverberated in his head that there were more important things in life besides accomplishments at work.

"No. I don't," Ian said quietly.

She leaned in and cocked her ear towards him.

He stared directly into her eyes. "I want you, Alexandra. I have wanted you since the night we were together."

She gasped, placing a shaky hand on the chair. She broke eye contact with him and looked towards the floor.

Her eyes slowly rose to meet his. The warmth was gone and replaced by a soft sheen. "You told me you didn't want me, Ian."

The sting of her words struck him hard. "I'm sorry." Ian breathed, knowing that those words weren't sufficient.

Alexandra stepped away from him. "We never ran into each other here. I thought you purposefully avoided me. I respected your decision and kept my distance."

Ian started biting at his lip. The conversation wasn't playing out the way he hoped. "I did try to avoid you. It was stupid. I thought that out of sight meant out of mind. But I couldn't get you out of my mind. I was wrong to deny what I felt for you. I was wrong to not try and make things work with you. I…I want to make things right, Alexandra." Ian urged, his fingers frantically tapping on his leg.

She started fidgeting. "The night we spent together touched me deeply. It took me a long time to move on, Ian." She looked down again. She wouldn't look him in the eye.

She inhaled deeply. "I'm sorry, Ian. I'm seeing someone."

His chest felt like someone had punched him and knocked the wind right out of him. He sat on the corner of his desk. "Oh," he murmured. He hadn't considered that possibility. At least not to the extent that she would be involved with someone seriously enough to deny him. He needed clarification. "So you aren't interested in me anymore?"

"Congratulations Ian." And with that, Alexandra exited his office without answering him.

Wow. He felt like a deflated balloon. He had spent nearly a decade of his life determined to make partner and yet he felt miserable. He sat in his chair and rested his face on his hand. Alexandra's scent permeated his office. The scent mocked him. It teased and taunted him as the source walked out of his office, and life, forever. He only had himself to blame.

He lifelessly sunk into his chair and dialed his parents on their home phone. His mom picked up. "Ian, what's wrong? Why are you calling in the middle of the workday?"

Ian rolled his eyes at his mother's over reaction. "Nothing is wrong mom. Relax. Can you put dad on the phone too?"

Ian could hear his mom yell for his dad to pick up the phone, as she never remembered to press mute.

His chest felt tight. He couldn't breathe. He was distracted and let the silence hang until his dad picked up.

"Ian? What's wrong?" His dad jumped right in.

"Great news. I made partner today." His tone didn't match the happiness of the news.

A whoosh of breath being let out was followed by a brief pause. "That's fantastic son. I'm so proud of you and the perseverance it took to get this!"

His mom added, "Congratulations! We have to celebrate. Let's have a family dinner tomorrow."

"Sure. Thank you." He wasn't in the mood to celebrate, but he wasn't up for the challenge of debating his mom, either.

"What's wrong Ian? This is great news. Why don't you sound excited?" His mom probed, questioned, and cajoled him until he spilled his guts about his conversation with Alexandra.

"I'm so sorry, Ian," his mother commiserated.

His dad interjected, "I wouldn't completely count out a relationship with her. You never know what can change. Whatever relationship she's in today could fall apart tomorrow." His dad's determination suited Ian well in the past. His dad's never-give-up attitude helped Ian earn a Division I hockey scholarship. Ian owed his perseverance at work to his dad, as well. But that attitude only applied to things within Ian's control. He couldn't control other people's feelings.

"Whoever she's dating is never going to let her go, dad. No one else could ever make the same stupid choice that I did." Ian's head fell back in his chair. He closed his eyes, berating himself for having made such a terrible choice.

Chapter 10

JD

JD hoped that Sasha's work wouldn't fuck up their plans to go to the hockey game. He was bummed when she didn't show up last Sunday. He'd texted her before the start of class.

JD—*Looking forward to seeing you again in class today (star-eyed smiley face)*—

Sasha—*See ya later! (smiley face)*—

JD admittedly awaited her arrival. At first, he assumed that she was running late. As the time progressed, he fretted over her absence. For two hours, he repeatedly glanced at her empty art stool in between helping all the other students in the class, but she never showed.

To put his mind at ease, he checked on Sasha after class. He debated the tone of the message. Concern? Disappointment?

JD—*Everything okay? I missed seeing you in class (one-tear sad face)*—

He sent the message, but was pleasantly surprised when the moving dots appeared.

Sasha—*Things went sideways at work*—

He snubbed his nose in the air. Her job sucked. It kept him from being able to see her.

JD—*U okay? (kissing smiley face)*—

Sasha—*Crap situation, dealing*—

No shouty capitals. Maybe she wasn't too upset?

JD—*Want a distraction? (smiling devil)*—

He crossed his fingers.

Sasha—*With you, yes! (smiley face) No time (super sad face)*—

Bummer! JD frowned.

JD—*Sorry to hear. Totally unrelated, I got two hockey tickets for Friday night? Want to go with me?*—

Sasha—*YES! (cheerleader girl) Gotta get back to work*—

Yes! JD fist pumped the air.

JD—*(kissing smiley face)*—

Her enthusiastic response about going to the hockey game encouraged him. He understood from his brother that shit often arose at work and fucked up plans. JD didn't take it personally.

Late Monday evening, JD couldn't shake thoughts of Sasha out of his head. Rather than driving himself mad, he sent her a text to mollify the desire to communicate with her. He purposefully kept it light and quick.

JD—*Better day?*—

Sasha—*(glass of wine) My glass holds about a half a bottle of wine (smiley face)*—

JD worried. Was work driving her to drink?

Sasha—*looking forward to our date on Friday (hockey player)*—

He smiled. He hoped that she actually enjoyed watching the sport.

JD—*Me too. Get some rest. Gnight*—

For fear she was having a particularly bad week, JD restrained himself from disturbing her with too many messages. He waited until Thursday to message again.

JD—*(coffee cup) special delivery*—

Sasha—*(heart eyes smiling face)*—

He smiled, but then wanted to smack himself for getting so excited about a silly emoji.

Friday finally rolled around; the night of the hockey game. JD prayed that Sasha wouldn't bail. He considered texting her late in the afternoon to confirm, but she beat him to the punch and thrilled him by texting first.

Sasha—*I can't wait until our date tonight! What time?*—

Halleluiah! JD tilted his head upward and mouthed, *thank you.*

JD—*6:30 work for you?*—

Adding a time pressure might put her in an off mood. His leg bounced rapidly while he waited for her response.

Sasha—*Yes! See ya*—

"Yes!" JD spun around in his chair.

JD arrived at Sasha's building right on time, but when her doorman called up, Sasha didn't answer. The doorman mentioned that he had seen her go up to her apartment a few minutes earlier. JD asked if he could go up to help her speed up the process of her getting ready to avoid arriving late to the hockey game. Either the guy recognized him from the prior week or he was a hockey fan, regardless, he let JD onto the elevator.

He could hear loud music coming from inside Sasha's apartment. No wonder she didn't hear her phone. He knocked between songs. Sasha opened the door and breathlessly said hello. She threw herself at him and squealed as she hugged him.

Wow! He could get used to greetings like that.

He kissed her. "It's good to see you too." She leaned back in and extended the kiss.

He pulled away and quickly eyed her from head to toe. Damn. She looked too good. *Maybe they could be late to the game?*

"I'm so excited to go to the game with you tonight." She clapped her hands. "Yay!"

He laughed. "I can see that." Her eagerness was precious. Getting to experience going to a game with her made the wait worthwhile. "I'm glad. I was a little worried that you were going to be too tired to go tonight. I know you had a grueling week at work."

She put a finger to his lips. "Shhhh. Let's not talk about that."

JD kissed the finger that touched his lips. He playfully grabbed her arm and placed another kiss on the inside of her wrist. He reminded himself that they would have plenty of time after the game for more kissing.

"Are you ready to go?" The longer they lingered in her apartment, the more difficult it would be not to undress her and skip the game. "No rush if you need more time."

"Absolutely. No, wait." She kissed him, again, on the mouth, much longer than a peck. "Now, I'm ready." They gazed at one another for an extended beat.

Her playfulness really turned him on, tugging at his jeans. "Let's go before I change my mind and tie you to the bed." Her eyes lit up. *Did the idea of bondage turn her on?*

Her legs bounced during the entire ride to the arena. The car vibrated at the red lights. "I'm so excited to go to my first game." Sasha smiled the entire way.

The driver dropped them off a couple of blocks

away as the mass of people converging on the arena crippled traffic. The temperature was unusually mild. Neither of them needed a warm hat or scarf. A lot of other people didn't even bother with coats. Of course, they were most likely intoxicated. JD and Sasha walked amongst the sea of red jerseys entering the arena.

Sasha asked, "Seems like all the fans are wearing jerseys. Why aren't you wearing a jersey like everyone else?" She quickly threw her hand over her mouth. "Shit, was that a rude question to ask?"

"It's all good." JD kissed her. He didn't want her to feel like she had stuck her foot in her mouth. "I love hockey. I always will, even if I don't ever play seriously again." Sasha smiled. Like a hammer to his head, her smile made him realize the truth in his words. He *would* always love hockey.

"I'm not wearing a jersey because I actually have buddies on both teams tonight and don't want to pick sides." He quirked an eyebrow.

She blushed and surprisingly shared, "You are damn sexy bare chested with no jersey."

JD tugged on her on her hand. "Let's go. Your teasing is making it difficult for me not to drag you back home now."

They walked hand-in-hand amongst the throng of people. Sasha stumbled, but JD quickly caught her. "You, okay?" He asked.

"Yeah, sorry. Did you *see* that woman? Who the heck wears a skimpy outfit like that to a hockey game?" She gestured with her head toward the woman. JD didn't turn his head. The only woman he cared to check out was Sasha. The image of Sasha naked took center stage in his head. Again, he pushed that thought aside. Well, at least he tried.

He stopped right outside the entrance and pulled out his phone. "We need to get a selfie here, to commemorate your first hockey game. I'm so excited that I get to be the one to bring you."

She didn't make a scene demanding several photos to capture the perfect look. She approved of the first one, which captured a natural chemistry between the two. "Can you text me a copy?" JD sent it immediately.

They took their seats. While the players warmed up on the ice, she continuously swiveled her head all around the arena. "I know this is your first game, but is this your first time at the arena?" JD wondered out loud.

"Yes," she commented while continuing to look around.

JD was taken-back. "I thought you just hadn't been to a hockey game. I figured you had been to a concert or something else here."

She stopped looking around the arena and looked at him. "Nope. No concerts, shows, or any sports for that matter." Her lips formed a thin straight line. JD counted himself lucky that she was willing to make the time to enjoy the game with him.

The lights went dark, and the music blared. They both stood, along with everyone else, and cheered loudly as the players took the ice. While the lights were down, JD took advantage of the moment, held her cheek, and kissed her deeply. He pulled away just before the first flash of light.

During the first period, they got a couple of beers and pizza. He pointed out a few of the teams' strategies throughout the period, but didn't bore Sasha with a barrage of statistics. At one point during the game, he got completely immersed in the game. After the intense puck exchange, JD caught Sasha staring intently at him.

She blushed. "Sorry. The lighting in here reflects off of all the reds mixed in with your brown hair. I never noticed before."

JD tossed his long hair back and forth. "Always thinking about color, huh?" JD smirked, loving the way her brain worked.

She continued, "And your hazel eyes remind me of a paint pallet. When you watch the game there is a buoyant spirit swimming in all that color." She smiled and nodded.

JD liked that she stole looks at him. Nevertheless, he redirected her attention. "Enough about art tonight, we're at a hockey game."

Sasha cheered appropriately and loudly as the first period continued. For a little thing, she had a big voice.

The second period started typically slow. JD noticed Sasha's eyes wander away from the ice. She fixated on a guy carrying snacks.

She leaned over and whispered in JD's ear, "What's that blue and pink stuff that the guy over there is carrying?"

JD laughed. "You don't know what that is?" JD's eyes widened.

"No," she murmured and shook her head with a cute pouty lip.

JD got the guy's attention and bought her a bag. She held the bag in her hand and stared at it. She opened it with reservations in her eyes. "Um, how do you eat it?"

JD pulled off a piece. "Open up," he ordered, setting the cotton candy on her tongue.

She smiled like a child. "Oh my god, this is *amazing*.

It dissolved on my tongue! I could totally devour this, but I probably would have a major sugar crash later." She grabbed some for herself and popped it in her mouth.

JD kissed her before she put another bite in her mouth. "You are adorably beautiful." He kissed her again. "I want to devour you." He kissed her sincerely without crossing the line of inappropriate public display of affection. But then she licked the stickiness off her fingers, and his cock sprung to life.

Between the second and third period, Sasha exhaled under her breath, "What the heck?"

Her voice was so low, JD almost didn't hear her. "What?"

Sasha's eyes widened and blushed. She slyly pointed to the ice. "That's the women I saw walking outside earlier. What is she doing out there with a stick in her hand?"

JD glanced toward the ice and turned right back to the beautiful woman beside him. "That's all planned beforehand." The woman on the ice didn't compare to Sasha.

Sasha scoffed, "What else is planned with her looking like a hooker on ice?"

"I guess it's like the girls in bikinis that hold up oversized cards with the number of the round in boxing." JD had never given it much thought.

The teams were tied at the start of the third period. Each team scored another goal within a minute of each other. JD focused on the game. The home team scored another goal, and the crowd went crazy. He loved the action and the display of skill on the ice. He didn't have any skin invested in the game and the outcome lacked significance, but *damn* did he love every minute.

The game ended and JD turned to Sasha. "Are you officially a hockey fan now?"

"I'm officially a fan of watching hockey with you." Sasha chose the best way to answer, of course. JD smiled devilishly. Damn he liked her.

The crowd slowly exited the arena. JD possessively kept his hand on her back as they dodged people in the crowd. He walked with his chin held high, proud of the woman at his side.

They managed to locate the car that they ordered, setting off to the local sports bar. She gripped her hands together, pinching the skin between her thumb and forefinger. JD inserted his hand between her knotted entanglement. "Why are you nervous?" His smile didn't even calm her.

"What if your friends hate me?" Her smile looked strained.

"Not a chance." JD reassured her with another kiss. Nonetheless, she remained unusually quiet for the rest of the ride.

When they entered Luxury Box, JD found all his friends congregating in their usual corner. He escorted Sasha directly to the bar, suggesting a little liquid courage before meeting the entire crew.

A few of JD's friends stopped them before they made it all the way to the bar. As expected, they welcomed Sasha. She laughed as everyone was most eager to find out if she was a hockey fan. One of the guys teased her that she must only be going out with JD to get an A in the art class. Sasha quickly corrected him that in a community class there weren't any grades, but that it had taken her all semester to muster up the nerve to ask him out.

Finally, they reached the bar and JD ordered a couple of shots. After they threw them back, Sasha excused herself to use the restroom.

JD stopped her before she walked away. "You aren't stalling to meet the rest of my friends, are you?" he teased.

Sasha shook head. "No, your friends that I have so far met are great. Most of the people I generally meet at Lawson's are judgmental assholes. Your friends rock. I'll be right back." Then she disappeared. JD chuckled to himself. Ian had mentioned something similar about the vibe of Lawson's compared to Luxury Box. *Ian and Sasha would probably get along.*

While she was gone, Kurt came by with a puck-bunny in tow. She was wearing a short plaid skirt with thigh high stockings and her top revealed a dramatic amount of cleavage. Kurt didn't waste time with introductions, but outright asked if JD was interested in a hook-up with him and the girl.

Before JD could tell Kurt to fuck-off, Sasha returned from the restroom. JD looked at the feral expression on her face. If she were a cat, her claws would have been extended.

He reached for her hand and tucked her into his side. "Kurt, this is my girlfriend, Sasha." The puck-bunny looked down her nose at Sasha. JD didn't acknowledge the woman and spoke directly to Sasha. "Kurt and I went to college together."

Kurt interjected, "Nice to meet you, Sasha. See ya, White Lighting." He didn't stick around to chat.

Sasha snickered. "Oh My God, was that the girl from the rink?" Her mouth hung open.

JD shrugged. "I don't know. I didn't really notice.

Want to get another drink?"

Sasha still looked a little shocked. "What did they want?" She looked in Kurt's direction once again.

"Unimportant," JD brushed off the question. "Want another drink before heading over to the table?"

Sasha put her hand on JD's chest. "JD, let me remind you that I am an attorney and I know avoidance techniques. And you are clearly avoiding the question. What. Did. They. Want?" Sasha articulated pointedly.

JD sighed and rolled his eyes. "The puck bunny wanted a Devil's threesome with two hockey players." He repositioned his feet into something that resembled a boxer's stance and braced for the questions sure to follow.

"What the hell is a puck bunny and a Devil's threesome?" Sasha threw up her hands in the air.

He didn't want a scene. "Puck bunnies are chicks that hit on hockey players and a threesome involving two straight men and one woman," he said in a clinical tone.

Sasha probed further, "So, Kurt walks into the bar while I'm in the restroom. And the first person he presumably turns to for a threesome, is you? Why would he come to you?" Damn she was good at reading between the lines.

JD took a deep breath. It was best just to answer quickly and not draw it out. "Kurt and I topped a few women together while in college." He didn't concoct a long story. He didn't play dumb. Everyone had a sexual past. He was sure Sasha did as well, but he preferred to remain oblivious to it.

"Oh." Sasha's mouth hung open. JD was thankful that she didn't respond hysterically, but he didn't move yet. "Were you and Kurt together," Sasha paused. "You know, together, together?"

"I'm heterosexual, if that's what you are asking." JD raised an eyebrow at her and peered at her.

Sasha's blush surprised him. "What's got you blushing this time, Sasha? You put me in the hot seat. It's time for you to fess up. It's only fair." He placed his chin on his fist dramatically and cocked his hip to the side. He wasn't going to let this one slide. The puck was on her side of the rink now.

The pink in Sasha's cheeks deepened. "Remember the other night when you asked me what was on my bucket list." She fidgeted.

"Yes. And I remembered you blushed then too." JD's smirk turned devilish. He wanted to know more.

Sasha looked down at the ground. "I…have always wanted a threesome with two men."

JD cupped her downturned head in his hand and made her face him. He kissed her hard. "I like knowing you have a naughty side. It's hot." He continued to hold her head in place so she couldn't turn away. "But, don't even think about asking me for a threesome with Kurt."

"No worries with that one. I think he's going to need a full course of antibiotics after tonight," Sasha chided and rolled her eyes.

JD shot her his most sexy smile. "Though I would be more than happy to pleasure you in ways that simulate being in a threesome."

Sasha raised her eyebrows, "Now, I have a lot more questions. Most of those I'll save for later when we are alone. But first, why did Kurt call you White Lightning?"

That wicked smile of hers was sexy as fuck. "I want to answer all your questions. Care to go back to my place?" All the talk of sex made him want *one* thing with only *one* woman. Sasha eagerly agreed. Thank God.

They said goodbye to the rest of JD's friends. Luckily, they didn't cross paths with Kurt again.

JD decided to make a slight detour before heading back to his apartment. It was easy enough to keep Sasha in the dark as she didn't know the actual location of his place.

She patted him on the leg. If she was trying to abruptly get his attention, it definitely worked on one member of his body. "Time to spill. What's up with the White Lightning nickname?" She pleaded.

Her curiosity was cute. "It kind of means two things. On the ice, I was the fastest guy on the team…"

"That's a cool nickname."

"Sure," he agreed. JD rolled his head and tilted it to the side. "But it also means illegally brewed whiskey."

"Ahh, so not your favorite nickname?" She frowned. "I can relate."

He tossed up his hands. "And the name stuck." He huffed. "Better than being called whiskey dick."

"I can vouch that one doesn't apply." She kissed him. "What do you prefer? JD or Jameson?"

He stared stupidly at her, noting that she didn't make assumptions about his preferences. "Jameson is too long to scream out when I make you come, and I plan on making you come again and again tonight."

"I can't argue with that logic. I'll stick with JD." She kissed him again. He liked her playfulness and how she freely kissed him.

She grabbed his hand. "I have another follow-up question to something you mentioned in the bar."

"So inquisitive," he mocked.

She cocked her head to the side and apologized,

"Nature of the job, sorry."

"No worries." He was used to the third degree from his brother, and his mother.

"Are you going to explain…" She blushed.

"I have a better idea." JD waggled his eyebrows.

Her voice pitched upward, "Really?" She raised an eyebrow back at him.

The car came to a stop. He reached for her hand as he got out. "Let's go. I promise to make it worth your while."

She took his hand and eagerly followed. Her trust in him touched him.

The lights for the adult toy store were still on. The great thing about adult sex toy stores in Chicago were that they were open late when you really needed to purchase something and didn't have time to wait for delivery. This one was open twenty-four hours. Sasha paused on the sidewalk and looked up at the store sign. JD pulled a hesitant Sasha by the hand into the store.

Inside the store, he took charge. "Some other time we'll shop casually. But for tonight, let's get a couple things and get to my place. ASAP." JD winked at Sasha. She blushed. "Damn. That blush is adorable. Fuck that, it's wicked."

The salesperson was extremely helpful. He directed JD and Sasha to the dildo section and helped them choose the material and size that suited their needs. When JD briefly explained what they were interested in, the salesperson also suggested a few other items.

Luckily, the walk to his place wasn't far. He was anxious to try out the new toys. As he unlocked the front door of his two-flat Sasha exclaimed, "This place is huge. Is it all yours?"

"No. The owner split it into two separate apartments." While they stood in the foyer, he pointed to the two entrances to the separate apartments. "This is mine." He unlocked the first-floor apartment door. No lights peeked out from underneath the upstairs door.

JD wasn't interested in giving a tour of his apartment. The only real estate he cared about was Sasha's naked flesh.

"You need to get out of those clothes," he commanded as he began stripping. Damn all those winter layers. JD took less care and shed his clothes much more quickly than Sasha. He grabbed the brown bag with their new toy collection, making a pitstop in the bathroom to unwrap and clean their purchases.

JD stood at the sink and was intently focused on cleaning the items properly yet quickly when Sasha's chilled hands landed on his belly. His abs tightened in response.

She began tracing her finger along the divots between his abdominal muscles. "You are incredible."

The feel of her hands was incredible. His cock started to harden. She ran her hands up his chest. His eyes closed as his head fell backward. His cock continued to swell. She scraped a fingernail over his nipple and kissed his shoulder blade. He hardened to full mast.

She sank to her knees. "Sasha...Oh hell, yes," he moaned.

JD moved to allow her access to his length. He watched as his cock disappeared in her mouth then reappeared glistening with her saliva. It was almost as hot as seeing his cock coated with her cum.

He was so lost in pleasure that he had almost

forgotten his promise of making her scream. He wasn't about to go back on his word. He had new toys at his disposal and he planned to use them. Most importantly, he intended on giving Sasha a night she wouldn't forget.

She looked up at him with half lidded eyes. JD rasped, "Fuck, that feels so fucking good. But I want to be in you. Go get on my bed. Now." He used one hand to help Sasha up off her knees and the other to grab the dildo.

Damn she looked beautiful on his bed. He stood staring at her image. She curled her finger at him, requesting him to come closer. "Don't make me wait," she taunted. Her seductive stare was hot as fuck.

"Good things come to those who wait." JD winked.

He reached into his nightstand drawer and grabbed a bottle of lube, preparing for stage two. Her lips parted as if she were about to ask a question, but JD kissed her deeply, shutting her up. While kissing her, he reached between her legs. Her moisture had seeped onto her thighs. She was wet and ready. He leaned back and inserted the dildo into her wet entrance. She rocked her hips against his strokes. Her moans became louder. Her sweet feminine scent filled the room.

He broke the kiss and her lazy dreamy eyes opened just enough to watch him. He opened the nearby lube, coating his finger and placing his digit at Sasha's star-shaped entrance. "Mmmm," she whimpered. JD soothed the opening with lube before pressing into her.

He removed the dildo from Sasha's greedy cunt. Her eyes popped open and narrowed at him. He needed to make her feel empty and wanting. Without his cock in her mouth, he was also feeling bereft. His single finger teased her as he spread the lube inside her.

Sasha pushed back against JD's hand, voicelessly asking for more. He graciously added a second finger in her backdoor. He began to fuck her with his fingers while slowly stretching her. Her whimpers grew louder.

He patiently ensured that she was well prepped. Extra prep time would heighten her desire and assuage his entrance. He was intent on enhancing her experience. While stroking in and out of her ass, JD implored, "Can I fuck you here? I want your tight ass gripping my cock"

"Yes. Please, JD!" She begged as her fists gripped the sheets.

JD gloved up, coated his cock liberally with more lube, and pressed his way into Sasha's opening. She pushed back onto JD, setting the pace for her to take him comfortably. She breathed through a second of resistance but then relaxed. He reveled in the persistent slow glide.

JD held Sasha's hips and kept her from hastening the pace, until she was begging. "JD, please," she whined. "I need more." He refused to give in to her desires. He wanted the need to build. In desperation, she reached to touch her clit, but JD grabbed her wrist.

That was the sign JD was looking for from Sasha. "Want to use the dildo too?"

"Yes," Sasha begged.

He handed the large red silicone replica to her. He gave her the control to adjust the tight fit. She didn't waste any time gliding it inside her. She moaned, "Holy crap." Her jaw relaxed. "Ahhh!"

"Too much?" JD worried, trying to read the expression on her face.

"So good, so full, so…" her voice trailed off.

JD paused his thrusting motion while Sasha took in every inch of the dildo in her channel. As soon as it was fully seated inside her, JD began to thrust again.

"Oh God, JD." Sasha was breathing hard. "JD," she chanted.

A flush spread across her skin and the muscles in her legs tightened. He was close to climaxing too. The sound of her throaty calls was more than he could handle. He leaned over and bit into Sasha's shoulder. She screamed in ecstasy. JD grunted like a wild animal as he came hard in a thunderous roar.

"Holy Crap," she panted. "That was amazing, JD." He gave her a quick peck on the lips then laid on his side, drawing with his finger on her hip.

"I told you JD would be easier to scream than Jameson," he whispered. They breathlessly laughed.

After cleaning up, Sasha fell asleep in his arms. JD stayed awake for a bit, enjoying the warmth of Sasha alongside of him, in his bed.

The next morning, he woke up before Sasha and decided to make breakfast for her. By the time she padded into the kitchen, he had plates of eggs and bacon ready on the kitchen island and was adding toast.

"What's this?" She kissed him and stole a piece of bacon from the plate. "Thank you."

"I'm hoping that my cooking will entice you to return to my place." JD smiled sweetly.

"Don't be silly, JD. Your hot body and the toys we didn't get to try out last night are more than enough." She laughed, which caused her braless breasts to jostle erotically under his t-shirt. *Was she wearing panties?*

"Oh, so last night you were adorably blushing at the bar and this morning you're all cheeky and insatiable?" JD teased. "Let's finish breakfast first, then we can see to your other needs." He said even though he really wanted to fuck her, there and then, in his kitchen.

They ate in silence until JD's phone chirped with a message.

Mom—*Don't forget dinner tonight at 5. Invite Sasha (heart-eyed face)*—

JD rolled his eyes.

Sasha paused midbite. "Something wrong?"

"Yes. My mom's use of emoji is disturbing." JD flinched. Sasha laughed.

"She would like me to invite you to dinner tonight at their house." JD looked at Sasha's face to gauge her reaction.

She gave away nothing, immediately donning a poker face. "Do you want me to meet your family tonight?"

JD debated how to answer. It was early days in their relationship, but he had never felt so close to any other woman. Logically it seemed to soon, but it felt right. "I do. I would really like for you to come to dinner tonight and meet my family." JD watched Sasha carefully, waiting for her answer.

Her face softened as she smiled. "Great. What time's dinner?" A sense of tension in his body released.

"Five." He took a second glance at his phone to make sure he remembered the time correctly.

"Oh jeez, I better get out of here so that I can get work done and be ready in time." She jumped out of her seat. "I need to get back home, shower and change, and get into the office." Sasha frantically started hunting for her clothes that had been unceremoniously discarded about his living room.

"Woah, woah, woah. I didn't mean to make you rush out here," JD protested. He tried to grab her, but she was moving intently. His chance for after-breakfast sex had slipped away. Instead, he planned to line things up for later. "After dinner tonight, would you want to come back here for the night?"

As she picked up her clothes, she brushed by JD and answered his question with a kiss. "Yes, that's great."

He wished she would slow down so they could talk for a minute. "Maybe you should consider packing some clothes to save you the hassle of running home before work tomorrow morning." As soon as the words left his mouth, he realized that would probably be a hassle for her. He flipped strategies. "Or maybe you'll invite me to your place where it would be easier for you. I can easily throw a few things in a gym bag."

She finally stopped and looked at him.

"I like that idea. You are full of great ideas." She smiled and formally asked JD in a dramatic fashion, "Would you do me the honor of staying at my place tonight." She blushed.

This time he knew what that blush meant. "Yes, and I won't forget to pack the other toys." JD smiled all too pleased with himself.

"Hot and devilishly smart. You, JD, are the total package." The compliment surprised JD. Sure, woman usually admired his body, but not his intellect. Sasha kissed him. She was nearly fully dressed. She spritzed herself with some fresh perfume and threw her hair up in a messy bun.

They lingered in the foyer while waiting for her rideshare. Passing the time, they fooled around like teenagers.

After Sasha left, JD changed into running clothes. He was fueled from the breakfast and energized from a night with Sasha. Buzzing with enthusiasm, he stretched before hitting the pavement.

Ian's door opened and JD turned and looked up the stairs at his brother. Ian sluggishly closed and locked his door. With heavy footsteps, Ian trudged down the stairs. JD greeted, "Good morning, hot shot! Congratulations on making partner!" He embraced Ian in a manly hug.

Ian grunted, "MmmHmm."

Ian's bloodshot eyes, drooping head, and lack of speech told a whole story. His brother was hungover.

"Fun night celebrating?" JD mocked.

Ian leaned his head against the wall in the foyer. "Too many drinks. Everyone pushed more and more alcohol my way."

"Admit it man, you're too old for that kind of drinking. You aren't in college anymore. You aren't even in your twenties." JD felt it was his duty as a brother to give Ian a hard time, but he was considerate enough not to speak too loudly.

"No kidding. I threw up several times last night." Ian closed his eyes.

"You aren't driving to work in your state?" Ian shook his head back and forth. He clutched his head and moaned. "Good luck getting any work done with your hangover." Ian moaned again. "Well, this has been an enlightening conversation," JD joked. "Hopefully, you'll be feeling better later when we get to celebrate with the rents tonight. Oh and yeah, I'm bringing Sasha tonight."

Ian nodded in the affirmative, inhaling deeply. *Was he going to throw up again?* His eyes drew together like he was in pain. JD offered Ian a reprieve from conversation and shoved off for his run.

Chapter 11

Sasha

Sasha set an alarm at work for late afternoon. She met JD at his place. Fearing being late and making a terrible first impression, she skipped stopping at home to change her clothes. Instead, she wore a new dress that she hoped looked appropriate for work, attractive for JD, and suitable for his parents.

She eyed the front door cautiously as JD parked the car in his parent's driveway. She needed a moment to compose herself. The passenger door opened, and JD extended his hand inside. She accepted it, murmuring quietly, "Thank you." She appreciated the chivalrous act.

JD squeezed her trembling hand as they walked toward the door. "Stop worrying. Everything is going to be great. My parents are going to adore you." They paused before the door, JD kissing her on her head. Sasha silently prayed for that to be true. Her mouth felt parched.

"You look beautiful, by the way." He gave her one last peck before he knocked on the front door. Sasha forced a smile on her face.

Mrs. O'Malley opened the door and welcomed her with a beaming smile, pulling her into a hug. She exuded the same kind of warmth as JD. "Please come in. I'm so glad you were able to join us for dinner, Sasha." Sasha relaxed a smidge.

She handed Mrs. O'Malley the bouquet of flowers that she picked up on the way. "Well, aren't these lovely. Thank you so much Sasha. I'm going to go put these in water and put them on the table to spruce it up." Sasha wiped her sweating palms on her jacket, before JD took it and hung it up.

JD placed his hand on her back and guided her through the house. The feel of his hand comforted her. She was delighted that JD didn't refrain from such contact in front of his parents. He made everything feel more carefree.

They entered what was presumably the living room, where the older gentleman rose out of his chair. JD introduced his dad and Mr. O'Malley greeted her with a firm handshake. He was more reserved than Mrs. O'Malley, but his mannerisms were still sociable, not standoffish.

Sasha looked between JD and his dad; the resemblance was uncanny. They both had amazing hazel eyes. "Nice to meet you Mr. O'Malley. I can see where JD got his good looks."

Mr. O'Malley laughed and turned to JD. "I like this one. She's a keeper."

"Thanks dad," JD mocked and brushed his hand reassuringly along the side of her arm.

Mrs. O'Malley entered the room and exasperatedly asked, "James, have you offered Sasha a drink?"

"I was about to, honey." Mr. O'Malley rolled his eyes. "Can I get you something, Sasha?"

"Thank you, Mr. O'Malley, that would be nice." She needed a drink. She had never done this meeting the parents thing. It was nerve wracking.

JD asked, "Want a beer?" Sasha nodded yes. "I'll go grab a couple from the fridge.

Sasha turned to Mrs. O'Malley. "Is there anything I can do to help in the kitchen?"

"No thank you, everything is all-ready. We are just waiting for JD's brother to arrive. He texted a few minutes ago that he was running late." She didn't seem surprised or annoyed by her other son's tardiness.

JD handed a beer to Sasha and explained, "My brother is always late because of work."

Mrs. O'Malley shooed-off JD's comment. "Never mind that."

JD also handed a beer to his dad.

"Thanks Jameson." Mr. O'Malley tipped his beer to JD.

"I notice you are the only one that calls JD, Jameson," Sasha pointed out and sipped her beer.

"That's because it is a great name. Son of James, what could be more fitting, right?" Mr. O'Malley claimed. He went on to explain how he had named JD. Although she already knew the story, she didn't interrupt. It was heart-warming to hear him sound so proud.

"It is a great name." Sasha turned to JD with a conspiratorial smile.

Mrs. O'Malley patted her husband's leg lovingly. "I agree it is a good name," she conceded. "I just hated all the whiskey related nicknames that it spurred."

"I can fully appreciate that Mrs. O'Malley. My last name is Smirnova. I suffered through too many vodka jokes once I moved here from Russia. I know that nicknames can sometimes get tiring." Sasha commiserated. "But I do like JD as a nickname." JD winked at her. Her cheeks grew warm.

Mrs. O'Malley pushed for more information. "JD tells us that Sasha is a nickname that your father and mother call you."

"Yes. It is actually a very common nickname in Russia. Even boys named Alexander are called Sascha. It's just spelled differently," Sasha began to explain but then a noise came from the front of the house. It sounded like a door opening and closing.

Mrs. O'Malley ignored it and continued, "What is your full name?"

Sasha kept her focus on JD's mom as she answered, "Alexandra Smirnova."

"That's a beautiful name," Mrs. O'Malley commented and looked over Sasha's shoulders.

Sasha heard footsteps approaching her from behind. Mrs. O'Malley beamed, "Oh good, Ian, you're here. Come meet Sasha."

Did she hear Mrs. O'Malley correctly? JD's brother's name was Ian? Must have been a bizarre coincidence. She must have misheard. Sasha placed her half-empty beer on the coffee table and slowly turned to verify.

"Alexandra!" Ian screeched like a record coming to a halt. Towering over her as she sat in a chair, he scowled at her.

"Ian?" Sasha looked up and whispered. She turned cold. Her hands and feet went numb. She began to shake.

"What are you doing here?" Ian turned to his mom and barked. "Is this some kind of a joke?" If it was, this was the worst kind of joke Sasha had ever heard.

"Ian! You're being rude," Mrs. O'Malley chastised. JD got out of his chair and stood between Sasha and Ian.

"Alexandra, what are you doing here?" Ian accused.

Sasha stood up. She stilled and stared at Ian, blinking to see if her eyes were fooling her. Realization crashed into her. *Ian* was JD's brother. *JD* was Ian's brother. Fuck. She had unknowingly slept with two *brothers*.

"What the hell is your problem, Ian?" JD accused, partially blocking Sasha from Ian's view.

"*This* is Sasha? The Sasha that you have been dating?" Ian challenged, his gesticulations increasing in intensity.

"Yes, I told you this morning that I was bringing her tonight." JD moved closer to Sasha and put his hands on her waist.

Ian glared at JD's hands. His nostrils flared and his breathing was clearly audible in the midst of everyone's silence. The fists at Ian's side concerned her. *Was he going to hit JD?*

"That is *Alexandra*. The Alexandra that I told you about." His voice sounded strained. His body curled inward and he hung his head. "The Alexandra that I'm in love with."

Sasha's jaw dropped. *What the hell did Ian say?* He loved her? Was this a dream? She must have been seeing and hearing things. She felt lightheaded. What was happening? There was no way for this to be real. It was too much to process. This was unbelievable.

Mrs. O'Malley took Sasha's hands in her own. "Sasha, I think you might need to sit down." She helped her to a chair.

"Her name is *Alexandra*," Ian repeated. The irritation in his voice confused her. *The whole situation was confusing.*

JD knelt in front of the chair where she was sitting and begged, "Sasha?" He held her hands in his, staring at her.

Ian took a step closer to her.

"Back up, Ian!" JD warned and put out a hand in warning.

"Fuck off JD!" Ian escalated, leaning over JD.

"Boys!" Mrs. O'Malley shouted. "Both of you, sit down." She pointed to two seats away from Sasha. "Give Sasha some space. James, why don't you go get her a glass of water."

Mrs. O'Malley approached Sasha, and asked softly, "Are you okay?"

"No, I don't think so." Her voice quivered. She glanced at the two men. JD looked confused and Ian appeared crushed. The tears began to spill from her eyes. "I don't know how this happened. How-How could this have happened?" She mumbled.

"It's a *bleedin* mess," Mr. O'Malley overstated the obvious.

Sasha agreed; it was a fucking nightmare. She closed her eyes tightly and prayed that she would wake up.

"James, that isn't helpful," Mrs. O'Malley corrected.

"Sasha," Mrs. O'Malley started.

"Her name is Alexandra," Ian enunciated each word.

Mrs. O'Malley scowled at Ian, and asked politely, "What name do you prefer, Alexandra or Sasha?"

"I prefer Sasha," she mumbled. She could barely think and her voice was hardly intelligible.

Ian harumphed! He crossed his arms in front of his chest.

JD slouched in a chair and covered his face with his hands.

All while Sasha struggled to breathe, feeling like an elephant sat on her chest.

Mrs. O'Malley began, "I don't want to offend you, but I think we all need to be on the same page here."

Sasha nodded in agreement. She didn't argue. As painful as this discussion was going to be, both brothers needed to understand.

"I know this is hard for all three of you. I love my boys." Mrs. O'Malley sent each of her boys a death glare making it clear that they should not even consider interrupting her. "Let's try and start at the beginning. From what I understand, you met Ian last Fourth of July." Sasha nodded and Mrs. O'Malley continued, "Then you realized you worked at the same law firm." Sasha nodded again. "But then you both decided not to see each other."

Sasha looked to Ian, knowing that it was Ian who had made that call. Ian hung his head knowingly.

JD didn't hold back, firing at Ian, "No! Ian didn't want a relationship with Sasha."

Ian's head popped up. "Fuck off JD. That's not it." Ian's knuckles turned white as he gripped the arms of the chair in which he was sitting.

JD continued, "Really? Did you ever call her again? Did you do anything to continue a relationship? Did you not tell her you didn't want to see her again?" JD argued like an attorney. Sasha was shocked by JD's articulation as he was normally so laid back.

"Shut. The fuck. Up, JD." Ian cursed.

"Great argument coming from a man that just became a partner at a law firm," JD insulted Ian.

Oh my god. This was supposed to be Ian's

celebration dinner. She looked at Ian again. He should be riding a high and celebrating. But no, he sat there looking miserable. Sasha needed to get out of there. She'd ruined everything between JD and herself. She'd ruined Ian's big promotion. *It was all her fault.*

Standing up, Mrs. O'Malley faced both JD and Ian, and bellowed, "Boys! You're not helping."

Sasha attempted to stand, her legs wobbling.

"Sasha, please." Mrs. O'Malley gingerly captured Sasha's hands. "Please sit. I can't imagine how painful this is for you, but could you please elaborate on what happened. Better than my two hot-headed sons."

JD and Ian didn't respond to their mother flinging shade in their direction.

Sasha hesitated. "I didn't think that Ian would ever consider having a relationship with me because we worked together." Sasha dropped her head. The disappointment hurt. Her chest squeezed tightly; her admission crushed her.

JD hopped to his feet and yelled at Ian, "See! It was over between you and Sasha."

"Sit down Jameson!" Mr. O'Malley ordered. JD obeyed his father's command. JD's leg bounced rhythmically. Was he going to spring out of the chair again like a jack-in-the-box?

Ian held his head in his hand, looking at the floor.

Mrs. O'Malley began again, "Then you met JD?" Sasha nodded. "And then you and JD started dating?"

She nodded again, smiling softly as she looked to JD. "Yes." JD returned her smile. She wanted to kiss that smile and comfort him.

"I can tell by your reaction, but let's just be clear here: You didn't know that Ian and JD were brothers?"

Mrs. O'Malley looked around the room.

"No. They don't really look alike. Ian is taller and JD is more rugged. And their eyes…I mean I guess I can see the resemblance now with everyone sitting here. And O'Malley is a common name. No offense. I didn't put it together." Sasha's chin quivered as the tears started streaming down her face. "I-I didn't mean for this to happen."

"Oh honey, nobody is accusing you of intentionally creating this situation." Mrs. O'Malley offered Sasha a comforting hug. "And no one is to blame for this situation." Mrs. O'Malley looked at JD. "Don't go blaming Ian for this either." Then she turned and pointed to Ian. "And don't you think about blaming JD, because he's not clairvoyant."

Mr. O'Malley remained in his chair, adding, "It's obvious that both Ian and JD care for you." Ian had professed his love to her in front of all of them. Mr. O'Malley continued to speak calmly, "And I assume, that since you came here today with JD, that he is important to you as well. And from reading the concern all over your face, that you still have some kind of feelings for Ian too?"

She looked at Ian and whispered, "Yes." A glimmer of hope lit up in Ian's eyes.

She turned to JD. "I'm so sorry." JD looked like she had kicked him in the stomach.

"I should go," Sasha muttered and stood up once again, prepared to walk out the door. "I can't believe this is happening. I really should leave. I'm so sorry. I didn't ever mean to make a huge mess, but that's exactly what this is. There is no way in the world that I would ever choose between Ian or JD. I could never do that." Sasha looked at both men. "As if either of you would ever want to be with me after this." She started for the door.

"Sasha," JD pleaded, following her.

"Alexandra, please," Ian implored as he walked beside JD.

As she put on her coat, she added, "I'm sorry I ruined your dinner, Mrs. O'Malley. I realize that this was supposed to be a celebration dinner for Ian. I'll leave now, so you can celebrate his great accomplishment. Again, I'm so sorry JD."

"Sasha, don't do this. Don't leave. Please," JD begged, reaching for her but she stuffed her hands in her pockets.

Mrs. O'Malley stepped between Sasha and the men. "While I love my boys Sasha, I'm worried about you as well. I know you mean a lot to both of them. I understand why you want to leave right now and I'm not going to stop you. I know this is equally difficult for all three of you. You all need time to think. Can I ask one thing of you right now? Can I call and see how you are doing tomorrow?"

Sasha didn't respond.

Mr. O'Malley offered to drive her home, but she declined. She wanted to get away.

JD and Ian made another gentle attempt to beg Sasha not to leave as the rideshare approached. Sasha looked out of the rear window of the car as it drove away. JD and Ian stood on the stoop looking in her direction.

Tears streamed down her face.

Chapter 12

JD

JD stared at the car as Sasha drove off. He gripped the back of his neck and rubbed at the tension in his muscles. The view morphed into a sad, gray water-color. The image of Sasha faded away like bleeding paint. He re-entered his parents' house. Despite having grown up in the house, nothing appeared recognizable. Everything was upside-down and inside out.

"You motherfucker!" Ian roared and shoved JD.

The aggressive move knocked JD out of his stupor. He adjusted his posture defensively.

"Fuck You!" JD retorted. How dare Ian yell at him. Ian wasn't going to accept his blame in this whole debacle? JD was the one getting screwed. The girl of his dreams just drove away.

"I can't fucking believe you!" Ian yelled, standing with his body tensed.

"I can't fucking believe you," JD threw back at Ian. "What the fuck? You fell in love after one date?" With Sasha, JD totally understood how that could happen. He screamed, intentionally provoking his brother. "I can't fucking believe you let her go!" JD was wrong about his brother. He used to think he was brilliant. In fact, he was a fucking moron.

"FUCK YOU!" Ian's fist flew through the air and

connected with JD's face.

JD didn't see it coming. The connection stung. He threw his fisted hands up in front of his face, guarding his head from another blow. In a hockey game, JD would have fought back, but he and Ian weren't on the ice. They never competed directly against each other. The few years of difference in their age had kept them in separate age divisions. He wasn't about to fight his brother now.

"God dammit stop!" His mom shouted. Her use of God's name in vain jolted his awareness. Things were serious on the very rare occasion when she swore.

"The two of you need to stop," his dad said, adamantly stepping between the men. He was shorter than both Ian and JD, but his place as the patriarch of the family made him more formidable. "We are going to talk about this as a family. Let's all go sit down." They all followed his dad back to the living room.

"Yeah, sure, that's going to work." JD heaved on the sarcasm. Well, he wasn't going to physically fight, but that didn't mean he was ready to talk constructively.

"Yes. We. Are," his dad barked. "Your mother and I are not going to allow this to become something that breaks up our family." His parents nodded toward one another.

"There is nothing more important than this family and we are going to solve this issue." His mom handed him a bag of frozen peas. The swelling had already started. "And don't think you are walking out of here until we come to a resolution." JD placed the cold package on his eye.

"There isn't a solution, mom." JD complained. "I never met someone I cared for as much as Sasha." If Ian bowed out gracefully that would be a convenient resolution. Easy-peasy. Why not? He had done it already months ago.

"Her name's Alexandra," Ian argued again.

"She said she likes being called Sasha. So stop arguing about her name as if that is important," his mom reasoned. His brother's arguments lacked strength. Wasn't he supposed to be some hotshot attorney?

"Isn't that how we got into this situation? She wasn't clear about her name?" Ian complained.

No way was JD going to allow him to blame Sasha. This wasn't her fault. "No. You got into this situation because *you* declared you didn't want her," JD both defended Sasha and accused Ian.

"Stop!" His dad stood and emphasized. "The snarky comments are not helpful."

On the contrary, the comments kept JD's anger at bay. He hadn't punched anyone, yet. He shifted the bag of frozen peas as the warm pool of blood underneath the surface of his skin defrosted one side of the bag.

"Oh, King Solomon are you going to suggest we cut her in half?" JD challenged. "Because I'm not conceding to giving her up. She's too important."

"I love her. I can't give her up," Ian said in a more reasonable tone. The temperature of the room began to cool.

All of a sudden, after months, he realized he loved her? Did JD feel that same level of connection with Sasha? Yes, but he preferred to share that thought with Sasha, and not his family.

"I'm not expecting either of you to prove your love by showing a willingness to let her go." His mom's response surprised JD as she usually pushed her biblical ideas on them. "I know the two of you love her. JD you may not have said the words but the way you have been speaking about Sasha since you met her makes it very clear."

"There aren't many other options here," Ian pointed out. "Can't cut her in half. So do we flip a coin?" Ian reached into his pocket theatrically.

"Best of two out of three?" JD seconded Ian's cynicism.

"Of course that wouldn't work. The two of you choosing would only drive a permanent wedge in this family. That is not an option," JD's dad declared his position.

"Well, we are out of options," Ian grieved, "You heard her. She isn't going to choose either."

JD felt beaten down, as well. The situation was hopeless.

"That isn't the only other option," his mom said quietly. Ian and JD both turned to their mom.

JD recalled his previous conversation with Sasha about having a threesome. He chuckled under his breath.

Ian looked at JD as if he lost his mind. "You find this funny? Because I don't. If it is so funny to you, then maybe you don't really care for her the way I do."

"Fuck off, dumbass. I laughed because I imagined that mom was suggesting we both date Sasha." This conversation sounded like a multiple car pile-up on a highway. It transformed from bad to insane. He just mentioned threesomes in front of his church-loving mother. *He was sure to burn in hell.*

"That isn't funny either. Don't insinuate that our mother would suggest something that would go against God." Ian acted like a righteous ass. When was the last time he joined his parents at church?

165

"Your mother is a religious woman. She is also a thoughtful woman that loves her two sons. Do not *ever* mock her religious beliefs," his dad demanded.

"Yes, Sir," JD and Ian murmured together, both looking abashed.

"And yes, I was suggesting that you both date her." Ian and JD twisted their heads toward their mom. Silence hung in the air. His mom could not have possibly said what he thought he heard. Maybe he needed to get his hearing tested by an audiologist? If it wasn't his hearing, maybe something was wrong with his mom?

"What the holy fuck? Have you been drinking?" JD worried that his mom had lost her mind.

"Watch your mouth JD. Apologize to your mother." His dad didn't tolerate speaking against his mother in his house.

JD apologized, but remained concerned about his mother's sanity. He refused to believe his mother was suggesting they both in fact date the same women.

"What, are you both suggesting some kind of competition to see who can win her heart?" Ian asked. "We could have a shoot out on the ice and whoever misses the goal first, loses the girl?" Ian's absurd suggestion made JD laugh.

His mom frowned. "No, Ian. I'm not," she declared. "From what I saw, you both have already won her heart."

JD knew his mom was observant. But was she right? Hope creeped into his chest.

"Looks like we are completely out of options." Ian threw his hands up in the air. JD's moment of hope evaporated as he commiserated with Ian.

"I guess we both move on without her." JD hung his head at that thought. A painful tightness amassed in his chest. "Fuck."

"No. You aren't," his dad argued. "Your mother was suggesting, and I agree, you both should date her."

JD's eyes practically bugged out of his head. His parents' proposal stunned him.

Ian shook his head. "Seriously, who are you two? Our parents pushed their religious beliefs on us since birth. Taught us all the bible lessons. You know, like 'don't covet thy neighbor's wife.' And now you are suggesting that we date the same woman? Last week, you were spewing the sanctity of marriage and how divorce is a sin." Ian's eyes drew together as he stared at his parents.

JD stared in disillusionment.

"Yes, I believe that when you make a commitment before God, you must keep that commitment." His mom reconciled her beliefs by adding, "We are not talking about marriage here. We are talking about a commitment to Sasha, to our family, and to each other."

"What are you suggesting, a time-share where Sasha is a real estate investment?" Ian balked, crossing his arms over his chest.

"I think the details are something the three of you would need to work out amongst yourselves," his dad clarified.

JD was confused by his parents' willingness to suggest such a situation. "I don't understand where this is coming from? Honestly, I would think that any type of scenario where Ian and I were dating the same woman, you both would find it appalling."

"Grow up Jameson," his dad deadpanned. "We are religious, not old fashioned. We are very clear on the priorities in our life. You and your brother's health and happiness are the most important things to us. We love you equally and want you both to be happy."

"And to be honest, after meeting Sasha, she seems like a woman that is worthy of both of you. I think you both should find a way to fight for her, but I want you to find a way where both of my sons win." JD's mom was starting to sound less crazy.

JD reserved a lot of skepticism. To the best of his knowledge, Ian had never even engaged in a threesome. Even though JD had participated in several, that didn't necessarily mean he wanted to share Sasha in any way with his brother. He questioned the practicability. Would Sasha be able to give JD and Ian equal amounts of affection? Would she be able to treat two men equally? Could he trust his brother to share a woman that he loved? Those were much more crucial questions than the actual issues of sex.

Ian remained unusually quiet. A relationship of this sort required a lot of communication. Was Ian capable of being forthcoming in such a personal way? He usually kept his cards close to his chest when it came to those he dated.

JD's mom proposed, "You two have a lot to talk about, but why don't we all sit down and eat. You can't have a serious discussion on an empty stomach. And, I made a great dinner to celebrate Ian making partner."

JD sat at the table but had no appetite. His mother had obviously gone to a lot of trouble to cook an amazing meal and he didn't want to offend her any more than he already had with his derision. Ian professed his gratitude to his mom for the meal that included some of his favorites. The four of them sat in contemplative silence during the majority of the meal.

After dessert, JD proposed to Ian, "Do you want to go home and maybe discuss things?"

"Sure," Ian murmured.

Chapter 13

Sasha

Sasha grabbed a bottle of vodka when she got home. Good thing she had several bottles on hand as she might need all of them. She downed a couple of shots, curled up on the couch, and wrapped herself in a blanket. She held her legs tight to her chest. The news shook her to the core. She needed to physically hold herself together.

The alcohol only slightly released the tightness in her chest but didn't slow the rapid-fire circling of thoughts racing through her head. The fact that JD and Ian were brothers was unbelievable.

Ian's proclamation of love had completely broadsided her. Her head ached as if she had been smacked upside the head. She had an amazing time with Ian. Although it had been months ago, she hadn't forgotten a minute of it. The intensity of his eyes was something remarkable. Admittedly, she had felt a pull towards him since they had been forced to work together. But until yesterday, she thought there was no chance in hell of her ever being with him again. And today, he professed his love to her. What the hell? She had no idea he had such deep feelings for her.

Had she used JD to get over Ian? Kat had joked about that scenario. Sasha didn't pursue JD until after resigning Ian to her memory. She didn't hop in bed with him as a quick rebound. They'd flirted for weeks. When they finally went out, their connection intensified. When she was with JD, she felt free. She felt validated as a person and as a woman. And God, did she enjoy being with him in bed. She craved his touch.

How did she not know that they were brothers? She considered every detail of information she knew about each. She didn't find any connection. It wasn't like they looked alike. Their hair and eyes were different colors. The red strands in JD's long hair made it appear more reddish brown. Ian wore his hair short and clean cut with gel so any red in it never caught the light. Even their bodies were built differently. Ian was a tall looking six foot two, whereas JD was a thick muscular six foot even. She scrutinized if JD had subconsciously reminded her of Ian.

After hours of beating herself up over the issue, the only resemblance between JD and Ian was how happy she felt with both. She firmly decided there was no way to choose to be with one brother over the other.

Thoughts of them were relentless. And, the more she thought about both Ian and JD, the worse she felt. Thoughts of both used to give her joy. Their absence left her brokenhearted. They were forever gone.

Eventually, she cried herself to sleep.

Sasha's alarm sounded loudly. Her head throbbed. Her vision was blurred as her eyes were bloodshot and her eyelids were puffy. Her body rejected the notion of getting out of bed. It felt like she was buried under a ton of bricks. Unlike the expression, things didn't look brighter in the morning after a night's sleep. She was still alone. She had lost two great guys in her life. And the thought that she would ever be lucky enough to someday find another great man was improbable.

Mr. Stein messaged Sasha while she showered.

Stein—*Meet me in my office as soon as you get in today—*

Fuck me. Sasha's day turned from bad to worse. She wanted to skip going to the office and work from home. That plan blew up. What if she ran into Ian at work? "Fuck!" She grunted.

She dashed by Ian's office, moving like a cat burglar trying not to get noticed. The lights were out. No one was inside. She sighed in relief and headed towards Mr. Stein's office.

"Good morning Mr. Stein." Sasha mustered the strength to say it with cheer.

"Good news, Ms. Smirnova." Mr. Stein's smile didn't meet his eyes.

"Oh?" She asked hesitantly. Thank goodness he wasn't announcing bad news. She had already hit her maximum tolerance.

"As you know, Mr. O'Malley was made partner last Friday. The firm decided that as a partner he should move to the real estate group in the firm. He will no longer be working for me. For now, you get the opportunity to temporarily fill in for Mr. O'Malley's previous role. This is a great opportunity for exposure for you and a critical step for eventually becoming partner."

The tension in Sasha's shoulders eased knowing that she wouldn't run into Ian. But there was something about the look on Mr. Stein's face that seemed off.

"Wow. I wasn't expecting this Mr. Stein." She tried to balance the appropriate amount of enthusiasm and professionalism.

"Fair warning Ms. Smirnova, it involves a lot more

work," Mr. Stein cautioned.

"Thank you, Mr. Stein." Sasha smiled and walked out of his office.

She appreciated knowing that she wasn't going to run into Ian while at work, which eased her burden. She threw herself into her work and tuned out her dating problems.

The weekly alarm for her art class caught Sasha off guard. She pressed stop on her phone and shut her eyes in annoyance. She berated herself for forgetting to delete the alarm. She easily dismissed the notion of going to class. She didn't want to see JD and she used her workload as an excuse to skip class.

Unlike Ian, when Sasha finished her work for the day she preferred to leave. Ian had intentionally ensured that he was the last to leave in the group. Sasha didn't intend to adopt his habit.

She was eager for a drink at Lawson's. More than the alcohol, Sasha needed Kat. She wanted to talk about the fucked-up situation with her best friend. She knew there wasn't any answer to her problem, but she hoped sharing would ease her pain.

With a lighter Sunday crowd, Kat had time to talk. "Long time no see. You and the hot artist run out of lube?" Sasha didn't laugh. "Tough crowd tonight. What's up? Need a glass of wine to turn that frown upside down?"

"Vodka, straight up, please," Sasha stated flatly.

"Sure thing." Kat ran off to pour the drink. She returned with a double. Lucky for her, her friend read her well. "Okay, spill the tea." Kat started rubbing down the bar with a towel.

"Fuck, Kat. I don't know how to talk about this."

Sasha was at a loss for words.

"Maybe I should have brought over the bottle?" Kat was an outstanding friend and bartender/therapist.

"Okay." Sasha threw the vodka back in one swallow. "JD and Ian are brothers."

"Shut the front door!" Kat hooted and threw the towel down on the bar.

Sasha recalled to Kat what happened the previous night. She noted that Ian professed to love her and she admitted that she would never be able to unhear those words. Sasha emphasized her stupidity for not knowing they were brothers.

"I feel so bad about this. I didn't mean to hurt anyone," Tears bubbled in Sasha's eyes, once again.

From all that, Kat remarked, "Well, I'm hurt. You never told me you preferred to be called Sasha." Kat had great comedic timing.

Sasha grinned and clarified, "I was thrilled when you called me Alex. It was so much better than the jokes about my last name. And, when I moved here, I liked having a more American nickname. But since I've graduated, I learned to appreciate my Russian background while loving the great things about America."

"So do you want me to call you Sasha or Alex?"

"Either is fine, Kat. I'm just happy we are friends." Kat was Sasha's rock.

"Well *Sasha*," Kat emphasized her name, "Just for the record, I've seen both of them and I would never have guessed by their appearance that they were brothers. And I consider myself an expert in observing people as I people-watch all day long," Kat bragged.

"Thank you. That does make me feel a little less

stupid. But still, maybe if I had asked more questions, I would have known?" Sasha continued to blame herself.

"What? Should you have questioned them like a deposition?" Kat raised her eyebrow.

Sasha shrugged. "If I had, I wouldn't feel so terrible right now." Sasha grabbed another shot of vodka. "Maybe I don't have the instincts to be a good lawyer." She buried her face in her hands.

"I realize that everyone in this bar is fixated on the law firms at which people work, but that isn't a question that typically crosses the mind of others. JD probably didn't ask you because he wasn't assessing how he felt about you based on your firm's status." Sasha didn't even remember if JD mentioned that his brother was a lawyer. Kat wiped the bar repeatedly with the towel.

Shit. Had she offended Kat? "True. You are always more perceptive than me." Kat's mouth turned upward in a slight grin.

"I'm sure those muscles of his were very distracting." Kat waggled her eyebrows and Sasha laughed in response.

"Even if this wasn't caused by my own stupidity, there's no solution here. I'm not going to choose one of them and rip apart their family." Sasha pushed her empty glass towards Kat, silently asking for a refill.

"I know you wouldn't want to hurt them intentionally." Kat left the consideration that Sasha was unintentionally hurting them hanging in the air. "Have you considered dating both of them?"

"What? Ah, no. I obviously can't date two people." Sasha looked at Kat like she was crazy.

"Why not? I know it isn't the most traditional thing to do, *but* it isn't unheard of either." Kat paused, before continuing, "During law school, Seth, Dylan, and I were all dating." Like a mic drop, Kat turned to grab the bottle of vodka to fill Sasha's glass and one for herself as well.

Sasha's jaw dropped. "What the heck? How did I not know?"

Kat threw back a shot of vodka. "It was all about sex at the time; we never made a big deal out of it. Besides, who people choose to fuck doesn't need to be news."

"Wow. I can't believe I didn't know. I assumed you were all just study partners. I guess I really am stupid." Sasha shook her head and rolled her eyes at herself.

Sasha finished off her drink and Kat continued, "No, you aren't. People aren't always observant. And during law school, everyone was solely focused on trying to keep up with the workload." Kat paused, then redirected the conversation. "Listen, this isn't about me. My point was that you have the opportunity to consider having a relationship with both Ian and JD. And before you go down the road where your dirty mind is spiralling, the way you set up the relationship with them is up to the three of you."

Sasha contemplated Kat's suggestion. She didn't think it was a good suggestion but she hadn't overruled the notion. "What happened between you, Seth, and Dylan?" Sasha was curious about the ability of a threesome lasting.

"Dylan moved to California for a job. Seth and I aren't compatible as a couple. We are still friends though." Kat didn't elaborate and Sasha didn't think it was appropriate to pry.

"Ask yourself, who is benefitting by you choosing to be with them or you choosing not to be with them?" Kat asked questions just like a therapist.

"Hmmm. That's an interesting way to look at the matter." Sasha felt bad that Kat seemed to be wasting her amazing mind by only running a bar. "I will have to think on that one. You never cease to amaze me Kat." Kat smiled and got back to serving other customers.

Sasha turned off do not disturb on her phone when she got home. She faced all the previously muted messages from Ian and JD.

Late last night Ian texted:

—Are you okay? I'm sorry. That was a total clusterfuck—

Sasha rolled her eyes at the understatement of the century.

In the morning Ian messaged:

—I heard about your temporary promotion. You'll be great. When they told me I would be moved in the firm, I suggested you for the role—

Was she supposed to thank Ian? She wanted to yell more than show gratitude.

After the conclusion of the art class, JD messaged:

—I guess I wasn't surprised that you didn't come to class, but I wanted you to know that I missed you—

She frowned as guilt washed over her.

A couple of hours later, JD messaged, again.

—I've been trying to give you space to think, but I would really like to talk—

Sasha shook her head, knowing she wasn't ready to talk.

Ian—*JD and I would really like to talk to you. Can we please come over?—*

No way!

JD—*Ian and I promise not to argue with each other. Please give us a chance to speak with you—*

Damn, JD was persuasive, but Sasha still refused to respond.

Her phone rang. The doorman announced, "There are a couple of pizzas for you at the front desk. Would you like me to send the delivery up?"

"I didn't order any pizza. It must be a mistake," Sasha replied and flipped the phone around to hang up.

The doorman continued, "There is also a card with the pizza addressed to you."

"Sure," Sasha answered hesitantly, giving the doorman permission to send up the pizzas.

Sasha opened the door to find Ian holding a couple of pizzas, almost entirely obscuring JD. In her quick glimpse, JD was apparently holding a couple of six packs of beer. She froze.

She didn't know what to say. She stood still in the doorway, unable to move. Her face went slack. She lacked the energy to fight. She refused to look them in the eyes.

"I'm going to take the fact that you haven't slammed the door in our faces, yet, to be good sign," Ian argued, but held the door open with his foot.

JD pushed and took one step inside. "Let us come in. We want to talk."

Ian gently guided her toward the kitchen. The clank of JD locking the door triggered a feeling of being trapped. They set the pizza and beer down on the table. She looked at the food as if it was a giant pandora's box. Once they opened the discussion, they would be faced with all the complicated problems once again. That was a lot to confront. Would it be a repeat of last night's disaster?

JD took her hand and pulled her to sit next to him at

the square shaped kitchen table. Ian sat across from her. She fought to avoid eye contact with both of them.

Instead, she stared at her hand intertwined with JD's. She had missed his touch. She missed his smile. She mustered just enough bravery to look him in the eyes, and gasped. "JD, your eye!" He had quite the shiner. Sasha turned toward Ian and accused, "Did you do that?"

Ian threw his hands up in surrender and declared, "No one is here to throw punches, physical or otherwise."

Sasha looked back at JD's swollen eye. "Are you okay?" Sasha worried. His eye was a terrible shade of purple and red.

"My eye is fine. I have had a lot worse on the ice. But no, I'm not okay Sasha." JD spoke unusually softly, while sandwiching her hand between both of his. "I'm worried about you. I understand why you walked out last night. Are *you* okay?"

"We are both worried about you, Sasha." Sasha noted that Ian's willingness to refer to her as Sasha was much less antagonistic than the previous night. "And I'm sorry for making the situation worse," Ian offered with pleading eyes.

A pregnant pause lingered in the air. What was she supposed to say? They initiated the discussion. It wasn't her choice. She hadn't prepared herself for this confrontation.

Ian started talking. Of course, he initiated control of the conversation just like he dominated legal negotiations. "We understand that you aren't inclined to choose either one of us. We aren't pressing you to do that now." The tenderness in Ian's voice and the concern in

JD's eyes alarmed her.

Sasha's chin began to quiver as a feeling of doom swept through her. Tears welled up in her eyes. "Are you both here for closure's sake?"

"Fuck no!" JD swore, clasping her hand more securely. "I have no desire to end things with you."

A tear slid down her cheek. Sasha started biting her lip. Did JD think she was going to choose him over Ian? Her head started to spin. Nausea brewed in her belly.

Ian leaned in closer. "Neither of us wants to end things with you. Well, I suppose our case is a little different." Ian extended an open hand. Her free hand itched to reach out and accept Ian's offer. Uncertainty made her hesitate.

"I'm totally confused." Sasha looked back and forth between the two. Neither of their faces gave her a clue. What were they suggesting?

Ian clarified, "I'm asking for you to forgive me for putting things off between us. I know I was wrong. I can see that now. And I realize that there were ways to have made things work."

"I don't blame you for the choice you made. I respected your motivation. It's not about forgiveness, but I'm not going to choose you over JD." Sasha didn't want to keep repeating herself.

JD interrupted, "Let me simplify. We are not asking you to choose between us. Both of us want to date you. And we wanted to propose a scenario where we both date you."

Sasha's brow furrowed as she stared at JD.

"I know it sounds a little crazy, but we are really hoping that you would consider such a scenario," Ian admitted and reached his hand across the table toward

Sasha.

She cocked her head to the side in consideration, then interjected. "Huh. Kat suggested the same thing to me."

JD chirped and smiled at Sasha and then Ian. "Really?" His voice lifted.

Ian pushed like in a closing argument. "What do you think, Sasha?"

Sasha refrained from spewing all the random thoughts in her head. Instead, she summarized, "I can think of dozens of reasons that it is a ridiculous idea and a million awkward situations that we would encounter." Sasha analyzed the situation methodically. That's what she was trained to do. She looked for potential problems and pitfalls. Protecting clients and predicting vulnerabilities was her job. This scenario was a bottomless pit of challenges.

"Does that mean you don't want to be with us?" JD gripped her hand tighter and she looked him in the eyes.

"No," Sasha whispered unsure of her feelings about attempting such a relationship.

Ian pushed for commitment. "I know it won't be simple, but I think we all can agree that the alternative of ending things completely isn't going to make anyone happy. Please, say you will give us a try." It was difficult for her to argue with Ian when he made such strong points.

"Please Sasha. Please don't say you would prefer to end things," JD begged, pulling on her heart strings.

"To be honest. It is a lot to consider," Sasha equivocated.

Ian jumped on her wording. "That isn't a no. So would you consider it?"

"What is there to consider? Nothing has changed about our situation, Ian. We still work at the same firm. How is that going to work when it goes against everything you have been saying for months?" Sasha hadn't forgotten how this mess started. Had Ian?

"I was wrong. I think we can hide our relationship from work. *And,* I think you are worth the effort. I can only hope that you think the same of me." Ian's words hit Sasha hard. His unexpected vulnerability knocked her sideways.

JD piled on, "I know I don't work there, but I don't see the problem. The place is huge and you aren't in the same area. It's almost like you are working at different firms." Damn them for being so convincing, Sasha was losing her battle with resisting them. Ian looked hopeful, but then she turned to look at JD.

She gestured to JD's face. "Look at your blackeye. What's going to happen the next time one of you loses your temper with each other?"

"Brothers fight occasionally, Sasha. But this," JD pointed to his eye, "isn't going to happen again."

Ian laughed. "Call our mom. She's a great referee. She's been doing it for years." Sasha wasn't amused. "Or not," he muttered.

JD tagged on, "How about this? For tonight, don't say no. We don't have to agree on how everything should work. For tonight, just consider the option that we work together to find a way to make a relationship work between us." Ian smiled proudly at JD. Sasha could feel her walls crumbling.

"Do you want to be with us? If yes, don't you think you should consider it?" Ian hammered home the point. Sasha reached to grab Ian's hand. A warmth spread through her as the tension in her muscles relaxed. He gently closed his eyes for a moment, then looked at Sasha, while he wore a bright smile.

Holding one of each of their hands, Sasha answered, "I think we should all consider it."

"Thank fuck." JD sighed.

Sasha let go of their hands and put up her palms to halt them. "There is a lot to discuss." She wasn't going to let them off the hook. She needed to leave herself an escape clause.

"We don't need to contemplate every issue and scenario tonight." Ian diffused the issue like a pro, putting his legal skills to good use.

"What is the biggest issue on your mind?" JD was very sweet to consider her feelings.

Sasha blushed. "Honestly? Your very religious parents to start." Sasha raised her eyebrows.

JD and Ian hooted like a couple of laughing idiot hyenas. JD went into detail about how the idea of them all dating was originally their *parents'* idea.

"I think that might be more shocking than finding out the two of you are brothers." Sasha laughed.

Ian opened a beer for each of them and raised one in a toast. "Cheers to giving it try."

JD lifted his beer. "To the three of us and agreeing to being open and honest with each other about our feelings."

Sasha raised her beer. "To going slowly." She clanged bottles with JD and Ian.

"Here. Here." The brothers said in unison.

JD stood up to open the pizza boxes and grabbed a slice. "I'm starving. I haven't eaten all day." He shoved a piece in his mouth.

"Hang on, let me grab some plates and silverware." Sasha got up to grab the essentials. JD continued to eat the slice with his hands. "By the way thanks for the pizza. I can't believe my doorman didn't announce you."

"I gave him a nice tip." Ian winked.

Between bites, JD added, "I hope to do this more often."

Ian took a plate from Sasha and joked, "If this relationship is ever going to work, we are going to have to come to some kind of an agreement about where we order pizza."

Still chewing, JD argued, "Bro, this place has the best pepperoni, hands down."

Damn, the O'Malleys were really serious about their pizza. "Maybe we should try them all and rank them together."

"I hear pizza and many dates in the future, so it sounds good to me." JD smiled.

The three of them finished off the pizza, JD and Ian devouring it in equal measure. Sasha looked at the empty boxes before her and an unease settled in her gut. *What came next?*

Ian stood up and while he cleared the table, he announced, "JD and I are going to head home. As much as we would both like to stay and spend the night with you, JD and I agreed that going slowly will help us all get our footing."

Sasha's hackles flared. "You two discussed this before arriving on my doorstep?"

JD took Sasha's chin in his hand to force her to look at him. "Ian and I had to discuss things in order to consider whether we thought this was a possibility that we could consider. Going ahead, every decision will be between all three of us."

Sasha looked to Ian to read his expression. "Promise," Ian agreed. She believed he was being sincere.

All three stood by the door to say goodnight. Sasha looked back and forth between JD and Ian. JD bent to kiss Sasha. It wasn't overly dramatic. It wasn't even an open mouth kiss, but his kiss tasted like relief. With his arms wrapped around her the stress of the past day melted away, temporarily at least.

When they separated, Sasha turned toward Ian. She wasn't sure how he was going to react. There wasn't any anger whatsoever on his face. On the contrary, he looked a little gun-shy. It had been a long time since their last kiss. Sasha hadn't explicitly forgiven him.

JD placed an encouraging hand on her shoulder. "Sasha. It's okay if you want to kiss Ian goodnight."

Sasha questioned JD with her eyes and he nodded accordingly.

She then looked at Ian's beckoning eyes, closed the gap, and kissed him soundly.

Ian hugged Sasha back, whispering into her hair, "I've missed your kisses, Sasha."

Being in Ian's arms felt so good. *Was it too much to hope that their little experiment could work?*

"Goodnight Ian. Goodnight JD." Sasha smiled timidly. An empty uncertain feeling jostled her belly.

"Goodnight Sasha," the men chimed in unison. The meshing of their two voices and their image together were sure to be good fodder for her dreams.

Sasha had barely started washing up in her bathroom when her phone buzzed. JD had set up a group message for her, Ian, and himself.

JD—*Thank you Sasha for trying. I was terrified of losing you*—

Ian—*Thank you for taking a chance on me again*—

Sasha was pleasantly surprised by their effort to be open and honest.

Sasha—*You both are worth the effort. Goodnight*—

Chapter 14

Ian

Ian woke up in the morning feeling better than he had in months. He had a chance at a relationship with Sasha and that was a hell of a lot better than her being completely severed from his life. Cautiously, he refused to allow himself to assume that getting back together was a sure thing. The fact that she was willing to try was great, but he knew she still harbored a lot of apprehension.

He chose to avoid thinking about all the things that would fuck up the relationship. The list was long and frightening. This wasn't a work issue and he shouldn't treat the relationship with the same skepticism. Instead, he focused on relishing the kiss he shared with Sasha the previous night. Even though it was chaste, it was invigorating. He felt like he had been awakened after months of melancholy.

He looked forward to the possibility of seeing Sasha at work, although the likelihood of them crossing paths was slim. The prospect made him smile.

Ian texted in the group message:

—*Looking forward to possibly running into you at work, but I think we need to keep things on a professional last name basis there*—

He hoped that didn't piss off Sasha, remembering

the previous times that she had injected sarcasm into his last name.

JD—*Morning beautiful. I hope that after a good night's sleep you are still interested in trying with Ian and me—*

JD's message caught Ian off guard. While the message popped up in the group thread, Ian hadn't yet fully embraced all the nuances of this threesome. He hadn't forgotten what he had agreed to in terms of the relationship, but that was different than feeling comfortable. Unchartered territory was awkward.

Sasha responded quickly. Ian checked the time and imagined she was awake and getting ready for work. Thoughts of her naked in the shower had him smiling with hope.

Sasha—*Ofc Mr. O'Malley & Yes, I'm still interested TBH I have trepidations—*

His smile turned bitter. Getting a message from Sasha pleased him greatly, but the use of his last name made him cringe. And, her second thought fell short of encouraging. Were her revelations about her concerns with potential obstacles or the construction of a protective barrier? He hoped for a more positive response first thing in the morning.

Ian reminded himself that he had a lot to atone for in terms of the time away from Sasha. Nonetheless, he considered his cup half full.

JD—*I think time will help. Can we all do dinner Friday?—*

Ian credited JD with a great idea. Sasha and Ian both reacted with a thumbs up on the message.

Friday would be a good time to address the apprehension. He had concerns and assumed that Sasha and JD would have their own issues as well. Although, JD was much more easy-going than he and was probably handling this better than him. Ian worried about reestablishing something with Sasha. Would she always have trust issues as a result of him essentially dismissing her? And it was hard to admit, but he worried if she might prefer being intimate with JD more than she would be with him. He really needed to be with her again to know if they still had fireworks. Did he need to ask JD for permission to be alone with Sasha? How did all the logistics and planning work?

In the late afternoon, a message came up in the group thread. There was picture of a cup of coffee with legs, arms, and a red superhero cape flying through the air.

What in the world? He remembered catching a glimpse of that same image on Sasha's phone the other day.

JD—*here's a late afternoon pick-me-up*—

Sasha—*Do I ever need some coffee right now! (kissing smiley face)*—

Ian's stomach felt queasy from essentially eavesdropping on someone else's romantic gesture. Was he jealous of their banter? Was he supposed to go bring Sasha a real cup of coffee? It would appear suspicious if he brought coffee to Sasha at the office. He tried not to stress over a cup of coffee and responded more lightheartedly.

Ian—*taking orders? I'll take a double shot of espresso*—

He expected that his brother would probably tell him to fuck off for the sarcastic comment. He deserved it.

JD—*(red-cheeked face)*—

Perhaps he shouldn't make assumptions about how everyone else was feeling or that JD had it easier than him. This situation was new for all of them. There were a lot of little kinks to iron out between them. Perhaps, not all messages between them needed to be in the group thread.

Apparently, Sasha had a better grasp on when not to use the group thread, she messaged him directly later that night.

Sasha— *Did Stein expect you to do all his work?*—

Ian—*Why do you think I was working late all the time?*—

He checked the time. It was past 11 p.m. Ian messaged Sasha in the group.

Ian—*Are you planning on leaving the office soon? It's very late and I would prefer that you don't walk home alone at this hour*—

Ian braced for a feminist comeback from Sasha.

JD—*I don't mean to be an overprotective ass, but I agree with Ian. I hate the idea of you on the streets alone this late at night*—

Ian appreciated the back-up from his brother.

Sasha—*I'm a big girl and am very capable of taking care of myself*—

JD—*Agreed. This isn't about your capability but about my sanity. Please let Ian walk you home*—

Sasha—*Fine*—

Wow, she acquiesced easier than Ian anticipated.

Ian—*Text when you're ready*—

Ian was very careful not to show any sign of affection toward Sasha as they walked out of the building. They intentionally rode down on separate elevators. They didn't speak in the lobby of the building.

They didn't even acknowledge each other's existence until they were a half a block away from the building.

As they neared her apartment building, Ian tentatively took Sasha's hand like he was holding a fragile, yet sweet, French macaron. Her tiny hand felt delicate within his. She looked down at their joined fingers and then looked him in the eyes. He tried to hide his apprehension. "Can I come up and talk? I feel like we never really had a chance to talk about how things went down between us. I know that it was my fault. But I think it would be best if we talk about how you felt so that we can move forward on a good note."

"I agree. We need to start out on a clean slate." She broke her eye contact with him and looked aside. "Should we let JD know? Do we need to ask him?" Sasha stuttered.

Once again, Ian disliked the awkwardness. They meshed so well months ago. Would they ever regain that unimpeded intimacy?

"We don't need permission to talk Sasha." Ian exhaled and worked to calm the irritation bubbling inside.

"Hey, I'm just trying to navigate this relationship. I'm sorry if I'm doing it all wrong," Sasha snapped and narrowed her eyes at him. *Shit.* He didn't mean to put her on the defensive.

"I apologize if I sounded exasperated. I'm having growing pains here too." Ian looked down and searched for a better approach. "Maybe you are right. Let's call JD and let him know and see if he wants to talk too. If the shoe was on the other foot, I wouldn't want to be left wondering."

Sasha nodded in agreement and dialed JD as soon as

she and Ian got to her apartment, putting the call on speakerphone. "Hey, I wanted to let you know I'm home safely."

"Thanks for calling me to let me know. It's nice to hear your voice. I know you don't have time to talk during your day,"

"I appreciate your understanding. Truly. I also wanted to let you know that Ian is here and wanted to talk a little. Would you like to come over?" Sasha offered while looking at Ian with soft compassion in her eyes.

JD responded without hesitation, "Thanks for asking. In all honesty, I would love to come over but I think that you and Ian do have some issues that may be best if you talk by yourselves."

Ian leaned closer to Sasha's phone. "Thanks man."

Sasha added, "Goodnight JD."

"Goodnight, beautiful." JD hung up.

"Feel better?" Ian asked, raising his eyebrow.

Sasha's body relaxed. "Yes."

"I think we will be able to figure this all out in time," Ian encouraged her, and helped her take off her jacket. He felt more positive than the last time he entered her apartment, but not confident by any stretch of the imagination.

"Do you want to share some wine or just talk?" Ian pulled Sasha toward the kitchen, hoping that some wine would ease the awkwardness.

"I'll pass on the wine. Would you like a glass?" Playing the role of an overly polite hostess, Sasha stiffly walked over to her small wine rack.

Desperate to ratchet down the formalities, Ian suggested, "Let's go sit on the couch."

Sasha tucked her feet underneath herself and

covered her lap with a blanket. She physically closed herself off from him. Ian insisted that she allow him to rub her feet while they talked. He planned to pry her open if it required.

At least she didn't shy away from meeting his gaze with her soft brown eyes.

"It's late and I'll cut to the chase. I'm sorry for making a decision that affected both of us and not giving you a chance to help me find a way to make things work. I thought I would be able to get over you since it was only one night. But as it turns out, you are unforgettable." Ian winked and flashed her his well-perfected, jury-charming smile, which elicited a smile in return.

"Seeing you at work was tough. I kept imaging you with your hair down and free spirited. When we started to work *together*, I thought enforcing rules of professionalism would help me to only think of you in that type of way. But your damn perfume fucking drove me nuts. All I wanted to do was be near you in order to smell you." His eyes drew together as the thought hit, "Holy crap, I just realized I could smell your perfume the other morning at our place. That wasn't my imagination, was it?" His heart hurt a little as he awaited confirmation.

"Maybe not. I left Saturday morning." Sasha played with her hands. "I'm sorry. Let me be clear. I'm *not* sorry for being with JD; I'm sorry if it troubled you."

Ian took Sasha's hand in his. He swallowed, mustering up his strength and determination. "I don't think you should feel sorry about being with JD and I'm glad you aren't sorry. I don't blame either you or JD. It's difficult not to blame myself." Ian looked down.

He took in a deep breath to steel his courage. "Fuck.

This is hard to say." Ian paused and finally looked at Sasha directly. "Did I push you into the arms of my brother?"

Sasha jerked her hand away from Ian. "JD was not a rebound if that's what you are suggesting," Sasha hissed. "He's much more to me than that."

"Shit. I'm sorry. I think the world of my brother. I didn't mean to demean your relationship with him. I feel guilty like I caused this whole problem," Ian admitted, hanging his head as his tongue acted like a noose around his neck.

Sasha took back Ian's hand. "I was worried that *I* caused the problem. Why didn't I realize? After speaking with Kat, I finally concluded that blaming isn't going to help us go forward. We need to be thankful for what we have found in each other," Sasha reminded him.

Ian raised his head to look at her again. "I agree, but…I also feel bad, because a few weeks ago my dad was suggesting that I should have tried to find a way to make things work if I cared so deeply for you. He was right. But in my own defense, I think my feelings continued to grow. This may sound nuts, but when I read your brief at work and I got to see an inlet to your brilliant mind, it really turned me on. And, I recognized how you always supported my decision to remain professional. You respected my choice and that meant the world to me." Ian's inner insecurity called to him as he rubbed small circles in Sasha's hand. "Were you not that into me? Was that why it was so easy for you to give me space and move on?"

Sasha tightened her grip around his hand. "Easy? Not at all. I had an amazing night with you. I woke up thinking I may have a new boyfriend. But I understand respect. That's something that I expect and I will always give to someone I date. I respected your choice to move on, but that didn't make it easy for me. Seriously, the sex was incredible. I never forgot."

"Incredible, huh?" Ian prodded and smiled mercurially.

"For me, it was…" Sasha trailed off, casting her uncertain eyes downward.

"Trust me the feeling was mutual." Ian punctuated his remark with a kiss, but he wasn't done discussing his concerns. He needed to get them all out there in order to fully move on. "I'm sorry I didn't find some way to work around all my concerns about working together, sooner."

Sasha balked. "If you are insinuating before I started with JD—"

Ian interrupted, "No, that's not what I meant. I just wish I hadn't lost that time with you."

"Good. Because I refuse to regret having started a relationship with JD."

Ian held both of Sasha's hands. "Can you forgive me for the past so that we can go forward? All three of us." Ian feared her denial.

"Yes—" Sasha attempted to continue.

"Thank fuck!" Ian interjected, allowing his body to relax forward in a heap.

"Can I ask you a question now?" She didn't wait for a response. "Did you mean it when you said you loved me the other night or was that just an attempt to argue your case?" She looked expectantly at him.

Ian scooted closer to Sasha and looked her in the eyes. "I love you, Sasha. I hadn't realized until that moment. But the feeling hasn't gone away. I know it to be true. If I didn't love you, I don't think I would have the strength to try and make this situation work. I don't expect you to say you love me. But I don't want to hide the fact that I love you. Well, except while we are at work, which is something we are going to have to deal with but not this minute." Ian closed the gap further so that they were only inches apart. He stared into her eyes. "I love you, Sasha."

Sasha's mouth hung open but nothing came out. She stared back at him compassionately. "Ian, I'm sorry."

"Sasha, it's okay, you don't have to say anything." Ian didn't want to put her on the spot. "I'm glad we were able to sit down and talk." He stood and headed for the door to leave. Donning his jacket, Ian's confidence slipped. Looking Sasha in her eyes, he asked, "May I kiss you goodnight?"

Sasha leaned in until her lips were touching his. The kiss started off slow. Two people contented to be in each other's company. Both satisfied to hold each other. Then, the scent of Sasha's perfume hit Ian and all the dirty thoughts of her being with him raced through his mind. "Oh god, Sasha," Ian moaned.

Ian intensified the kiss. He pushed Sasha up against the wall. Sasha opened her mouth for him wantingly. Months of pent-up energy were released in that single kiss. A longing passion. A bursting need to consume her surged in his veins. His body pinned her against the wall, preventing her from ever possibly escaping.

She rocked her body against his, reaching and pulling his head closer to her. The push of her hips and the pull of her hands made his cock impossibly hard.

"Oh Ian," Sasha implored.

"Sasha, look at me," Ian directed her. Her dilated eyes stared back at him. He saw the desire deep within.

"I want you."

"Yes. Oh God, yes," she assented, kissing him intensely.

Sasha and Ian began to tear at their clothes as if the items were on fire. Ian's desire blazed. Tremors of excitement caused him to fumble with buttons and zippers. They ungracefully grabbed at each other.

Somehow, they managed to stagger toward her bedroom area. Ian lifted Sasha's naked body to the bed, laying her on her back. She inched toward the center but Ian dragged her ass back to the edge.

"Condoms…nightstand," Sasha stuttered, pointing to the furniture positioned a couple feet away from them. He didn't have the forethought to bring condoms with him. He hadn't planned this moment with her. Ian had never indulged the actual hope of being with Sasha again. The best he had allowed was the mere fantasy. The reality was far better than his dreams.

He grabbed a condom and reached between Sasha's legs. His fingers found her sex spilling with desire.

"Ian, please!" Sasha begged. "Don't fucking tease me. I need your cock in me. Now." She pushed his hand away and directed his steely length to her entrance. He pulled her legs over his shoulders and stared at her until their bodies and eyes were mutually connected. "Ian!" Her voice coaxed him and the demand propelled him to slam his cock deep inside.

It was fast. It was furious. Ian fucked her with all the energy that had been building for months. He hovered over her, wanting to be closer. He lusted for the sensation of being inseparable. He leaned over her petite body, bending her legs back towards her own shoulders, the angle allowing him to grind his pelvis against hers.

"Ian! Ian! Oh yes, Ian!" He clearly hit her in the right spot. Her eyes began to close.

"Look at me, Sasha," he demanded.

He felt the connection with her on a more intimate level as her dilated eyes begged him for more. He thrusted faster. Harder. He wanted to climax with Sasha. He was consumed with the need to fill her.

"Oh fuuuuck," Sasha screamed as her core pulsed around him.

Ian buried himself all the way inside her and came in a massive eruption.

He kissed Sasha tenderly as his heart rate slowed. After they each calmed, Ian disposed of the condom in the bathroom. He caught a glance of himself in the mirror. Relief and gratitude stared back at him. He braced his hand on the counter and hung his head as an unexpected release of tension overtook him. "Thank fucking god, she forgave you," Ian mumbled to himself. He inhaled deeply and rejoiced. A joyful smile spread across his face.

He returned to the bedroom only to find Sasha pacing back and forth, dressed in an oversized t-shirt that fell to her mid-thighs. She played with her hands. She wasn't smiling. She didn't even look at him.

"Are you alright?" Ian worried and approached her to offer a comforting hug.

Sasha shunned Ian's advance. "Um," Sasha grabbed at her shirt and avoided looking him in the face. "Uh…JD."

That felt like a slap to the face. He didn't want to hear about another man moments after being with a woman. He took a beat and a deep breath. Rather than make assumptions, he asked, "What's on your mind?"

"Are we supposed to tell him? Do we need permission for you to stay the night?" Sasha fretted, continuing to bore a hole in the floor.

He was relieved that the stress was over concern for his brother rather than remorse for being with him. But he needed confirmation. "First, I need to tell you, it felt amazing to be with you."

"Absolutely," Sasha affirmed verbally, but motioned her hand dismissively. Ian forced Sasha to allow him to console her with a hug, which she accepted.

"As for JD, I think that it may be best if tonight, I don't stay here. I don't want him to feel like I tricked him into being excluded. It's new between all of us and we probably need to discuss arrangements." Ian didn't want to be the one to fuck up the arrangement.

Sasha countered, "I don't want to pretend that nothing happened tonight. I don't want to pretend that we only talked. We need honesty." Sasha nervously played with her fingers. "I can't help but feel guilty right now. I feel like I betrayed JD."

"Part of being honest means stating how you feel. I think you should call JD." Ian noticed Sasha didn't seem gratified by the suggestion. To help matters along, Ian grabbed his phone, sat on the bed, and pulled Sasha onto his lap.

"Hey JD," Ian started, putting JD on speaker.

"Everything okay?" JD worried.

"Listen, I think that Sasha needs some reassurance from you," Ian continued and kissed Sasha on the head.

"Of course, anything. Is she with you?" JD asked.

Sasha remained quiet. Ian kissed her on the cheek in encouragement.

"Hey," Sasha mumbled.

"What's going on, beautiful?"

Sasha clammed up.

Ian summed up the situation as quickly and neatly as possible. "I was with Sasha tonight and she's afraid that you're going to be angry."

Sasha shot Ian a horrified look, but he hugged her tightly back.

JD responded, "Please don't stress over this Sasha. I wouldn't have agreed to try this with you if I didn't feel confident in my ability to handle knowing that you were going to be with Ian." Sasha sighed in relief. JD jokingly added, "But I'm not sharing you with anyone else, got it?"

Sasha laughed. "Agreed."

"Good. Anything else? If not, goodnight beautiful."

"Goodnight JD," Sasha said with relief and hung up.

Ian kissed her on the cheek again. "Feel better?" He needed verbal confirmation.

"Yeah," Sasha paused, swiping away a tear, "I guess I'm surprised by JD's reaction."

"Hey, this is new for all of us. I don't expect it to be smooth sailing all the time. But JD and I are going to try our best to make this work," he reassured her.

"Does that mean you are staying tonight?" She looked at Ian questioningly.

"I would like to but I actually need to be in the office early tomorrow. I think it might be best if I head home. Are you okay with that?" He kissed Sasha.

She nodded.

Sasha walked him to the door and stepped up on her tippy-toes to kiss him. The kiss lingered. She wasn't pushing him out the door with a quick peck. He held her and enjoyed the feel of her in his arms. It felt almost as good as his orgasm moments ago. Different but equally as satisfying.

He hummed to the song about happiness on his way home.

Chapter 15

Sasha

Sasha's hands lay on top of her keyboard unmoving and her bleary eyes stared at the screen. She must have read the last sentence ten times and she still wasn't able to dissect the meaning. It was only Tuesday, but it felt like a Friday. The new workload under Mr. Stein was kicking her ass. The added emotional stress over the weekend sucked out all her extra stamina. The sex was great with Ian the previous evening, but the loss of essential sleep was hurting her ability to focus. She tried to medicate with coffee, but the jolt of caffeine lacked the capability of compensating for her mental capacity failure. Her brain amounted to a pile of mush. It was time to throw in the towel for the day.

She left the office around 6:30 p.m., which at most places would be considered a reasonable time to leave, but at her firm it was considered cutting out early. The other associates at the firm most likely would disapprove of her leaving at such a time. Leaving early went against an unspoken comradery where they all battled together like comrades in arms hitting their extremely-high, yearly-required, billable hours.

Knowing that she didn't have anything to eat at home, she stopped by Lawson's to grab some dinner. She didn't care if she ran into anyone from the firm at

Lawson's and they thought less of her for leaving work early. Fuck it. She worked hard.

Sasha took refuge at the bar with her best friend. Despite Kat's tasty skills as a bartender, Sasha planned to only drink water. If she had any alcohol, she probably would have fallen asleep with her head on the bar.

"Hey Sasha," Kat greeted her with smiles. "Woah, calling you Sasha feels weird."

"It's okay if you want to continue calling me Alex." Sasha didn't want to cause people issues.

"No, no, no. I'll get used to it. If I can get used to eating kale, I can get used to calling you Sasha," Kat quipped, wiping down the bar an additional time.

"Speaking of kale, can I get a salad? I'm starving." Sasha knew the food was good at Lawson's but she rarely arrived during mealtimes.

"Sure. Want an apple pie martini with that?"

Sasha yawned. "Water only tonight."

"Dating two men wearing you out?" Kat teased. Sasha had sent her a text to update her on the status of things between Ian, JD, and herself.

Sasha sent Kat a death glare. This may have been Kat's place of work, but many of Sasha's colleagues frequented the bar. Sasha wouldn't risk people at work knowing about her situation.

"Oops," Kat mouthed and whispered, "Can be exhausting." Kat added a smile and a wink for emphasis.

"Kat, while you are taking your time amusing yourself, your best friend is sitting here starving to death." Sasha grumbled and glared.

"I'll hurry up on the salad. I wouldn't want to have to deal with a dead body at the bar." Kat ran off to the kitchen.

Sasha perked up when she received a text from JD.

JD—*better day at work?*—

Sasha snarled as she didn't want a reminder of work.

Sasha—*Exhausting! Grabbing food at Lawson's*—

JD—*If it is an early night for you, can I stop by?*—

Sasha wanted to see JD, but if she were honest, she really wanted to go home after her food and hit the hay. Despite JD's full understanding about being with Ian last night, Sasha felt a little guilty. Did she need to split her time evenly? Did she have to agree to see JD?

Not trying to overthink it, she stuck to the facts.

Sasha—*My food will probably arrive soon*—

JD—*I could meet you at the bar by the time you are finishing dinner and walk you home*—

Sasha was unable to think of a polite way to say no to JD.

Sasha—*See you soon (smiley face with heart eyes)*—

The smiley face in the text looked much more energetic than how she felt.

Kat returned and brought out the salad for Sasha. It was loaded with a variety of vegetables and seeds. A hearty salad was exactly what Sasha needed. "Looks great, Kat. Thank you." She dug in as soon as the plate was placed in front of her. She wasn't exaggerating when she told Kat she was starving. She gobbled the first few bites so quickly that she barely registered the taste.

Kat served other customers while Sasha ate her salad as it was busier than usual. Sasha appreciated the moments to herself. She didn't have the energy to engage in friendly conversation. By the time Kat returned to Sasha, half of the salad was gone. Sasha complimented Kat, "I forgot how good the food is here. I think it has been a while since I've eaten here. The salad is great. Thank you."

"Well thanks for the compliment. I appreciate it. One of my cousins is now helping out in the kitchen and it seems to be working out well." Sasha was happy for Kat. She deserved a break.

Sasha was almost finished with her salad when JD arrived. "Hey, beautiful." He gave her a quick innocent kiss on the cheek.

Then he took a sip from her glass. "Only water?" JD teased.

"I'm too tired for alcohol." Sasha tried to smile as she was happy to see JD, but she was fighting shear exhaustion. Dark circles showed under her eyes despite her attempts to conceal them with make-up earlier. She knew she was looking less than her best.

"Wow, you do like you are going to pass out." JD noted. She felt like it too. She wanted her pillow more than JD. He threw some money on the counter. Sasha waved goodbye to Kat.

Sasha remained quiet the entire walk back to her apartment. Her brain had turned off. She wasn't even paying attention to whatever JD was talking about. When they were in front of her building, she headed in.

"Aren't you going to invite me up?" JD nudged Sasha with his elbow.

She hadn't even considered it. All she wanted was sleep. "JD, I'm exhausted. I don't mean to be rude. You're hot and incredible but that notwithstanding, I'm going to be out like a light within two minutes of crossing the threshold of my apartment." Sasha didn't bother to stop walking towards the elevator. She didn't have the energy to debate.

"I can see that, beautiful. I have no expectations of anything going on," he claimed while tugging on her arm.

"JD, I need sleep." Sasha yawned.

"Listen, Sasha, I miss you. Please let me stay. No nonsense. I just want to hold you." JD crossed his finger across his chest in an "X" motion. "Cross my heart." Then he held out a fisted hand, extending one finger. "Pinkie-swear."

He proved to be too cute to deny. "Fine." Sasha wasn't trying to be rude, but she made no attempt to speak to JD while she got ready for bed. JD waited for her in the bed with the comforter drawn back for her to crawl in beside him.

Sasha climbed in beside him. He spooned her, wrapping his arm around her and placing a single kiss on her shoulder. "Goodnight beautiful."

Sasha felt his length hardening against her ass. "No and goodnight," Sasha spit out in frustration.

"I'm a man Sasha, some things I can't help. But I'm not animal, I can control how I choose to act," JD explained, but didn't shift away from her.

His voice faded into the distance before she dozed off.

Sasha's alarm went off early like always, but she didn't feel as groggy as usual. She had slept soundly. No nightmares about work deadlines. She stretched her body and sat up. Wait. The light in the kitchen was on. She smelled coffee brewing. JD! She remembered that she had spent the night in bed with JD.

"Morning beautiful." He walked in carrying a hot cup of coffee, wearing only his boxers.

"Am I awake or am I dreaming about a hot guy

bringing me coffee?" *This was the right way to start the day.*

JD set the coffee down on the nightstand and kissed Sasha. "Does the guy in your dream kiss like me?"

"Not sure, maybe you should try again," Sasha spurred.

JD bent down to kiss her. Sasha reached up to pull him closer. She tugged hard enough that he lost his balance and fell on the bed. They continued kissing. "I need to get to work early," Sasha murmured between kisses.

"Mmm hmm," JD mumbled, not stopping.

"I only have time for a quickie." She began to stroke JD's cock that was already long and hard. "Did you hear me, JD?"

"I can't think about anything except your fingers wrapped around my cock." JD slipped off his boxers and moaned when she once again stroked his length. "Fuck."

She wanted him and his body indicated he felt the same. She needed to take matters in her own hand. She grabbed a condom and pushed JD onto his back. He fell back allowing Sasha to take the lead. She climbed on top of him, straddling his hips, and allowing his hard cock to slide into her slick channel.

"Fuck," JD moaned. "So wet for me."

She arched back in pleasure. JD took her breast in his hand, thumbing her erect nipple.

Sasha began to buck vigorously, focusing on getting herself off on top of JD. She reached behind and began to massage JD's balls, wanting him to come as well.

His balls began to draw up tight against his body. The tingling sensation hit her quickly. She was about to lose control. "JD, I'm about to come. Come with me!"

Sasha yelled, rocking faster on top of JD. Hurling herself over the precipice of climax.

"Oh fuuuck, Sasha." JD groaned as he exploded into her.

She looked down at him. Damn, he was gorgeous, even with bedhead. She imagined sitting and marveling at his delicious body for hours.

Another alarm went off on her phone. She reached out for it and realized that she had accidently pressed snooze earlier. Damn phone. She looked back at JD and frowned.

"What's wrong?" He worried, stroking away the tension in her face.

"I really need to get work, but you look incredible lying there." She sighed.

He sat up and all those sections of abs flexed. *Mmmm.* "Let's get going. I don't want to make you late. Next time, hopefully, we can take our time." JD smacked lightly on her ass as she walked to the bathroom.

"Promise?" She turned back to JD with a cheeky grin.

"Absolutely, beautiful." JD kissed her again.

****

Ian

The next evening, Ian agreed to meet up with a few of the younger attorneys at the firm. They offered to take him out for drinks and he didn't want to be a jerk and turn them down. They mentioned wanting to pick his brain on how to improve their shot at making partner too. It wasn't easy to pick up tips along the way and he wanted to help. He would have appreciated more advice from new partners about the process. However, spending the evening at Lawson's Bar wasn't his first choice for how to spend the evening. Being at home with Sasha would have been a hell of a lot better.

Ian didn't need to scan the restaurant to find his friends as they were sitting at their usual table at Lawson's. They were also unusually boisterous and stood out in comparison to the other subdued patrons. He wasn't in the mood for their exuberance.

He sat down with a view of the exit in his sight and the bar to his back. Jonathon caught him up on the gossip that had them all celebrating. Apparently, some guy they went to law school with and had cheated his way through law school, was disbarred. He didn't know their friend as he had gone to a different law school, but after years of playing sports, cheaters in general pissed him off.

The waitress brought over a round of shots of vodka. With glasses in the air to toast Ian, the group loudly yelled cheers and they all threw back the shots. He recognized the brand immediately and started scanning the bar for his little Smirnova. He peered at the bar, where he had originally found her that night back in the summer. Not only was she there but she was looking right back at him. His lips naturally lifted into a smile. He turned back to the table casually so as not to call attention to himself. He had trained himself not to gawk in her presence over the past few months.

The group decided that they needed another round of drinks. Marcus turned to find the waitress. "Isn't that Sasha over there at the bar? We should invite her over here to toast to Ian," Marcus suggested. "I know she usually hangs out with Kat, but we should ask her to join us."

Cromwell chimed in, "She's probably busy. She was

here last night and then left with some really hot guy last night." She acted like a chatty schoolgirl. Ian turned to Cromwell, waiting for more details.

"Who was the guy? What firm does he work at?" Jonathon begged for details. Ian was irritated that the topic of Sasha continued. His hand fisted underneath the table.

"He wasn't in a suit. I don't even know if he is an attorney. I've never seen him here before. Because, let me tell you, this guy was so hot I would definitely have remembered him," Cromwell fawned.

Marcus was more observant than the others at the table. "Huh." He looked at Ian. "I always thought you and Sasha had something going on between the two of you. It felt like some kind of sexual tension. I guess I was wrong."

Ian confirmed with a stone face, "No, there isn't anything going on between Ms. Smirnova and myself." Ian used her last name to punctuate a distance between he and Sasha. He tamped down the anger that began building inside him. If it weren't for Ian's skills as an attorney at knowing how to never show your hand, he would not have managed to contain the rage. Even with all his experience perfecting the discipline, he wasn't sure how long he would be able to continue to hold it inside.

After a few rounds of drinks, Ian thanked his colleagues and called it a night. On the way out the door he shot a text to JD and Sasha in their group message. He was fuming.

Ian—*WHAT THE FUCK DID THE TWO OF YOU DO?! YOU FUCKING OUTED YOURSELVES AS A COUPLE LAST NIGHT. YOU GUYS COMPLETELY*

FUCKED ME!!!—

JD—*Dude, calm down. We didn't tell anybody anything at all—*

Sasha—*What are you talking about? Where are you?—*

Ian—*I'm heading home. As if either of you actually care—*

Ian knew that Cromwell wasn't going to let the story go. She probably had exaggerated it even further after he left. Ian's ire burned.

JD—*We absolutely do care. Obviously, we need to talk. I'm already home. Sasha can you come over?—*

Sasha—*Yes. I'll be there ASAP—*

Ian stormed through the entrance of the two-flat. He slammed the front door so hard the windows shook. He stomped up the stairs to his apartment and slammed that door shut too. He threw his suit jacket over a chair and loosened his tie and began pacing back and forth across his apartment, running his fingers through his neatly coiffed brown hair, not caring if he looked like a madman.

"Fuck, fuck, fuck," he muttered over and over again.

He turned towards his front door shutting. Both JD and Sasha strode in together like a couple, holding hands. A neat little couple that didn't include him. "Don't you two look adorable together," he mocked.

JD entered the room with his chest puffed up ready to fight. "Dude, I know you are angry about something but you better fucking watch your tone," he warned.

Ian wasn't scared of his brother. He had an extra inch on him and the means to strike first. He gripped the counter tighter until he started losing feeling in his fingers. He wanted to hit JD even more than he did last weekend. This was worse. JD knowingly hurt him.

Sasha's eyes were wider than he had ever seen, but he chose to look away. He didn't want to look at the woman that had just knifed him in the chest.

"Ian what is going on?"

He looked her way. She stepped toward him but he stepped backward. He used the space as a protective barrier.

Ian felt like he was going to vomit as he regurgitated the story. "The two of you went out on a date. Alone. In public. But not just anywhere in public but to Lawson's where everyone we know hangs out. They all saw you there. You made it clear you were a couple. And now I have no place in this relationship. You two fucking cut me out," he screamed. Ian bent over heaving. The implication of what they had done knocked the life out of him. "I thought we were going to try." He lost his intensity and had lost his will.

"We didn't go on a date Ian." Sasha inched her way closer.

JD cut in, "I would never do something like that to you. I know we need to discuss things like this all together." JD shoved his hands in his pockets, unprotectively. Unlike Ian, JD wasn't there to fight.

"Abby Cromwell saw you at the bar. She saw you kiss Sasha. She saw you walk out of the bar together. One plus one equals two," Ian stated as if it were as codified as law.

"That's all circumstantial, Ian," Sasha qualified as she placed her hand on top of his.

Ian pulled his hand away and shot back, "Are you denying the facts?"

"I'm denying the premise. JD and I were not on a

date. We did not arrive together. We did not eat together. Although I did eat a salad at the bar alone. We did not share a drink together either," Sasha retorted with equal lawyerly sass.

"Did you kiss Sasha in public?" Ian fired at JD, taking an aggressive step toward JD.

JD held his ground but deflected Ian's aggressiveness. "I gave her a peck on the cheek as a hello."

"We did walk out together," Sasha admitted, looking guilty.

"We weren't even holding hands when we walked out," JD filled in the gaps.

"That situation could have been interpreted many different ways, Ian. Abby is a bit of gossip and probably just wanted to spice up the story," Sasha grumbled, crossing her arms over her chest.

"I'm not a lawyer, but even I could have interpreted the situation differently. What if you and Sasha were out as a couple dating. As your brother it would be very conceivable that I would kiss Sasha on the cheek and ensured that she got home safely." JD sat down in a chair.

He had a well-reasoned argument. Ian's fiery anger reduced to smoke rising in the air.

"I denied that there was anything going on between Sasha and I." Should he have diffused the situation differently? "Marcus accused me of having a relationship with Sasha on the sly and I denied it."

"What does that mean? You always intend to deny having a relationship with me?" Sasha stammered and sat at the table next to JD. JD put an arm around her shaking shoulders.

"I don't know." Ian acknowledged his uncertainty. "It's not that simple. For me. For you. For all three of us. This is fucking tricky." Ian took a swig of the vodka. "Did I fuck this up?" Ian sat down and took another drink.

"Listen this was a minor little incident. All of it could be explained away fairly easily. First, it's really nobody's fucking business." JD was the man of reason. *When had he become the more logical one?*

"It does bring up a lot of potential problems of how we present ourselves in public." Sasha reached for the bottle of vodka.

"Bro, I would never fuck you over. I didn't even punch you back when you hit me the other night." JD's words stung. Ian felt guilty for hitting JD and he almost did it again as he did the other night. He needed to reign in his quick-trigger anger. His feelings for Sasha were driving him mad.

"I'm sorry you thought we had done something to exclude you, Ian. You must have felt very hurt." This time when Sasha approached Ian, he didn't back away. "I'm sorry it happened." Sasha kissed Ian sweetly.

"I think we are going to have to come up with a game plan about how we act in public. We need to be in agreement on this so no one gets hurt." JD pulled out his phone. "And I think we should order pizza because I'm starving."

"Yes, to both," Ian agreed. He needed pizza to absorb all the shots he had consumed.

"Order me a salad, please. I'm not a guy, I can't live on pizza multiple times a week," Sasha reminded them.

"Really, I hadn't noticed. Here I was thinking you were just one of the guys." JD teased, leaning over and kissing Sasha.

Ian laughed. He wanted to say she should have to strip to prove that she was actually a girl. Sasha naked with both he and JD was a whole other can of worms. That issue needed to be tabled for later.

The three of them sat down on the couch together. Their relaxed postures were much more amenable to a nonconfrontational discussion.

Unlike Ian's usual take-charge attitude, he asked, "So how do we start?"

Sasha turned to Ian. "I have a question. Why did you definitively deny to Marcus, Jonathon, and Abby that you and I aren't dating?"

"I suppose because you and I work at the same firm and I think that people knowing that we are dating is a bad thing. It's what kept us apart before. Those issues really haven't changed."

"I suppose you're right," Sasha conceded and leaned into Ian's side. Ian liked the feel of Sasha leaning on him, not just in the physical sense.

"Yet you were pissed off when your coworkers were under the impression that I was dating Sasha? Does that mean all of this needs to be on the down low?"

Sasha took JD's hand, as Ian looked over to his brother.

Ian attempted to explain, "I think what bothered me most was the fact I thought you two had made a decision without me. Or worse, I thought that maybe you two had decided to exclude me. I know I was wrong." Ian rolled his head as all the muscles in his neck were strung tight.

Sasha put her hand on Ian's knee. "I'm sorry. Again."

JD threw out another option, "Now that you know

differently, how would you feel if they thought Sasha was dating me and not you?"

This was a big question. Dealing with emotions in this type of relationship was key to whether or not there was a potential for it to work. "I think I might feel jealous, but I think I could learn to deal with it if it means the three of us can make this work. It might not be easy, but I think it will be worth it in the end." Ian reconciled the issue in his head. He laid his head on Sasha's head in exhaustion.

JD turned to Sasha. "How do you feel about denying that you are dating Ian?"

Sasha pointed out a more important distinction, "I completely understand at work. We have had to keep a professional distance for months. So going forward would be more of the same, but easier knowing how we actually feel about each other. But I don't want to keep Ian, or you, on the down low all the time. I think some people are going to know. Like your parents and Kat. I don't want Ian to become the dirty little secret." Ian smiled at Sasha blushing and leaned into her.

JD nodded in agreement as if they hadn't considered that scenario yet. Ian loved that Sasha was so thoughtful. It made him feel safe when he worked in and amongst a pool of vipers. "I appreciate your consideration, Sasha."

"Bro, I would never think of you as anything less than me in the relationship even if Sasha and I are out to your friends," JD added.

Things seemed simple for a minute, until Sasha confessed, "I have to admit that I am leery of being out to everyone. Most people aren't going to understand. And let's face it, as a woman, I am going to be accused of being a whore." Sasha's shoulders slumped forward.

"Don't ever refer to yourself in such a negative way again," JD demanded and kissed Sasha earnestly to hammer home his point, but she barely grinned.

Ian conceded, "I think initially, we should probably keep it a secret as much as possible." Ian waited to see what JD and Sasha thought. He was slowly realizing that making assumptions for others wasn't that great of an idea. *Another mine to avoid in the relationship.*

"Let's go to Lux this weekend. They're all cool and won't care," JD suggested. Ian considered it, but was uncertain.

"I met the team last weekend. They already think that you and I are a couple, JD." Sasha reminded him and mouthed the word sorry to Ian. Ian wanted to punch something, but he felt bad for Sasha's concerns and kissed her head.

"Oh yeah, I forgot." The options were starting to seem very limited.

"So, in public, I play the role of only JD's girlfriend?" Sasha frowned.

"And I can't ever take Sasha on a date myself?" Ian's gut tightened.

"Maybe we need to keep things simple with very little PDA." Ian doubted the hopeful look on JD's face.

"I still feel like Ian is getting the short end of the stick here?" Sasha advocated on Ian's behalf again.

"I think the bigger worry here, is if you think you're getting the short end of the stick in the relationship." JD winked with sarcasm.

It took a second for Sasha to get the joke, but then she turned red faced. "Well, there's no chance of that."

In a sudden change of subject, JD said to no one in particular, "Where the hell is the pizza, I'm starving."

His brother was incapable of thinking when he was hungry.

The issue wasn't going to be solved in a singular discussion. Ian turned on the hockey game to help pass the time until the pizza arrived. He and JD got hooked on the game and decided they would all eat in front of the tv. Sasha didn't object. They finished eating early in the second period. Everyone helped clean up during intermission and resumed their positions on the couch with Sasha sitting between Ian and JD.

Sasha dozed off halfway into the third period. When the game finished, Ian and JD debated if they should wake her.

"Damn, she's so tired lately. Last night she looked like she was going to fall asleep at the bar. She was a walking zombie by the time we got to her place." JD whispered to Ian as they both gazed at her sleeping body on the couch.

"Stein is really giving her a hard time and passing off way too much work on her. He's a prick that way. I was thrilled to get away from him. Unfortunately, there's nothing I can do about the situation," Ian informed JD, regretting if he had inadvertently put Sasha in a bad position by highlighting her exemplary capabilities.

"What a dick!" JD noted and quietly attempted to rouse Sasha. "Bro, she's out cold."

"Let's let her sleep here. Then, in the morning, I can drive her back to her place so she can grab a clean suit for work." Ian gestured toward Sasha. "Help me get her undressed and into my bed."

JD kissed Sasha goodnight and headed to his own apartment down below.

Ian was content to be able to hold Sasha and fall asleep beside her.

Chapter 16

JD

JD checked his phone several times while he was out with his friends on Thursday. Nothing. Sasha hadn't replied to a single text message. His buddy caught him sneering at his phone and poked fun at him. His buddy's razzing didn't bother him, but her lack of response did. He understood how busy she was during the day, but he took it personally that she didn't bother to send him anything after normal work hours.

He enjoyed their playful banter. It was more than just meaningless messages to him; it was a form of connection. He craved connectedness, physical or otherwise.

Around 11 p.m., she finally texted one word in the group message with Ian.

Sasha—*Goodnight*—

That's it. One lousy word. No emoji. No emotion. It didn't take more than a minute to write a sentence or two.

Was she trying to cut out JD? Was she in contact with Ian and not him? He texted Ian.

JD—*Hey, have you heard from Sasha at all today?*—

Ian—*Only thing I got was goodnight in our group chat*—

JD needed to vent.

JD—*It really bugs me when she doesn't reply—*

Ian—*She's had a really hard week—*

JD—*Emoji, something—*

Ian—*Some of the other first years are literally working and billing hours while they are in the bathroom dude. It's tough this time of year and her boss is a nightmare—*

JD—*That's fucked up—*

Ian—*It takes time to get more efficient. I'll check on her in the morning and give you an update—*

JD—*Thanks man—*

Ian—*Np—*

JD woke up at the ass crack of dawn like he did most days. He threw on some running gear and set out for his morning run. His days of being a professional athlete were over, but running was something he always enjoyed. He hit the pavement at his normal pace. It was cool, but the sidewalks were dry. No big snow had yet fallen. He didn't have to watch out for black ice, which was great because he didn't want to slip and reinjure his knee.

He would have been grateful for the mental distraction, but thoughts of Sasha consumed him. Fury burned inside. Her lack of replying to his messages was inexcusable. He started running faster. He clenched his jaw tighter as he wasn't able to outrun his anger.

Messaging was something he needed in this relationship. Was she not capable of providing it or unwilling?

His phone rang and he answered on his earbuds. "Hello?" He didn't slow his pace for the call.

"Jesus Christ. Please tell me you are out running and not doing something else to make you breathe that hard."

Ian choked.

"Fuck-off Ian."

"I just wanted to let you know I stopped by Sasha's office this morning."

"Did you talk to her?" *And...?*

"No man. First off, she was already working by the time I got there and I'm usually the first one in the office. She was typing at a break-neck pace when I stopped by. Her keyboard strokes were so loud it was like she was brutalizing her keyboard."

"I get it, she got to work early. What did she say?" *Jesus, couldn't Ian just get to the point?*

"Nothing. She didn't even acknowledge that I was there until I knocked on her desk. I asked if she was okay. Then she told me she had a lot of work to do and didn't have time for idle chit-chat."

JD's mood shifted from upset to ticked off. "That's rude."

"I agree. But I don't think today is the day to discuss the issue. She's really having a hard time at work," Ian defended Sasha. "I'm worried about her. Think about what we can do to turn this around. I need to get back to work."

"Peace."

JD had an art history class to teach later in the morning. He preferred to use the class time for discussion and practice among the students rather than straight lecture. He wanted his students to learn to feel, to think, to describe, and to mimic all styles. The topic of the day's lecture was Celtic art from 500 BC to 100 BC. JD joined his students while they worked on their own after the discussion.

Sketching out a triskelion, with three connecting

spirals, had him thinking about his relationship with Sasha and Ian. The triskele represented forward motion. The three of them needed to move forward together. Ian and Sasha worried about outside perceptions. They needed to work together and not worry about outsiders. A strong foundation required work inside in order to secure the outside facade.

He kicked around a few ideas for how to put a good plan in place. He messaged both Ian and Sasha.

JD—*Maybe rather than going out tonight, we eat in, all together? I'm even willing to eat something besides pizza. Greek food?*—

JD received a direct text from Ian. He didn't like talking behind Sasha's back. She had already complained about it before.

Ian—*I thought we were going to test the waters at Luxury Box?*—

JD—*She's tired. Let's stay in and tempt her with a two-man massage to help her relax? I massage her neck and shoulders? You can give her a foot rub?*—

Ian—*Great idea. She can't say no to that*—

JD might not fully appreciate the difficulty of the work that Sasha and Ian did, but he did understand that everyone once in while needed a break.

Ian—*If the massage goes well, we should probably discuss some other guidelines. NOT VIA TEXT!*—

JD knew that Ian had never had a threesome and he obviously had some reservations. He rubbed at his eyes. Why did people get so fixated on the details of sex in a threesome? Sex wasn't meant to be some kind of paint by numbers picture. Sex was the easy part. The relationship stuff was complicated.

JD—*I hope she reaches out at some point today*—

Ian—*I'm not letting her leave the office by herself tonight. She's not sneaking out. I'll text you—*

JD—*Thanks bro—*

Finally, shortly after 8:00 p.m., JD's phone buzzed with a message in the group chat.

Sasha—*I'm in (smiley face)—*

Thank fuck! JD fist pumped the air.

Ian—*Meet in the lobby downstairs? I'll drive—*

Sasha—*See ya in 5?—*

Ian—*Perfect (kissing face)—*

JD released the tension keeping him wound like a top all day. He cursed himself for being overly dramatic. He didn't want to fight or have to convince Sasha to make time for them tonight. And, he was giddy over an emoji. If his hockey buddies saw him at this moment, they would give him a boat load of shit.

About fifteen minutes later, his phone rang. It was Ian. "No," he said before answering the phone. Did something go wrong? Did she bail? He looked up, hoped, and swiped to answer.

"Hey Bro. Did you catch our fugitive?" He crossed his fingers.

"Am I a fugitive?" Sasha asked and JD smiled at the sound of her voice.

"Hey beautiful. You're coming home with Ian?" He forced himself to sound more chipper than desperate. It came out a bit strained.

"I hear that my very sexy boyfriends are offering to give me a massage and feed me. So, hell yes. Sounds like heaven." Sasha sighed.

"Perfect. I already put in the order for dinner. Cool with you guys?" JD prayed that he was starting off the night on a positive note.

"Thanks for skipping a day of pizza," Sasha acknowledged.

"I agree with Sasha. Seriously, even I can't keep up with your predilection for pizza." Ian laughed. JD knew that his brother loved his pizza, but appreciated him supporting Sasha.

"Pizza or no pizza, I'm looking forward to seeing you Sasha." JD hoped for an amazing night.

"Me too, JD. Sorry about not texting back."

Her apology made him feel two feet tall. He had driven himself crazy over the fact that she didn't text for one day. He knew she had been busy with work. All he wanted was to see her and feel her.

"See ya soon." Ian hung up the call.

The sound of the front door had his heart racing. He wasn't expecting them home so soon. They must have gotten lucky finding a spot to park on the street, a rarity on a Friday night. With long strides, JD strode across his apartment to greet her at his door.

The inner door to his apartment opened and her smiling face sent shivers through his body. He closed the gap between them. He grabbed her face between both of his hands and eagerly kissed her. He didn't want to let go. She stepped closer into his kiss, crushing his arousal between their two bodies. Reluctantly, he broke the kiss. "Hey beautiful."

"Mmm, hello there." Her cheeks reddened. Between the kiss and her blush, he needed to adjust himself in his jeans.

"Dinner should be here in about thirty minutes," JD announced. "Sasha, I put some sweats and stuff on my bed. I thought you might prefer to get comfortable before we eat." JD wanted to suggest that she should start keeping some of her clothes at his place. It was very inconvenient when Sasha needed to run home in the early morning to grab fresh clothes. And, it was seriously a pain when her work hours were extreme.

"Aww thanks." Sasha kissed him and went off to his room to change. He stared at her ass as she walked away.

"That's a great idea. I think I'll go run upstairs and change too." Ian returned readily with a couple of bottles of wine.

JD went to grab a few glasses from his cabinet. The three chatted while waiting for the food. Sasha remained unusually quiet. He hoped that her lack of conversation was due to exhaustion and not anything related to them. He and Ian had no problem carrying the conversation while including Sasha sporadically without pressuring her.

Sasha's eyes widened when they started opening all the containers of food. "Oh my god, the food smells so good. Thank you for doing this JD." She dug into the food and ate more than he expected.

Finishing the last bites of food on her plate, Sasha looked like life had been reinfused in her body. Her eyes were brighter and her smile looked content. "Thank you again for dinner. It was really good. I haven't had a decent meal since Wednesday."

Ian held up the bottle wine. "Want to top off your glass?"

"Yes, please."

Ian emptied the rest of the bottle into all the glasses.

JD rose from his chair and offered Sasha his hand. "Why don't we all go sit on the couch."

JD turned on a basketball game as he wanted some kind of noise on in the background. He had considered putting on music. Relaxation music seemed out of place since he wasn't trying to recreate the ambiance of a dentist office. Romantic music was too cheesy. He avoided the hockey game that was on because he tended to get too involved in watching the game. Hence, basketball was the choice, as inappropriate as it seemed. Ian gave him a look like he was crazy.

Sasha took her designated spot between Ian and JD. Ian grabbed her legs and brought her feet onto his lap. On the opposite end, JD saddled up behind Sasha so that her back was against his chest and that he was in an ideal position to massage her shoulders and neck.

She continued to sip on her wine, as he and Ian worked her muscles. Her moaning increased as the wine slowly drained from her glass.

JD watched the pace at which Ian dug his thumbs into Sasha's aches with little circles. He mimicked the movement on her shoulders. He wanted her attention spread equally between himself and Ian. The point was to stroke away all of her stress, not escalate a competition between the two men.

Ian was methodical and thorough in his ministrations. They were both familiar with foot fatigue from years of playing hockey. After spending hours and hours on the ice, days often ended with their feet in an ice bath. Ian started on one foot and eventually moved to the other.

A sigh escaped Sasha's mouth and made the blood rush to JD's cock.

All the while, JD continued to massage her shoulders, maintaining a delicate touch. He aimed to relax her, not perform a deep tissue massage. He was very careful not to grip her too firmly and elicit flinching.

He wanted to make her sigh in pleasure, again and again.

"Did I die and go to heaven?" Sasha murmured, setting down her empty glass and relaxing back on JD's chest. "This feels too good to be true."

"I'm glad you are enjoying it, beautiful." JD kissed her head and Ian kissed the inside of her ankle, causing her legs to slightly open up. JD's cock thickened.

JD continued to work up and down Sasha's spine and then up her neck. Her head fell forward. He kissed the side of her exposed neck, loving that sexy feminine angle.

"Mmmm," Sasha purred, twisting her neck and revealing more kissable surface.

Ian moved from massaging Sasha's feet to her ankles and calves. The massage started to change from a form of relaxation to an appreciation of Sasha's form and skin. JD worked his muscular hands down Sasha's arms, gently kneading her muscles. He followed the firm strokes with light touches that sent goose bumps down her arms.

"JD...Ian," Sasha contentedly breathed. Her voice was thick and sultry.

As soon as Ian's hands moved closer to her knee, Sasha's legs fell open wide. The scent of her arousal permeated the space. JD inhaled deeply. Fuck, she smelled fantastic.

JD's fingers lightly grazed the sides of her breasts as he lightly touched her arms. Ian hadn't moved his hand northward of her knees. She began to wiggle.

Her nipples were firm and clearly visible under the thin t-shirt. JD reached for the firm peaks on the outside of her shirt. He thumbed them gently. "JD," Sasha begged, thrusting her chest upwards.

Ian began to slide his hands up her thighs. His fingers danced along her inner thigh but never reached the apex of her legs. "Ian…" She attempted to inch herself closer to his touch.

JD pinched her nipple through the shirt firmly enough to make her cry out. She bucked her hips in response. JD repeated the firm touch on the other nipple. "Pleeeease," she cried. "Stop teasing me."

"Baby, we're not joking here," Ian mocked, smiling devilishly up at her.

JD ran his nose along the sexy curve of her neck. He continued by running his tongue over the shell of her ear.

"Pleeease," she cried out louder.

JD scraped his teeth on her ear lobe. Ian placed a kiss near her sex, on the outside of the sweats she was wearing. They continued to tease and tempt her. JD wanted to rip off all her clothes, but waited for her to beg. The scent of her arousal made him want to fuck her.

"God damn it! Make me come," Sasha wailed.

JD and Ian were ready and willing to respond accordingly. JD ripped her t-shirt over her head, while Ian stripped off her sweatpants. JD carefully extricated himself from behind Sasha and kneeled beside her on the floor, allowing Sasha to gently fall onto her back. She looked beautiful, naked and laying on his couch.

Ian was still at the end of the couch leaning near her spread legs.

"Oh Fuck, Sasha. You're so wet." Ian stared hungrily at her swollen sex weeping on her thigh.

"Ian, please I need you," Sasha beseeched. Ian complied and lapped at her cum dripping from her core.

JD ran his tongue over her nipple and teased. With an eye on Ian, he waited for Ian to insert his fingers. He waited for the opportune moment to bite down at the same time Ian's fingers disappeared inside her.

"Uhhhhhh," Sasha called out, pushing her sex against Ian's hand.

JD wanted to taste Sasha too. He kissed her on the mouth and took over, opening her mouth and kissing her as if he were kissing her sex. His hand palmed her breast aggressively. She moaned deeply when he squeezed. She responded appreciatively to the roughness.

Sasha bucked and groaned. "Ian…JD…oh…yes." Ian sat up for an instant, continuing to finger her. JD took advantage of the opening and used his fingers to apply pressure to Sasha's clit. "Fuuuuck." Sasha screamed as she climaxed hard.

JD watched her as the waves of her orgasm rushed through her, leaving her flushed.

"I can feel the walls of your pussy squeezing my fingers." Ian approved.

JD wanted to feel the warmth of her cum. He needed her. Her entire body called to him.

"Damn you are beautiful," Ian gushed.

"So, god damn beautiful," JD reiterated the sentiment. He didn't want her worry to set in again. He seized on her moment of bliss. "What do you think about continuing this in the bedroom?"

Sasha hummed in agreement.

Ian picked up Sasha from the couch. It was possessive, but JD wasn't bothered by it. The three of them headed to his bedroom. JD in one grandiose movement removed his comforter and told Sasha to hop up on her hands and knees in the center of the bed.

Ian was going along well with JD's plan, in spite of their lack of experience together. JD knew that driving up Ian's arousal by satisfying Sasha on the couch first, would force him to be brave enough to go beyond his comfort zone in the bedroom. He would start thinking with his cock and not be inhibited by his brain.

JD had given this a lot of thought on how to best ease both Ian and Sasha into a threesome. He stepped-up to take a commanding role. "Ian, our girl looks very hungry. I think you should help her out."

Ian looked at JD with uncertainty. "Yeah?" It wasn't clear if he was asking JD or Sasha. He needed a little bit of a push to help get him started.

JD gave Ian what he needed. "Yeah. Sasha, do you want to suck Ian's cock?" She nodded enthusiastically. "Keep her busy while I go gather a few things." JD directed Ian to help him along. JD stepped into the bathroom to give Ian and Sasha a moment alone. He figured that a moment with Sasha solo would help Ian through his reservations and help him gain his confidence.

JD grabbed a condom and the lube from his bathroom.

When JD returned to the bedroom Ian and Sasha were in the perfect position for him to join. She was on all fours with her mouth wrapped around Ian who was kneeling in front of her. JD climbed on the bed behind her. He began to apply the lube at Sasha's back entrance. He knew she enjoyed anal from the other night they had spent together. He began to loosen up her opening with his fingers. She moaned around Ian's cock.

"Fuck. When you moan, you send shivers through me." Ian groaned.

"Oh, I'll make her moan." JD entered her star-shaped opening. Sasha moaned intensely.

"Holy fuck." Ian groaned like he was fighting off his orgasm.

In time, JD found a rhythm with Sasha. He held her hips tightly so he didn't push her to take more of Ian than she was able to manage without choking.

JD thrusted faster. Sasha mewled loudly.

Delicious ecstasy extended through all JD's nerves. Thoughts of a threesome weren't on his mind. Pleasure consumed all his thoughts, sensations, heart.

"Fuuuck, Sasha," Ian cried. "I'm going to come!" JD slowed his movements for Ian's sake and allowed Sasha to focus on Ian. Sasha mouthed Ian's cock as she stroked the base. "Oh fuck, fuck, Sasha," Ian cried out as he came down her throat.

When JD was certain that Sasha had finished swallowing, he began to fuck her hard and deep. It was JD's opportunity to completely focus on Sasha and his pleasure.

Ian initially laid in a breathless heap on the bed. He slowly came out of his mesmerized daze and began to fondle Sasha's breasts. Ian pinched her nipple.

"Oh god," Sasha yelped.

"Are you close beautiful?" JD prodded for an update.

"JD!" Sasha screamed, "Yes…please…yes."

JD let himself go in fast quick movements. Sasha screamed again until she and JD climaxed together.

JD shuffled off to the bathroom to clean up. When he returned, JD asked Sasha, "Do you need a minute alone in the bathroom?" She kissed Ian, who was still laying on the bed, then kissed JD on her way to the bathroom.

The bathroom door closed. JD found himself naked

along with his brother. An awkwardness darkened the room. JD saw panic wash over Ian. He whispered to his brother, "Don't, bro. If you panic, she'll panic. She's feeling fabulous right this minute. Don't fuck that up for her because of some nerves."

Ian got off the bed and started gathering his clothes.

Sasha returned to the bedroom and saw Ian dressing. "Wait, you're not leaving, are you?" Sasha turned to JD. "He doesn't need to leave, does he?"

"Not at all," JD agreed with Sasha's train of thought.

"Please Ian, don't go," Sasha pled in a tone that no man could say no to.

Ian stopped putting on his pants. "You want me to stay here? To sleep here? All three of us in the bed?" JD saw Ian struggling.

JD wanted to tease his brother that he wouldn't spoon him, but he knew Ian was trying his best to warm up to the newness of the situation. He didn't want to mock a man that was sincerely trying.

Sasha went over and kissed Ian. "Please, Ian, don't go. We agreed to try."

JD offered an olive branch and attempted to ease some of Ian's hesitation. "How about we impose a boxer brief requirement in bed." He hoped that eliminating the accidental touching issue would help Ian.

"Does that rule apply to me as well?" Sasha asked.

"No!" Ian and JD responded in unison.

"Okay. I'm going to go take a quick shower." Ian noted. Sasha kissed him again and he stood a little taller. He teased, "Don't go running off while I'm in the bathroom."

JD smiled at his brother's ease.

"Not a chance," Sasha reassured him and started

making the bed with JD.

As JD climbed under the sheets with Sasha, he wanted to make sure Sasha was okay as he wasn't adept at reading her. "You okay, beautiful?"

"Are you kidding? I couldn't be better. I thought it was amazing." Sasha glowed. Suddenly, her face turned to concern. "Did you enjoy it?"

"Every time I am with you, beautiful, it is amazing." JD kissed her deeply.

The bathroom door opened. Ian looked much more relaxed than he did a few minutes prior. Sasha looked at Ian with concern. "Did you enjoy tonight?"

"After a few minutes, to think and rehash it all in the shower, I can say yes. I think at first, I was surprised to have liked it. If that makes any sense. Then, I felt a bit of guilt for doing something untraditional. And then I decided that idea was fucking stupid. When we were on the couch and JD and I were able to work together to turn you on and make you scream, it was probably the hottest experience of my life."

"I'm not sure I can agree," Sasha said flatly. Ian's jaw dropped. Then she smiled. "I think the three of us on the bed was the hottest experience of my life." She patted the empty part of the bed. "Now come here. I'm tired."

Ian eased into the bed, his breathing resumed a languid rate when Sasha started running her fingers threw his hair. JD smushed the front of his body up against Sasha's back.

"Oh, now this is heaven. Goodnight O'Malleys." Sasha dozed off quickly.

For the first time, JD felt confident that the three of them had a real chance of making this relationship work.

Chapter 17

Ian

Ian woke early on Thanksgiving morning. He lingered in bed with Sasha's head on his chest. She stirred slightly at the sound of his alarm, but nestled back in to him. He never truly had the opportunity to savor this moment in the morning. JD's presence in the bed as well no longer bothered him. The fact that neither he or JD sprawled out across a bed mitigated Ian's concern for boundaries. They all kept to themselves while they slept and didn't form a crazy puppy pile. And, Sasha handled being in the middle well. She rolled onto each of her sides, offering Ian and JD equal affection. He cherished the moment of calm, as he and Sasha's law firm had ordered all employees not to come into the office.

His addiction to morning coffee nagged at him. He carefully extracted himself from Sasha's touch and walked slowly to the kitchen. He enjoyed the unhurried pace. Even his brain appreciated the break from focusing on rushing through a to do list first thing in the morning.

While the coffee percolated, Ian saw JD's mail sitting on the counter. The letter from the owner of their building was sitting on top of the stack unopened. He knew what was inside as he had received a copy as well. The owner of the building planned on selling it and gave them three-month's notice to move out. Ian reconciled the notice to the terms of their lease and the owner had supplied adequate notice.

Moving was a pain in the ass and the thought of it was unpleasant. On the other hand, maybe this provided a perfect opportunity for him, JD, and Sasha. Bouncing between the three apartments was burdensome. Maybe this was exactly what they all needed to prompt them to discuss the issue and consider options. Should they all get a place together? Where should they consider living? Ian needed to get more information about the status of Sasha's lease situation. It was very early days in their relationship to discuss living together. Ian planned to prepare a few options to discuss with them at a later date. Timing was often the key to selling an idea.

He was pouring himself a cup of coffee when Sasha joined him in the kitchen. She had thrown on an oversized long sleeve t-shirt. *Had she bothered with putting on underwear?* Ian loved that she slept naked at night.

"Mmm. Good morning. Can I get me some of that?" Sasha implied a double entendre.

"Me or the coffee?" Ian teased. Her cheekiness turned him on.

"Both." Sasha's eyes brightened.

"Come here." Ian opened his arms and beckoned her to come closer. As soon she was within reach, he used his long arms to pull her closer and caged her tightly against him. He kissed her neck and whispered, "Happy Thanksgiving."

"You too, Ian. This might not be my native holiday, but if this holiday means more time with you in the morning, I plan on adopting it." She kissed him.

Ian looked her in the eyes with adoration. "I have a

lot to be thankful for this year."

"Mmmm, me too."

"I am so very thankful that we found a way to be together again." Ian hugged Sasha warmly. The thought of being without Sasha was unthinkable. He appreciated the fact that he was lucky to be with her again. The pain of being away from her for months had been building day by day. Ian felt himself falling into the dark tunnel of memories.

"Ian, you need to let it go." She kissed him. "Look at me." She used his own tricks on him. She stared him in the eye. "I am here. I am with you. Let's enjoy today. Be thankful, not dwell." She kissed him again. "Can you do that?"

She was right. Ian depended on Sasha's reassurance while they figured the lay of the land in the relationship. She centered him emotionally. His desire for her erupted. Feelings of gratitude and lust overwhelmed him.

He kissed Sasha again and pulled her against him tightly. His pajama pants did nothing to hide his erection. He wanted to take Sasha, right then, in the kitchen. "I want you, Sasha."

She reached into his pajamas pants and started stroking him.

"Fuck Sasha." Ian kissed her, grabbing her hair tightly. Her locks of hair twisted around his fingers as he tugged. "Condoms. Bathroom. Let's go." They all needed to make some decisions in order to stop needing condoms.

Throwing the drawer open, Ian grabbed the essentials. He bent Sasha over the counter and began fucking her from behind. Ian was ready to blow the second he was inside Sasha. "Sasha, I'm close. Get there with me."

She reached between her legs and rubbed her clit. Their breathing quickened. Their moans became louder. They screamed each other's names. "Fuck!" Ian shouted as he came inside Sasha.

For the first time, Ian found morning sex to be appealing. He typically hated the instant that the blissful moment was ruined by the urgent need to run to the office. The extra time today to savor the dopamine rush made all the difference.

A knock on the partially open door tore Ian from his state of ecstasy. "Hey, can I get in the bathroom?"

"Damn, did we wake you?" Sasha's cheeks flushed.

"No worries, beautiful. It's nice to see you here in the morning as opposed to merely seeing you run out the door to work early." JD kissed her. His brother always knew what to say to smooth over the awkward bumps in the road of their relationship. "But seriously, can I get in the bathroom, please." Sasha and Ian stepped aside for JD. Ian raised finding alternative living arrangements higher on his priority list.

Sasha got started on putting together a bunch of items that she ordered for a charcuterie tray. Ian and JD had claimed that it was completely unnecessary to bring something to their parent's house for Thanksgiving as their mom always went overboard with too much food. Sasha had chastised both of them and told them they should act like adults and not walk into a holiday meal empty-handed. It was great to see Sasha not willing to back down to both of them. She wasn't a push-over. Ian ran upstairs to his apartment to get dressed while Sasha busied herself.

By the time he returned to the kitchen, all the fruit

was cleaned, the meats were chopped, the variety of cheeses were sliced, the crackers opened, and the vegetables washed. Ian saw Sasha arranging the food on the wooden bread board. She had done quite a bit of work but hadn't even started to get dressed. He worried that all three of them would be late.

"All that food is making me hungry. Can I help?" JD quickly snagged a piece of salami.

Sasha looked at JD with pleading eyes. She hesitated. "If by help, you mean eat everything that I've prepped, then no thank you."

JD asked rather than offered, "Can I help arrange the food on the tray? I won't just dump it out and I won't eat all of it, either." Ian respected the way JD was careful not to offend Sasha by taking over her project.

"Actually, that would be really helpful. It would give me a chance to put on my make-up. Maybe we can even leave on time." Sasha thanked JD with a kiss.

"Did I hear you were going to get ready on time?" Ian feigned shock. "JD and I will stay out of your way."

JD spoke quietly to Ian as he continued to organize the charcuterie tray. "You know, it isn't easy for all of us to get ready with only one bathroom here."

"Are you upset that we were in the bathroom earlier?" Ian voiced his concern.

JD continued with his arranging. "No, I just really needed the bathroom. We are tight on space," he clarified.

Ian sighed. He hadn't grown comfortable with all the etiquette of sharing Sasha. Rather than linger, Ian changed topics and pointed to JD's stack of mail. "Hey, I saw you didn't open your mail this week. There's a letter from the building owner." He resisted the urge to comment on JD's lack of responsibility in not opening his mail. "We need to find a new place to live."

"Oh man! Moving is a pain in the ass," JD whined.

Ian ignored JD's comment. "I think we should discuss options with Sasha."

Sasha returned half-dressed with two dresses on hangers. Ian's mouth fell open at the sight of her in a bra and panties. All worries about apartment issues were forgotten. She was beautiful and extremely tempting. *Perhaps, being a little late wasn't terrible.*

JD took two strides in her direction like a lion going after his prey. Apparently, he shared the same thought as Ian. Sasha held up her hand. "Stop right there. I have already done my make-up and I don't have time to redo it so get those naughty thoughts out of your head."

Damn! Ian's shoulders slouched. "Then why are you teasing us?"

"I came down here to ask for your opinions on which dress to wear." Luckily, for all their sakes, Ian and JD pointed to the same dress. Putting Sasha in a situation where she had to choose one of their opinions over the other was unfair. Ian made a mental note to discuss that concern with JD at another time.

To Ian's pleasant surprise, they all arrived at his parents' home on time. Both of his parents greeted them with hugs.

Carrying the charcuterie tray, JD asked, "Where should I put this?"

"Oh, that tray looks fabulous," his mom gushed, taking the tray.

"JD was instrumental in making the arrangement look so good," Sasha bragged.

His mom patted Sasha on the arm. "I know my boys,

and this idea has you written all over it. Thank you for that, and enlightening my boys on the art of growing up and contributing to a meal." His mom shot a look of derision at Ian and JD.

Ian was still holding the wine bottles, his mom asked, "Ian, can you open the bottles. And, JD why don't you go grab some wine glasses." His mom was obviously trying to distract him and JD. Ian worried about her intentions. She proceeded to corner Sasha. He remained in earshot in case Sasha needed someone to run interference. *What was his mom up to?*

"It is so good to see you again." His mom embraced Sasha in a big bear hug. "I was so worried about you when you left our house last time."

"I'm so sorry about that Mrs. O'Malley," Sasha apologized openheartedly.

His mom dismissed the notion with a flip of her hand. "Apologies are not necessary, Dear. Today is a day for being thankful, and I am grateful that you are here with both my boys. James, is happy you are here too."

"How are you doing? I imagine that dating two men can be a handful. And as much as I love my boys, I *know* they can be a handful." His mom laughed. Sasha looked at Ian over his mom's shoulder. "Maybe during the Thanksgiving meal, I can embarrass both of them with some childhood stories."

Sasha laughed. "Oooo, now that sounds fun!"

His mom pressed, "But seriously, how are you?"

"Things are really good with JD and Ian." Sasha smiled but then paused. "I don't want you to worry about us. And if I seem a little less bubbly than usual, I've been going at a near breakneck pace at work. I don't want you to think that it has anything to do with your sons. I'm doing my best to make them happy as well."

"Ian mentioned that you were having difficulties with your boss. I'm sorry to hear that. I hope that my sons are supporting you in the situation and not pushing you to overextend yourself. If there is anything that I have learned over the years, it is that you need to take care of yourself before you can give to others. Even if it is my boys." His mom hugged Sasha again.

"Mind giving me a hand?" Both of the women set off toward the kitchen.

While the women were out of the living room, his dad approached him and JD. "How is everything going with Sasha? I hope the two of you have not come to fisticuffs again."

"Not at all, dad." Ian freed his dad from the concern. He didn't mention the one moment after the incident at Lawson's when he actually wanted to beat the shit out of his brother. The three of them had worked through that. No reason to bring it up again.

"Things are good between the three of us," JD added, handing his dad a glass of wine.

Ian's dad wasn't clueless and knew how to extract the full truth from both of them. "JD mentioned you all went out the other night, how did that go?"

"Good," JD inserted reflexively. "We all had fun."

His dad read him easily and Ian wasn't in the habit of hiding his feelings in front of his family. "Did you have fun too, Ian?"

"We were at the Luxury Box. It isn't my favorite place to hang out. It was okay." Ian obfuscated and shrugged.

"I know you often hang out with JD there. Why didn't you have fun?" His dad took a sip of wine.

Ian looked at JD, worried that he may offend him. He was also nervous Sasha might overhear. But mostly, he worried that if he expressed his concerns that he would potentially blow up this relationship. Ian didn't usually pause when he spoke. His delay in answering was apparent to both JD and his dad.

"Bro, what's wrong?" JD shifted his weight and asked.

"Son?" When Ian didn't say anything again, his dad conjectured, "Things in private are great but not as great as you would like in public?"

Ian felt his body beginning to heat. His dad had hit on the heart of their problems.

"Huh?" JD sat down. "Ian? What's up?"

Ian sat closely to the other two men and lowered his voice. "Nothing was really wrong," Ian reaffirmed the positive in order to remind himself and bolster his own belief in the viability of the relationship. "The three of us are great." Ian intentionally left out the condition of in private.

"Ian, stop talking like a lawyer. What the hell are trying to say? We talked about the necessity of honesty for this to work." *When did JD become so mature and articulate?*

His dad looked at JD with a newfound pride, but didn't pile on as JD spoke.

"It is ridiculously minor. It's stupid to even mention." Ian tried to shrug it off again.

"That may be, but I want to know," JD said softly, leaning in more closely.

Ian sighed. "It's really little stuff. Like the fact that I can't put my arm around Sasha when we are in public. That *everything* needs to be platonic in public between her and I. I get it. I agreed to it. But when I see you make gestures, I can't help, but feel...*jealous*." Ian exhaled and took a long sip of wine.

"Jealousy isn't little, stupid, or minor, Ian." His dad put his arm on Ian's shoulder.

"It has to be when there isn't any other choice. We discussed this issue. I can't be dating Sasha at work. Sasha can only be dating one of us publicly. We all agreed," Ian sagged in his chair, repeating what he knew to be true. No relationship was perfect.

"That may be true, but your feelings are also valid," his dad acknowledged. "Also, I think you might be surprised that some of your friends may be more accepting than you think if you gave them a chance."

"Dad's right. You know, Sasha's friend, Kat, knows and supports us," JD pointed out.

"That's one. That's a start. I'm not suggesting you tell everyone, but maybe if you feel you can each tell one of your friends then you won't feel like the relationship is a secret. Secrets have a way of eating at you. Your mom and I know, that's two more." His dad crossed his leg.

"Also, maybe consider doing some other things together where you can be more open together." His dad counted out the number of ideas on his fingers. "Go to a movie. Go hiking. Go on a vacation where no one knows you."

JD nudged his brother lightly. When Ian looked his way, he noted, "You can't shove your feelings in a box. Dad has some good points, Bro."

JD added in a serious tone, "You need to share your feelings with Sasha too. You can't expect me to keep this from her. I won't, Ian."

Ian nodded. "I'll tell her," he said just as Sasha entered the room.

"Tell me what?" She asked.

All the men got out of their chairs. "I'm starving. Let's talk over lunch." JD took Sasha by the hand and pulled her to the dining room. The freedom with which JD took her hand looked natural. Ian didn't feel like he had that same liberty. The question remained; was it possible to create a situation where all three of them enjoyed the relationship without compromising beyond a point that was unhealthy?

His dad led grace at the table. "Bless us, O Lord, and these Thy gifts, which we are about to receive from Thy bounty, through Christ our Lord. Amen."

His mom cleared her throat to get everyone's attention and continued where his dad left off, "And bless the relationship between our sons and Sasha. May you help them find the fortitude to see through all challenges that they face."

"Amen."

Ian reached for the potatoes, hoping to avoid the conversation. He counted on JD's normal ravenous appetite and Sasha's desire for politeness as distraction. But JD didn't reach for any of the food. No one started serving themselves, except Ian. "Why isn't everyone digging in?" His mother's perceptiveness never failed.

"Ian?" Sasha shot a laser stare at him.

"Bro."

Ian poked at the potatoes on his plate, debating how to initiate the conversation.

"The boys and I were discussing some other date ideas for the three of you."

Yes. Fun ideas for dates sidestepped the real issue.

"Dad suggested going to the movies." Sasha squeezed his leg underneath the table and winked at him. He smiled at the fantasy of making out during the movie.

Out of the corner of his eye, he saw his mom looking skeptical. She remained unusually quiet. The silence at the table was deafening.

"Ian?" Ian winced at JD's prodding.

"What aren't you telling me?" Sasha placed her hand gently on top of Ian's that was still holding the fork. He released the utensil.

Ian took a deep breath. "We were trying to come up with date ideas where we all don't need to hide all the PDA."

"You mean between you and I?" Sasha's insightfulness impressed Ian. He nodded.

JD added, "We could also go away for the weekend."

Sasha grimaced. "I don't have time to get away for entire weekend. I'm barely managing to survive as it is at work."

"Listen. You guys need to be respectful of each other's time. And don't forget that people need time to themselves." His mom looked at him. Sasha looked down at her plate. *Was she feeling that dedicating time to two men was too challenging?*

"That being said, maybe the three of you could do a quick getaway to a bed and breakfast. There are plenty of places in the suburbs that are within an hour and a half drive, so it wouldn't be such as hardship timewise."

"That might work." Sasha gazed at her empty plate.

"We'll figure it out." JD served as the voice of reassurance.

"I'm sure you all will. But for now, please eat."

Everyone followed his mother's orders and filled their plates.

Ian had started the day positive and thankful. After visiting his parents' house, he had a lot of concerns about whether or not they had the strength to make it work.

Sasha didn't stay long after they ate as she had promised to stop by and see Kat and her family. Ian and JD had plans to join his parents at another gathering with all their extended family.

While Sasha slipped on her coat at the door, Ian's mom mentioned, "Thank you so much for coming. And if I'm not pushing my luck too far today, I would love it if you could come to brunch on Sunday along with Ian and JD."

Pulling her long hair out from her winter jacket, she answered, "Thank you so much Mrs. O'Malley for Thanksgiving. The meal was amazing. And thank for the invite, but on Sunday I'm going to mass with my friend Kat. Her father passed away about a year ago and her entire family thought Sunday would be a good day for a memorial."

"Oh, I'm so sorry," his mom commiserated.

JD put his arm around Sasha and added, "Ian and I are going to mass with Sasha, so we won't be able to make it Sunday, either."

"Oh my." His mom sniffled. "My boys going to Sunday mass. Do I ever have reason to give thanks today. Even if you aren't at our church, I'm thrilled that you will be at mass." His mom reminded JD that he agreed to stay and clean up.

JD kissed Sasha goodbye before Ian walked out the door with her. He held hands with Sasha on the way to his car. It was nice to feel free around his family. Ian drove to Lawson's and kissed Sasha before she hopped out of his car.

He made a mental note that while he was at church on Sunday, he should consider praying for a little help to make the relationship work.

Chapter 18

Sasha

At church on Sunday, Sasha walked up the nave with both Ian and JD by her side. She proceeded to the front row where she found Kat with red-rimmed eyes, breaking Sasha's heart. Tears rolled down both of their faces. Sasha choked back her sadness as she hugged her best friend.

She spotted a place to sit right behind Kat, near Seth and Dylan, her good friends from law school. Both men stood and hugged Sasha. Seth's eyes looked like he had been crying as well.

Seth placed a comforting hand on Kat's shoulders while peering over Sasha's shoulders. "And who are these two lovely lads?" Sasha grinned at Seth's remarkable ability to mourn and flirt simultaneously.

Then she froze momentarily, not knowing how to introduce Ian and JD. She fidgeted and stammered, "Um, JD, Ian, this is Seth and Dylan." The men all exchanged cordial handshakes, but Seth ogled a little too much. In an attempt to distract Seth, Sasha covered her mouth with her hand and faked a cough.

Unlike Seth and Dylan who both knew Mr. Lawson well, Sasha had no explanation of why Ian and JD were at Kat's father's memorial. The only reason for them to be in attendance was for Sasha's sake. She knew she made an idiot of herself, but Seth and Dylan fortunately didn't call her out on it.

When it came time to sit, Sasha sat between Ian and JD. It was another obvious move that her friends must have noticed. She wiped at her brow. She would have liked to have hidden under the pew at this point. She grabbed the bible in front of her instead. She needed something to hold onto as she didn't want to absent mindedly reach out and hold Ian and JD's hands in public.

Before the mass began the priest politely requested that everyone turn off their phones rather than simply placing their phones in silent mode. He preached that for one hour, God should be the priority. JD, Sasha, and Ian all complied as it seemed it was what everyone was doing.

The priest preached about focusing on the good memories. He reminded everyone of the importance of being thankful for those in your life today. The sermon left Sasha feeling more content.

Nearing the end of the mass, JD and Ian rose to get in line to take communion. JD stood right behind Kat and offered her a comforting squeeze on her shoulder. Kat mouthed a thank you to JD. The moment warmed Sasha's heart. She loved that he was so kind and considerate.

Sasha, Seth, and Dylan remained in the pews as none of them were Catholic. She kept her eyes fixated on JD and Ian, primarily on their backsides. She felt her cheeks heat as she thought about how good they each looked naked earlier that morning.

The mass concluded and the family planned to reconvene at Lawson's Bar for a brunch. As people headed out, Ian extended a hand to both Seth and Dylan and told them it was a pleasure to meet both of them but that he had to go in to work and wasn't able to stop by Lawson's. Ian gave Sasha a seemingly friendly kiss on the cheek goodbye before heading out.

Seth kindly offered JD and Sasha a ride to Lawson's as they had driven to the church with Ian and were without a car. While Seth maneuvered the car into traffic, Dylan, sitting shot-gun, wasted no time with chit chat and asked, "How long have the three of you been dating?"

Sasha paled. JD argued, "What are you talking about? Ian and I are brothers."

Seth hooted like he was cheering at a baseball game. "Bagged both brothers. Nice."

JD wore a murderous glare. "What the fuck?" JD muttered. Sasha put a hand on his leg but he shifted away from her touch.

"JD, Seth wasn't trying to be offensive. I know you don't know us, but I promise you we aren't here to judge. We're happy if Sasha is happy." Dylan's finesse calmed Sasha enough for her to risk being vulnerable.

She jumped all in. "I am happy. Very happy. And yes, I'm dating both JD and Ian."

"Sasha!" JD spit out and Sasha cowered, reflexively.

"I'm sorry. Was it a secret?" Dylan looked back at them from the passenger seat. JD scowled at Sasha.

"It's new. And only Kat and their parents know." Sasha worried her fingers together.

She turned to JD and whispered, "Sorry." She reached out for JD's hand, but he still didn't take hers. He folded his arms over his chest. Sasha whispered as softly as possible to JD, "We talked about possibly

251

dipping our toe in the water by telling some friends."

Seth tried to reassure JD as he continued driving. "I don't mean to butt in between you and Sasha right now, but if you guys were ever thinking about coming out to anyone as a threesome, you chose the least judgmental couple of people. Seriously, man, Dylan, Kat, and I were a throuple during law school. We understand keeping things on the down low. Don't worry. We aren't going to out you."

The corner of JD's mouth raised slightly.

Sasha grinned at JD and whispered, "See, no problem."

Dylan added, cocking an upturned eyebrow at Sasha. "I'm not going to tell you what you should or shouldn't do about coming out, but I will say you guys are going to have to up your skills for doing the introduction thing. Sasha blew it when she introduced you and your brother to us at the church. Sorry sweetie. Like I said, I don't care. I'm not one to pass judgment on what someone else does between the sheets."

JD relaxed his arms across his chest and asked calmly, "How do you think we could do the introduction thing better?"

"It depends on what information you are willing to share. I can tell you, people either don't want to hear anything or they want to hear too many details. Some people can be really fucking rude and want to know who is topping whom. My gaydar is telling me you are both straight, yeah?" Dylan pried, but not in an aggressive way.

"Uh yeah." JD faltered. Sasha reached for his hand, which was oddly sweaty.

"So I assume you haven't ever had to deal with

people questioning your sex life?" Sasha turned her attention to Seth. "It's a bit of learning curve. The three of us never had to explain. People always assumed we were all study buddies." Seth smiled devilishly.

Dylan added, "It's a little trickier for you guys. But when you go to something, like church, which isn't a casual thing, you call attention to yourselves."

"I hadn't considered church like that as I grew up going to church every Sunday. People were more concerned about the consistency of your attendance than anything else," JD qualified, fixing his grip on Sasha's hand.

"Fair enough," Seth agreed, tapping his fingers on the steering wheel. "What about the brunch right now? Perhaps you could spin it that both you and Ian are friends with Kat. You probably aren't aware of it, but both of you use your bodies in ways that indicate a connection with Sasha. And Sasha you do the same."

"But we didn't hold hands. It wasn't like we were playing footsies in the pews. Ian only gave me a quick peck on the cheek goodbye. Lots of people kiss goodbye, even friends." Sasha protested and looked to JD for backup.

"Sweetie, it's all the other little things. The way you look at one another. The distance at which you stand. Granted, my brain may be more attuned than most, but you all were obvious," Dylan leveled them with a stare of condemnation.

"So, what you're saying is that there's no way to keep this on the down low?" An ache grew in Sasha's belly. JD tightened his grip on her hand.

"Sasha, there are ways to get around it. One, don't bring JD or Ian to anything that requires a date or where it is anything more than a friend event. Or two, only acknowledge that you are dating one. But that's a fucked-up choice. The one you don't acknowledge is going to get hurt, bad. Being the dirty-little-secret is horrible." Dylan shook his head dismissively.

"Or three, don't fucking give a shit what other people think and admit you are dating both Ian and JD. Seriously, they are both hot! You are fucking lucky." Seth winked at Sasha while at a stop light.

"I don't know what to do." Sasha stared at her shoes.

Nearing the bar, Seth suggested, "You don't need to make any huge decisions before we enter Lawson's. Today is about Kat and her family, not about you. If you need to introduce JD today, just say he is your friend. It's the truth. If people assume boyfriend, that is on them."

"I guess I can do that." Sasha looked to JD for confirmation, who nodded.

"Try to keep the fuck-me eyes to a minimum between the two of you. Seriously, the three of you were lucky that you didn't get struck by lightning in church based on all the dirty thoughts that were obviously going through your minds." Dylan laughed. "And I was sitting next to you, JD. The bolt of lightning could have taken me out too. That's not cool, dude." They all laughed and the mood in the car lightened a bit.

Once she and JD were hanging out with Kat, Seth, and Dylan, it was easy to act like just friends. On this rare occasion, Kat wasn't working behind the bar so she was able to sit and chill with everyone. And, there was *a lot* of drinking. Everyone hung out until late afternoon.

JD stayed the entire time with Sasha as there wasn't a Sunday art class due to the holiday weekend. It was truly convenient as she was very drunk when she left the bar and needed some help making it home.

Later, JD answered the door of Sasha's apartment while Sasha remained sprawled out on the couch. She dragged her head up to see Ian enter. She lacked the energy and coordination to get up and greet him.

"What is wrong with the two of you? I texted you a bunch of times!" Ian growled, loudly shutting the front door.

"Damn. I forgot to turn my phone back on after church." JD reached for his phone and turned it on.

"Ian?" She slurred.

"What's wrong with Sasha?" Ian leered at JD.

Sasha didn't move on the couch but reached a limp hand out in his direction. "Ian."

"She had a lot to drink." JD raised his eyebrows. "Let's just say her bestie is a serious drinker. Even I struggled keeping up with the chick."

Ian sighed along with rolling his eyes. "How was it otherwise?

"The ride from the church to Lawson's got intense, bro." JD went on to share all the details with Ian. Then JD whispered, "I'm worried she's having cold feet about the relationship.

Ian slumped into a chair. "Well fuck."

Sasha drunkenly mumbled, "No dirty secret," and closed her eyes, again.

She felt Ian's kiss on her forehead. "I think you need to get some sleep, baby." He asked JD, "Did she take any ibuprofen for her head?"

"Yeah, I took care of it, bro." JD heaved.

"She's plastered, dude. How were you taking care of her?" Ian accused as he carried Sasha to her room.

"No fight," Sasha moaned, lying in bed. The room

started spinning, but eventually stopped.

Sasha woke to the sound of her alarm at 5:00 am. Her mouth was dry, but her head wasn't too bad. She recalled the mass amount of alcohol she consumed. The smell of coffee wafted into the bedroom and called to her. She grabbed her phone and padded her way into the kitchen.

Ian greeted her with a kiss and a cup of coffee. "How are you feeling this morning?" He asked. "You were really drunk when I came over last night. Do you even remember seeing me? I turned your phone on for you. You must have forgotten after church."

Sasha glanced at the phone in her hand and looked back to Ian. "Thanks. I wouldn't want to oversleep."

"I got you covered." He kissed her head. "JD made sure you took ibuprofen and drank lots of water before we put you in bed. How's your head?"

"I'm feeling better than I probably deserve. I'm lucky." Sasha took a long sip of the coffee.

She sat at the kitchen table and took another sip of the aromatic drink and opened her phone. She had dozens of unread messages. She took a longer sip before diving into the daunting task of reading through all the messages.

"Fuck!" she yelled, tears burned her eyes.

Ian jumped and spilled his coffee. "What's wrong?"

"Stein messaged me twenty times yesterday. First, he was telling me that I needed to come in and help him on something. Then he started getting angry at me for not responding. Now he's threatening to fire me. Fuck!" She started shaking.

"Didn't you tell him you were going to be unavailable yesterday?" Ian looked confused.

Sasha narrowed her eyes at Ian. "Of course! I asked for the time off days ago. And I reminded him about it several times last week." Tears streamed down her cheeks as she hastily wiped them away.

With shaky fingers, she typed out a text to Mr. Stein.

Sasha—*I will be in first thing this morning. As I told you, I was at mass yesterday and at a memorial.*—

Sasha pressed send and pushed forcefully out of her seat, sending her chair careening into the wall. As she ran to the bathroom, she crashed into JD's chest, which was like hitting a brick wall. He caught her before she bounced backward on her ass.

"What's wrong beautiful?" He attempted to swipe away the tears on her cheek. "Sasha?"

She tried to shove JD away. When he didn't actually move, she maneuvered around him. "I need to get going." Sasha tugged her shirt off and dropped it on the floor on her way to the bathroom.

She turned on the water in the shower and hopped in without waiting for it to heat up. "Fuck!" The icy water felt like she was being assaulted with an ice pick. "Fuck," she repeated over and over as the cold water pelted her chilled skin.

When she got out of the bathroom, both JD and Ian were dressed. It made her think that she was running even further behind rather than being a comfort to her.

While she was getting dressed, Ian reminded her, "You didn't do anything wrong. You gave Stein plenty of notice and he approved it."

JD handed her a pair of shoes, "It was a *Sunday* and you were at a *memorial*."

"Stop." Sasha barked at both. "None of that is going to matter. I'm probably going to get fired. Dammit."

More tears ran from her eyes.

Ian tried to offer her a comforting hug. "Stein can't fire you. HR will never let him fire you for this. It's ridiculous." JD wisely didn't interfere.

Sasha ignored Ian's comment. She didn't have the time to argue.

She kept her make-up to a minimum. Her hand was shaking and she didn't want to look like a child applied it.

On the way down to the lobby of her building, she allowed both JD and Ian to hold her shaking hands.

She counted her blessings that Mr. Stein was not there when she got to her office. Unfortunately, it was a brief calm before the storm.

Mr. Stein charged through her office door. His face was red and his eyes seemed to bulge out. He leaned over her desk and got uncomfortably close to her. He seethed, "I'll keep this brief Ms. Smirnova. This is a law firm, where clients' needs can be emergent. You turning off your phone so that you were unable to be contacted is unprofessional. You're Fired! Security will watch you pack up and escort you out in fifteen minutes." He dropped a box on her desk.

Sasha stood from her chair with her fists on her desk and fumed, "I had your explicit permission to be out of touch yesterday."

Her words had no effect on Mr. Stein as he ignored her and walked out the door.

Sasha clenched her jaw to keep from crying. She cursed under her breath as she placed a few items in the humiliating cardboard crate. The two security men demanded she turn over her access passes to the building and accounts. Sasha kept her head down and evaded eye contact with everyone as the officers literally walked her all the way to the building's exit.

She went straight home and dumped her box on the floor. She thought about throwing herself on the bed and crying, but she chucked that idea. She wasn't going to let some dumbass, entitled man keep her down. She pulled out her computer and updated her resume.

Around noon, she got a text.

Ian—*Just heard. How are you doing?*—

How did he think she was doing? She was angry. She was sad. She was pissed. She was scared. She was furious. She was humiliated. She was irate. She was spiraling in hell.

Sasha—*Don't want to talk*—

JD—*I can't believe this happened. There's got to be something you can do*—

He was right. She needed to do something. She shouldn't sit and sulk. Thinking about her feelings was unproductive, but everything was an emotional drain. She pushed past the distracting feelings. Thinking about Stein wasn't going to get her a new job. Thinking about JD and Ian wasn't helpful, either. After talking with Dylan and Seth, she wasn't really certain how she felt about being in a relationship with two men. Maybe that was destined for failure too.

Sasha needed to focus on getting her career back on track before thinking about her relationship. She took stock of all the things she liked about her job and the things that had frustrated her. She was very proud to have earned a spot in a top firm in Chicago. She enjoyed the prestige of telling people where she worked. But even before Mr. Stein, she hadn't really like the environment. She compared herself to Ian, who seemed to love it.

Argh! She needed to banish him from her thoughts. She focused on her inventory once again. Sasha found satisfaction in doing research and writing. She didn't like the necessity of trying to prove her loyalty to the firm by having no time outside of work.

She made a list of all the attorneys that she had met along the way that had solo practices. She thought that maybe someone might be in need of some assistance with their practice. With the list complete, she planned to reach out to every one of them over the next few days.

With no immediate task at hand, she fixated on her anger towards Mr. Stein. She needed to vent. JD, Ian, and Kat were out of the question.

Sasha called Hailey. While most attorneys never answered their phones, Hailey surprisingly picked up. "I heard the dick fired you too." Sasha's jaw dropped opened at Hailey's unexpected greeting.

"Uh, yeah. How did you know?"

"Bad news travels fast and I still have a lot of friends at the firm who are Stein survivors."

"Huh?" Sasha searched to understand what Hailey meant.

"You know. The women at the firm who managed to do all of Stein's work and finagle a better position at the firm. We all know Stein is unable to actually do anything on his own."

"Is that why you quit?" Sasha wanted the real answer to Hailey's exit.

"I tried to transfer out from Stein but he stonewalled me. I had no choice. I would have liked to stay at the firm."

"We should *all* file formal complaints to Human Resources." Sasha objected to Stein's unscrupulous behavior.

"Maybe. We need to be careful. Last thing I need is Stein talking shit about me outside of the firm while I'm looking for a new job." Sasha agreed with Hailey. Why hadn't Hailey found a job yet? She was more marketable than Sasha. Maybe she was too picky?

Not wanting to pry any further, Sasha changed the subject. "Hey, how's your recovery from surgery?"

"Okay, but a bit rougher than I expected" Hailey's answer confirmed Sasha's original concern about her returning to the office too early.

Commiserating with Hailey eased some of Sasha's pain, but weariness overwhelmed her.

Late in the afternoon, Ian and JD both called but she refused to answer. When she refused to speak, they texted.

JD—*Can Ian and I stop by tonight? Bring in some dinner?*—

She read the message and grunted, but didn't reply. She didn't have the energy to talk, and she didn't want to be rude and tell them no explicitly. Blowing them off was simpler.

Her phone rang in the early evening. The caller ID indicated that it was the doorman downstairs. He only called if there was a delivery or someone to see her. She didn't want to see anyone and she hadn't ordered anything. She didn't bother answering. Her phone rang again. She refused to answer, again.

Her phone rang a third time and she wanted to throw it across the room. The caller ID said Captain Coffee. "Fuck!"

He left a voice mail. "Beautiful, we are downstairs in your building. Please let us come up. Please let us be there for you." She didn't have the energy to do anything for them. She needed to take care of herself.

Kat sent her a message about an hour later.

Kat—*Your two hotties stopped by tonight looking for you. They looked worried. Everything okay?*—

Great! Did they tell Kat that she was fired? Sasha didn't want to worry her best friend. She also didn't want to complain about getting fired from her job. Sasha didn't want to burden Kat when Kat had no choice in stepping away from her law job to take over the bar.

Sasha—*No worries. Need some space from them*—

Another text came in.

Ian—*At Lawson's. Thought we might find you here. (sad face) Kat mentioned that Dylan and Seth really made our relationship seem bleak when they talked to you. I think they're wrong. I know you have a lot of other things on your mind. What can I do to help?*—

Yeah, they could give her some space to think. Sasha continued her silence until she went to bed.

JD—*Goodnight beautiful. (kissing face)*—

Why didn't they understand that she didn't want to talk? She had too much to do and her energy was already depleted. She muted her conversation with them. The messages were distracting and counterproductive. She pulled her blanket over her head and planned to attack the job situation the next day.

Chapter 19

Sasha

With a positive mindset, Sasha started her day. She outlined a strategy for the day. Rather than being angry and hurt by Mr. Stein firing her, she intended to take the opportunity to find a job that she found more rewarding. She sent out her resume to several firms in Chicago and scoured the internet for other opportunities.

When she exhausted her search, the impending wait-time frightened Sasha. She knew how to tackle a problem. She wasn't a sit-back-and-wait kind of girl. How long would it take for her to actually find something? December was only days away. No one hired in December. She calculated how long she financially could manage without an income. What if she didn't find a job with the same earning potential?

Adding to her list of problems, her apartment lease was up to be renewed. Her rent wasn't cheap. Working at a big firm meant she was able to afford a luxury apartment. Unless, she found something with a comparable salary, she would need to find a new apartment.

Sasha considered calling her parents for emotional support, but dismissed the idea. They taught her to be independent and tough. She imagined her father, speaking in Russian, telling her to fight for a job. She pressed forward on her search.

Midafternoon, Sasha's phone rang with a call from a number she didn't recognize. She recognized the area code as one from Chicago's northern suburbs.

She answered skeptically, "Hello."

"Ms. Smirnova, it's Thomas Lane." Why would her previous boss at the firm being calling from such an odd number?

"Oh, I'm sorry, I didn't recognize the number Mr. Lane."

"I understand. I didn't think it would be appropriate for me to call from my work number," he explained. "I heard about what happened with Stein. I can't really comment on what happened. I called to give you a heads up. You should expect a call from a Meagan Finch. She has a solo practice in the loop. I suggest you take the time to speak with her. Sorry again for what occurred. I need to get back to work. Good luck, Ms. Smirnova."

"Thank you, Mr. Lane." His comments bewildered her. True to form, he kept his words to a minimum. What did Mr. Lane mean? His comment was cryptic. Mr. Lane's assistance seemed to come out of the blue, but Sasha wasn't going to close a door unnecessarily on an opportunity. As such, Sasha looked up Meagan Finch online to investigate her practice. She was immediately impressed by the variety of clients that Ms. Finch represented. She even represented a few art galleries.

Of course, this reminded Sasha of JD. No matter how hard she tried to put Ian and JD out of her mind, they seemed to creep their way back into her head. There was a limit to the number of issues she was capable of addressing at one time. Dealing with their relationship was not at the top of her priority list.

Her research revealed that Ms. Finch was married to a woman, which piqued Sasha's interests. She contemplated the benefits of working for a liberal woman as opposed to a misogynistic man.

Finally, she needed a break from her job search. The walls of her apartment felt constraining compared to working in a large office. Some fresh air would do her some good. She considered stopping by Lawson's, but she didn't feel like telling Kat about losing her job nor seeing any of the attorneys from her old firm. She opened the door and stared in her barren refrigerator. She decided to go and pick up some groceries.

When she returned from the store, she fixed herself a salad and mustered up the courage to read the messages from JD and Ian.

JD—*How are you doing beautiful?*—

Sasha shook her head. What a dumb question.

Ian—*Your doorman is a hard-ass. He wouldn't let us up to see you. I even tried bribing him*—

Sasha made a note to increase the doorman's holiday gift.

JD—*We miss you*—

The mention of "we" made Sasha's chest tighten.

JD—*Do you want us to stop trying to get in touch with you? We aren't going to stop!*—

Ian—*Kat said that Dylan may have said some things to insinuate we shouldn't be in a relationship? Is this true? Is that what you are thinking?*—

Dylan had made it clear that a threesome was complicated. She was already dealing with enough complication by needing to find a job. It was too much. Why couldn't they understand that and stop piling on?

Ian—*Your doorman wouldn't let me come up again.*

That guy is starting to piss me off!—

JD—*There are only a couple of sessions left in the art class, I hope to see you this weekend*—

JD—*Please let us know that you are okay*—

Shit. She felt like crap for ignoring them. She knew she was being rude at this point. It didn't require that much thought or time to respond. In fact, avoiding them seemed to be more of an effort. She texted them back.

Sasha—*I'm okay. Licking my wounds and trying to pick myself up again*—

JD—*If you need someone to lick you, I'm available (smiling devil)*—

Sasha laughed. It felt good to smile. She even responded to the message.

Sasha—(*smiley face*)—

JD—*Goodnight, beautiful*—

The next day Sasha was pleased to see that some of the firms that she had reached out to had gotten back to her quickly. It looked promising. She was excited to set up a few phone interviews for later in the week.

To Sasha's pleasure, Meagan Finch reached out to her and scheduled an interview later that day. Sasha reviewed the formal job description before heading over to the interview.

Sasha's phone rang as she walked to the meeting. *Goddammit!* She forgot to turn off her ringer. Flustered, she swiped to answer. "Hello."

"Time to celebrate! Stein finally got what was coming to him!" Hailey skipped a normal hello.

"What?" Sasha abruptly stopped on the sidewalk.

"The firm stripped him of his title and demoted him to handling trivial issues like traffic violations. And, I got my job back, with a huge raise!"

"Whoa." Millions of questions raced through Sasha's head.

"I bet they are going to offer you your job back too."

"That's great news, for you and Stein. Listen, I can't talk right now. I'm happy for you." Hailey replied with a clipped goodbye.

Sasha strutted off toward the interview. An ease set in as she delighted in the justice of Stein's humiliation.

Her phone rang again and the caller ID indicated it was her old firm. "Ms. Smirnova, I'm calling about your improper dismissal. We would like to offer you your job back."

Sasha appreciated the heads up from Hailey. "Thank you. I will consider it, but I am busy at the moment and don't have time to discuss this further."

They hadn't offered her a raise, like Hailey. She must have negotiated for it. With that in mind, Sasha walked into her interview with her chin held high and a gleam in her eye.

She admired the interior design of Ms. Finch's office, preferring the modern and minimalistic black leather furniture to her previous firm's traditional and tired look. And, the office sported a great view of the Chicago River. While she waited for Ms. Finch, Sasha glanced at a magazine article about a recent endowment for the arts at a small university in the suburbs.

The receptionist escorted Sasha to Ms. Finch's office. Sasha refocused quickly. Ms. Finch greeted Sasha in the center of her office, gesturing for Sasha to sit on one her couches. Rather than placing a large wooden barrier between them, Ms. Finch sat on the other couch near Sasha.

Erasing the distance and offering a warm smile Ms.

Finch established an immediate connectedness with Sasha. "Thank you for making the time to come in today, Ms. Smirnova."

"You're welcome. I read up about you and your practice. I'm happy to have the opportunity to sit down with you Ms. Finch."

"Please, call me Meagan."

Sasha smiled at her informality. Another pleasant change. "Everyone calls me Sasha."

"Great. Well, Sasha, I won't waste either of our time. Mr. Lane had a lot to say in regards to your amazing skills as an attorney." Sasha closed her mouth, hiding her surprise as Mr. Lane typically was succinct. "I could truly use someone like yourself that doesn't need hand-holding. My partner, my life partner that is, would like me to take more time off, particularly this holiday."

Sasha caught Meagan's hesitancy. "Am I understanding you correctly that would you need me to start right away to spend time with your wife?" Meagan's eyes widened. Sasha returned Meagan's concerned look with a comforting smile. She wanted to allay any concerns Meagan had about Sasha's level of open-mindedness. Her smile also hid her awareness that Meagan's immediate need was a pressure point for Sasha to negotiate.

Meagan attempted to gain the upper hand. "I figured that since you are not currently working that you would want to start right away." Sasha held her cards close to her chest. Meagan detailed the position's duties, limitations, and benefits.

Sasha considered all the information Meagan presented and leaned in favor of accepting her offer rather than returning to her old firm. When pushed for an acceptance, Sasha smiled knowingly. "While I can see a lot of benefits of working here, your offer is a bit low. And as it stands, my previous firm has offered to reinstate me at an even higher salary than before." Meagan increased the offer by $10,000.

Sasha pressed, "Also, while I understand that working here does not offer an opportunity to become partner or share in the profits, I think that I should be entitled to bonuses based on bringing in new clients."

"Agreed. Mr. Lane was correct you do have a knack for negotiating aggressively and politely simultaneously. I look forward to working with you." Sasha and Meagan ironed out the rest of the details.

Sasha buoyantly walked out of Meagan's office, and what was soon to be her office as well. The tension in her back relaxed. The migraine that she had barely managed to keep at bay disappeared. The tightness in her chest eased too. Even the chilly temperature outside no longer felt formidable.

She felt strong enough to walk into Lawson's with her head held high. She deserved a celebratory drink for landing a new job. Who made the best drinks in town? Her best friend of course.

While walking, Sasha confidently called the HR representative at her old firm. "Hello Ms. Smirnova, great to hear from you. I wanted to apologize again for the misunderstanding and inconvenience." Sasha laughed at the representative's absurd description. "Are you available now to come in and complete some paperwork and get started?"

Sasha held her head high. "Actually, I am not interested in returning to the firm." The representative sweetened the offer but failed to sway Sasha.

The representative threw out a last hail Mary. "Is there anything that I can do to change your mind?"

Sasha didn't need any time to consider it. "No, but thank you."

"I understand. In recognition of your excellent work, the firm would like to offer you a severance package if you are willing to sign a nondisclosure agreement."

Sasha blinked her eyes repetitively at the hush money proposal. Despite Sasha's righteous objections, she accepted. She didn't plan on speaking ill of Mr. Stein and the firm owed her.

She hung up and fist-pumped the air, a mannerism that she had picked up from JD. With renewed strength, she walked to Lawson's. She no longer worried about someone confronting her about getting fired. Based on her talk with HR, her record would officially state that she quit. And most importantly, she had a job that excited her.

As soon as she entered Lawson's, Marcus confronted Sasha, "I can't believe what happened with Stein! I heard that it was a partner that filed a complaint with HR. Do you know who?" *Was it Ian?*

Abby pried, "Who are you going to be reporting to now?"

With an eyebrow cockily raised, Sasha announced, "I'm not coming back to the firm."

"What? Why?" Marcus's eyes widened.

Abby pushed for more details, "Where are you going to work?"

"I'm going to work for Meagan Finch."

Abby looked at everyone else at the table. Everyone looked dazed. "I don't recognize the name. What firm is she with?"

"She has a solo practice." Their jaws dropped to the table.

"Why in the world would you work for her instead of at a big firm?" Jonathon blurted out

Sasha was unphased by their inability to understand. Sasha realized she didn't care about their opinions. They had all succumbed to the brainwashed notion that all attorneys must fight to gain employment at the top firms. She refused to conform to those rules. Screw their expectations! She didn't bother answering.

Sasha looked over at the bar. "Oh, I see Seth. I'm going to say hi. Later." She hurried over and sat beside him.

She let out the breath she had been holding. "Wow, I didn't see you for months and now I see you twice in one week."

"Apparently, I'm having an exceptionally lucky week." He kissed her on the cheek. "Your firm is the talk of the bar tonight. Sounds like Stein got fucked."

"Not my firm. Not my concern." Sasha wiped her hands together indicating she was washing her hands of the drama.

"What?!" Kat exclaimed, sneaking up on Seth and Sasha.

"Hey Kat," Sasha recoiled and felt a knot in her stomach. She finally confessed to the situation that she had purposefully concealed from her best friend. "I got fired on Monday."

"What?" Kat dramatically put down her towel on the bar top.

"It's all good now. I actually accepted a job working for a woman in a solo practice." As Sasha said the words aloud, an enormous smile spread across her face and she took in a long cleansing breath. "I think it was all a blessing in disguise. I wasn't happy at that firm. I'm feeling better than I have in a long time."

"Well good for you. And fuck Stein for firing you." Kat clapped. It was great to know her friend always had her back. Besides, Kat understood what it meant to give up such an opportunity. "I have the perfect drink for the occasion, *Adios*, Motherfucker."

Sasha and Seth laughed. "Perfect!" Sasha agreed.

Kat sat the blue colored drink in front of Sasha. Seth raised his drink to clink his glass with Sasha's. "To fucking the status quo."

"Cheers to that!" Sasha raised her glass in response. Both the flavor of the drink and her success tasted delicious.

"Did you catch up with your hotties this week? They looked like a cross between sad puppies and growling wolves." Kat refilled Seth's glass.

"I have to admit, I'm a little jealous that you found two hot men." Seth took a sip of his drink. "Seriously, those two are *fine*."

Sasha's excitement diminished at the mention of JD and Ian. She had been feeling guilty about not having the energy to reach out to them the past few days. And, she hadn't yet called to let them know her good news. Why was she stalling?

"By the way, sorry for Dylan being a jerk the other day and being so negative about the whole threesome thing. He can be moody." Seth looked uncommonly serious and looked away. Sasha got the distinct impression that he was purposefully not saying something and it wasn't her place to probe further.

"Anyways, I hope he didn't cause a problem between the three of you."

"He didn't say anything that wasn't true," Sasha admitted, playing with her glass.

"He was overly pessimistic," Seth countered, placing a gentle hand on Sasha's back. "If you want to make it work, I'm a firm believer that there is always a way."

"Thanks for that Seth." Sasha kissed him on the cheek.

"We agree with Seth, we can make this work." Ian's deep voice came from behind Sasha. The sound of his voice sent a warm tingly sensation down her spine.

"Hi beautiful," JD greeted Sasha with a kiss on the cheek. She flushed with instant attraction to both JD and Ian. A smile spread across her face. Once in their presence, she was happy to see them both.

JD stepped out of the way and Ian kissed her on the cheek as well. Sasha's eyes went wide with the unexpected public show of affection. What was he doing?

Kat put another Adios, Motherfucker in front of Sasha. "This one is on the house. Don't be mad at me, but as soon as I saw you walk in tonight, I texted JD to let him know that you were here."

"Thanks again, Kat." Ian spoke over Sasha's head. "I owe you one."

"I'll hold you to that. As a bar owner, having an attorney on speed dial can be handy." Kat mimed pocketing an IOU for another day.

"From what your girl was telling me earlier, I think this little rebel is finally ready to stand up for what she wants." Seth stuck his nose in their business again.

"Is that so?" JD asked staring Sasha in the eye.

"I heard you accepted a job working for Meagan Finch," Ian stated with a small grin on his face. "You know the gossip mill runs full throttle at the firm."

"I did," Sasha said as she fidgeted with her hands. She worried how Ian might react as he was a staunch supporter of the conventional employment route.

"I have heard great things about her from Mr. Lane. I think you working for her will be great for both you and Ms. Finch." Ian smiled.

"When were you talking with Lane?" Sasha tried to piece together his story.

"After Stein let you go, I went to Lane because I knew he was well-connected. I may have leaned into the fact that his failure to protect you from Stein could have violated his compulsory duty and may have amounted to harassment vis-à-vis his actions. Anyways, he thought the world of you as an attorney and was happy to lend a hand." Ian popped a peanut in his mouth from the bowl on the bar top. He looked hot standing there tall, with good posture, and a huge smile on his face. Sasha blushed.

"Thanks for the help." The fact that he helped made her feel better about her choice of jobs, but also made her feel worse about ignoring his offer to help earlier in the week.

"I'm thrilled that you have found a job that seems to be a good fit for you." The expression on JD's face didn't match his words. He didn't look thrilled. The immediate relief on JD's face when he first said hello to Sasha had dissipated. He looked a little green. "I can't help but worry about the wall you have built up between us this week."

"Damn Sasha, give them a break. If you don't try to work things out with them, I'm going to try and get them to switch teams." Seth winked at JD, but JD didn't laugh.

"I want to tie you up so you can't run away from us again," Ian admitted his frustration and placed a possessive hand on Sasha's shoulder. She lightly placed her hand on top of his.

"Oooo, they're kinky too. Can I play?" Seth waggled his eyebrows. "Or at least watch."

Kat stepped in. "Give them a break, Seth. Not everyone is as open as you."

"As much as I appreciate Seth's enthusiasm for us getting it on, maybe we could finish this conversation someplace else?" Ian suggested in a tone that was more demanding than suggestive. He started to pull Sasha from her seat.

"Wait." JD picked up Sasha's drink and finished it off. "Damn, this is really good."

"Thanks." Kat turned to Ian. "See, some men don't find colorful drinks to be unmanly. Let me tell you, I saw three women ogling him drinking that and practically drooling. I wouldn't be surprised if they go ahead and order one for themself."

"My guys aren't on the menu." Sasha turned to Seth, "and that includes you."

"You wound my spirits, Sasha. You are greedy to take both of them off the market." Seth put his hands over his heart as if he was in physical pain.

Ian exhaled. "Can we get out of here?"

"Do you need some rope to tie her up?" Seth asked before they had a chance to step away. "I have some in the car if you need it."

"Nope, got some at home. We're all good. Thanks."

JD smiled wickedly at Seth.

"Sasha, you greedy bitch, why won't you share?" Seth whined.

"Okay, let's go." Ian took Sasha's hand urging her to speed up her process of leaving the bar.

As Sasha put on her coat, Seth called out, "Good luck kids!"

Chapter 20

JD

The strong cool wind did nothing to chill JD's mood. His heart had been racing since Kat had informed him that Sasha was at Lawson's. While she spent her time enjoying a drink, he had been frantically trying to get there before she evaded them once again. The vision of her happily chatting it up with Seth was a relief as well as a slap in the face. Seeing her and being able to touch her allowed him to release a lot of tension that he had been carrying the past few days. But the fact that she was able to enjoy herself without contacting him was insulting.

The three of them stood on the sidewalk, all the playful banter that occurred inside the bar vanished.

"You were eager to get out of a bar that was nice and warm with good drinks. Where are we going?" Sasha rubbed at her coat sleeves. JD shoved his hands in his pockets. Neither man offered to help keep her warm. Did she not understand how upset he was? *They* were?

Silence ensued. JD made her wait for a response. He was going to force Sasha to listen to them. Tonight, they ended her imposition of silence.

Ian broke first. "I think we need to talk. And, Lawson's is not the place to do it. With all the attorneys around from my firm and other firms, it is more like an extension of my office than a place to enjoy myself," Ian explained. "I feel like I can't be myself there. I have to be completely professional. More importantly, we need to talk among the three of us, without interruptions."

"That makes sense," Sasha conceded and looked back and forth between JD and Ian. JD remained stiff.

"Besides talking, I think we all need to take steps to prove that we can work. It's one thing to talk about hypotheticals, but we need to put the issues to the test." Sasha's eyes widened. JD knew she needed to get over the hurdles in her head that were giving her an excuse to pull away.

Ian bounced in the cold. "Here's what we are going to do. We are going to get some food, which will give us a chance to talk and will get us all out of the cold."

JD braced himself for Sasha's response. "After we eat, we are all going to Luxury Box openly...together." JD intended to make sure that Sasha understood where they stood.

Sasha fiddled with her fingers.

Knowing that this conversation had the potential to result in ending their relationship, JD was in favor of some good emotional eating. "I vote for pizza."

"Fine." Sasha didn't put up a fight.

"Sure." Ian didn't squabble.

At least they all saw eye to eye on that one. JD put that in the win category.

The pizza place was too far to walk in the cold, so Ian ordered a rideshare, which only required a two-minute wait. They all waited together: not touching, not talking.

When the car arrived, they all crammed into the back with Sasha in the middle. Ian kissed Sasha on the mouth. "I've missed you." She grabbed the back of Ian's head, holding him close. JD wanted to feel Sasha's hands on him.

Ian's words made JD sick to his stomach. If Sasha didn't come around tonight and commit to them in a real sense, how would he ever deal with missing her in his life forever. It was a real possibility.

JD cupped Sasha's face and forced her to look him in the eyes. He planted a firm kiss on her lips. "I need you, Sasha." JD didn't want to let go. If this was his last kiss, he focused on every detail as if he were painting a memory. She laid her hand on top of his.

"I'm sorry for the distance this week." She gazed at him, keeping their hands connected.

Those were pretty words, but not enough to satisfy JD. She had been downright inconsiderate, particularly at the point where she stopped to have a drink with Seth. Her apology inflamed his frustration. He pulled his hand back. "I'm not looking for an apology. I need you to promise that you aren't going to put up a wall again. I can't take it." JD held back his tears, his voice cracking.

Sasha attempted to speak, but he put a finger over her mouth to halt her. "Don't say anything this minute."

Ian kept his hands to himself. "We're going to talk and we are going to go out. And then all three of us are going to decide once and for all, if we are going to commit. I have been waiting for months. I don't want to wait anymore."

Sasha crossed her arms across her chest and argued, "I had a difficult week. You know getting fired was a big deal."

JD cut to the quick of the matter. "Life happens. Good and bad. We either share in both or this relationship doesn't mean much."

Sasha blanched.

Ian closed his eyes.

Silence hung in the car. She started twirling her hair. JD extricated her hand and stilled her . He didn't want to scare her. He wanted to be a rock for her. He wanted to be the man that she counted on and wanted to reach out to when she needed someone. He wanted her trust. Why hadn't she trusted him this week?

She looked at him with uncertainty in her eyes. He took her hand and rubbed small circles over her skin with his thumb. Ian gave her a quick kiss on her forehead.

Luckily, they snagged the last open table at the restaurant. Ian put a pizza order in before they seated themselves.

So as to avoid a ping pong style of conversation, JD sat across from Sasha at the square table.

"Why do I get the distinct feeling that both of you are pissed off at me?" Sasha worried her lip and went back to twirling her hair.

Ian took her fidgeting hand in his. "Pissed? No. Hurt? Yes." Ian kept it simple. "We aren't angry at you, but we feel that you need to understand how your actions made us feel."

Sasha didn't instantly rebut Ian. JD placed his elbows on the table and laced the fingers together in a casual praying position.

Ian leaned in closer. "When you block me out, it makes me worry that you don't respect how much I care about you. I love you and when you essentially ghost me for days, I feel like you don't care about me."

Sasha scooted her chair in closer to the table, leaned forward, and confessed, "I'm so sorry, I never intended to make you feel that way as it couldn't be further from the truth." She averted her eyes.

JD reached across the table and placed a finger under her chin to redirect her focus on him. Ian said his peace, but she needed to hear him too. "For me, your silence scares me. It's like you have one foot in the relationship and one foot out. I don't mean this as a threat, but I can't be in a relationship where I feel like this. I don't want to constantly worry if tomorrow will be the day you are going to end it." JD felt lifeless. Forcing her to choose them wasn't practical.

Sasha's jaw dropped open. "Did you come here to end things?"

Ian scowled at JD. "Sasha, we are here to get a firm commitment from you as well as a promise from you not to go radio silent again. We can respect if you don't want to discuss something with us or you need time to process.

"Listen, every couple argues. And my guess, our arrangement will probably cause more disagreements than in most relationships based on complications. We have to agree to *talk* them out between all of us."

Sasha rested her forehead on her hands. "I'm so sorry I made a mess of this. And I'm sorry I hurt you both. I could explain why I did it, but now that I can see it in a clearer light, I was being selfish. I could have told you that I was overwhelmed. That I was embarrassed that I got fired. I could have told you that I was angry about what happened. To some extent I was worried I was so angry that I would lash out at both of you." Sasha hung her head.

Ian placed his hand on her shoulder. "Sasha, look at me please." He waited for her to look his way. "There's no doubt that you got fucked at work. Are you angry at me for still working there?"

"No, I think you fit in well there. And, I know how you reached out to HR and put your name on the line for me. I can't believe you did that for me. And, your talk with Lane opened up a phenomenal opportunity for me. I can't thank you enough."

Ian sighed. "I'm not looking for a thank you. And, just so you know, I didn't reach out to HR. I did speak to Lane and I may have pressed on him. I suspect that he was the one that reached out to HR, he was irate about losing you. Listen. I didn't handle things well at the firm before. I wanted to make sure I got it right this time."

But JD wasn't going to let any issue slide. He butted into the conversation, "Did what Dylan say also factor into your silence? The fact that he didn't think we had much of chance of making this work?" Ian rolled his head to face Sasha and remained silent.

"I'll admit that I didn't have the energy to process what Dylan had said. I didn't have anything left in me to attempt to figure things out." Sasha sat back in her seat, putting distance between them.

JD folded his arm down on the table and leaned forward. "We aren't toys that you can put on a shelf and play with when it is convenient."

Sasha's mouth dropped open.

Ian snarled, "Bro, that's a little harsh. I don't think that's what Sasha was doing."

JD ignored Ian and stared at Sasha. "You can't just press pause in the relationship when it doesn't work into your schedule."

"I'm sorry for how I handled everything. Obviously, there were plenty of ways that I could have done it better," she said with glassy eyes. "Do you plan on holding a grudge? I'm not sure what else I can say to make things right."

JD wasn't moved by her apology or teary eyes. "I get that you guys have stressful and demanding jobs. I don't care how tired you are at the end of the day, I need to hear from you *every* day, even if it is a text before you fall asleep." JD laid it out there. Certain things he needed and he wouldn't compromise.

"That's very fair. And, I think my workload is going to be much more accommodating for me to be able to spend time committed to our relationship. That was a big part of why I accepted the position. I want to have more of a life outside of work. I didn't want a job that was draining all my energy. I don't want to be so tired that I fall asleep after only one orgasm," she teased.

"Heh!" JD snorted. "You didn't even blush that time."

"Now she is." Ian snickered. Even Sasha giggled.

JD flopped back in his chair. Ian exhaled. The thick tension diminished.

"Just so you know, my new boss is married to a woman. I don't see our arrangement causing an issue at work." Sasha smiled. JD half smiled as he worried about how much outside approval she needed in order to commit.

"That's good," Ian remarked. "Now, that you aren't forced to endure the wrath of the firm, I don't think our relationship will be an issue for me either. It was difficult for me not to show an interest in you while we were at the same firm. For now, it is none of their business who the hell I'm sleeping with. For all they need to know, I'm married to my job. I won't discuss my private life with them. It's none of their fucking business." Ian cocked his head to the side and Sasha nodded affirmatively.

JD preferred to return to the previous topic. He rolled his eyes and honed his attention on Sasha. "How many orgasms do you think you can handle before passing out?"

"Hmm. Four? Six? I think we will need to test it out?" Ian joined in the playful chatter. Sasha's blush deepened.

JD didn't allow himself to smile fully. He knew that a few words didn't guarantee that everything was fixed.

Sasha narrowed her eyes on him and pressed, "JD, are we good? I promise I will be better about communicating." She turned to Ian. "And I will never ghost you for days ever again."

"I don't know, bro. I think Seth was right, maybe we should tie her up so she can't run away." Ian sported a cocky smile.

"We are good, beautiful." JD leaned over and kissed her. At least, they were good for now. Only time would tell if she reverted to silence.

To all of their surprise, Ian followed JD's kiss with his own.

Sasha's eyes went wide. "That was bold."

JD looked around to see if anyone else had noticed. One girl had and she looked a little jealous. An older woman scoffed.

Ian shrugged. "Fuck it. I don't know these people. What they think doesn't mean crap to me."

"Your new attitude is sexy as fuck." Sasha smiled devilishly.

JD feigned pouting. "What about me? I'm not sexy as fuck?"

"I'm trying not turn as red as the tomatoes on the

pizza." Despite her words, Sasha was flushed from her face all the way down her neck.

"Too late. I think our beautiful girl is thinking some very dirty thoughts right now." Ian smirked.

Sasha lowered her voice an octave. "I'm happy to share my thoughts with you back at your place."

JD placed his head on his fisted hand. "As much as the thought of that is making me hard, you are going to have to hold onto those thoughts for a while. We are still going to the bar when we finish the pizza. I don't want any other big issues left as a question mark." He wasn't going to budge.

"Okay, but are you both ready to come out to your friends?" Sasha raised her eyebrows and looked quickly between JD and Ian.

"I am telling my friends that I am dating an amazing girl. That isn't scary." Ian winked at Sasha.

"And, they already knew I was dating a beautiful girl." JD's nonchalance mirrored Ian's indifference.

"And the fact that you both happen to be dating the same girl? What about that little issue?" Sasha clasped her hands together while twisting her fingers.

"We will all deal with it. Together." JD placed a hand on Sasha's squirming hands. Being nervous was a waste of energy.

They finished their dinner and caught a ride to the bar. JD slowed his steps before walking into Luxury box. He didn't worry about coming out to his friends in the same way Sasha and Ian did. He could see the tension in their bodies. It was fruitless to ask them to relax. Their entire relationship could blow up from this little experiment. For that reason, this was going to be trying for all three of them. He wasn't certain who he was most concerned for. All of their hearts were on the line.

"Any last rules for how we behave in front of all your friends before we walk into the bar?" Sasha gnawed on her lip.

JD took her left hand. "No. We are here to figure things out as we go."

Ian took her other hand.

"Even if things don't go perfectly, we work them out together. And no running. Got it?" JD squeezed Sasha's hand. She smiled weakly.

The three of them walked into the bar hand in hand in hand. JD scanned the room as they entered. Despite entering with their hands held together as if they were playing a game of Red Rover, he didn't think anyone even noticed.

His core group of friends was not at the bar yet as the team's hockey game finished only forty minutes earlier. JD led the way to the rounded booth in the corner where his teammates always hung out. There was plenty of room for friends to join them later. Just in case Sasha got nervous and decided to bolt, JD had purposely caged her into the booth by placing her between him and his brother.

Thankfully, they didn't have to wait long for a waitress to stop by the table and take their order. "Whiskey for you guys tonight?" Thankfully, the waitress didn't pester JD with jokes about his name.

"No, three vodkas straight up, tonight," Ian ordered with a smug tone. He winked at Sasha. She grinned back.

"Well okay then, mixing things up." The waitress headed toward the bar.

"You okay, beautiful?" JD placed a reassuring hand on her leg underneath the table. Sasha linked her fingers with his.

"Apprehensive but okay. Having each of you beside me makes all the difference in the world." Her smile appeared unnaturally tight. JD would accept baby steps as long as they were moving in the right direction.

JD and Ian watched the recap of the game on the television. It was always great when their friends won. JD leaned around Sasha. "Did you see that? That was a great play. They keep that up and they're going to go far this season." JD hoped a little sports talk might calm Ian's nerves.

Ian nodded. "Yup."

Loud cheering drew JD's attention away from the screens. Logan and his girlfriend were greeted with loads of congratulations as they entered the bar. Logan was dressed in jeans and a blazer while his girlfriend was sporting Logan's jersey. They joined the threesome at the table.

JD stood up. "Congrats man, another win, another good day." He fist bumped Logan. JD started to introduce Sasha and then stumbled. He quickly recovered, but avoided placing a title on Sasha. "Sasha, this is Logan and Emma. Logan and I grew up together. He just transferred onto the team last year. He used to play for some California team, but finally decided to return to the ice skating capital."

"You know it," Logan confirmed, placing his arm around Emma.

"Nice to meet both of you." Sasha cordially said hello and extended a hand to both Logan and Emma.

Emma asked, "Mind if we sit with you guys?"

Ian pointed with his open palm toward the other end of the booth, "Sure. Nice game by the way."

The waitress returned with the three vodkas. Sasha quickly put back the vodka, impressing JD. Ian took a regular size gulp.

"What the fuck are you drinking JD? I thought you only drank whiskey."

JD rolled his eyes. He wasn't in the mood.

Luckily, Ian spoke up, "I ordered the first round."

Sasha inserted herself in the conversation, "Next round is on me." Logan and Emma both ordered a beer that was on tap. And Sasha, Ian, and JD followed along.

Logan faced Ian. "I hear congratulations are in order. JD told us that you finally made partner. That's great news, dude."

"Thanks. It's like getting into the playoffs for hockey. It's great, but that's when you need to dig even deeper and work even harder." Ian's genuine response sounded heartfelt and not condescending like most attorneys.

"What do you do?" Emma asked Sasha.

"I'm also an attorney. How about yourself?"

Emma shrugged. "I'm between things since the move. It seems like everyone in the hockey world knows one another. Did you know Ian through law stuff?"

Sasha squeezed JD's hand beneath the table. He calmly stroked the back of her hand with his thumb. "Ian and I met last summer." Sasha smiled timidly. Ian polished off his vodka and his fingers started tapping on the table. JD wished his brother could relax.

"Isn't it funny how small of a world it is?" Emma laughed. "So, you met Ian before you started dating JD?"

"Yes," Sasha agreed, but didn't elaborate.

Someone needed to speak up. Emma had thrown the pitch and one of them needed to swing. JD, an athlete at heart, stepped up to the plate. "Actually, both Ian and I are dating Sasha."

Everyone stilled. No one drank. JD forced himself to breathe. Sasha looked like a deer in headlights and Ian like a mannequin in a wax museum. Emma and Logan had a look on their face like they were having difficulty solving a math equation.

Logan's eyebrows drew together. "I heard through the grapevine that you were dating Sasha?"

Sasha took an audibly deep breath. "It's a long, long story. But I'm dating *both* Ian and JD."

"Mmmm. You'll have to share the long version of the story some time. You should come out with me and the other WAGs. We'll get the whole story out of you. And I'm guessing it's a good one." Emma smiled sweetly and offered a conspiratorial wink.

JD squeezed Sasha's hand. A comfortable warmth spread across his face. Their first interchange had gone over without any fuss. Ian finished off the vodka.

"Thank you, it would be nice to get to know the other wives and girlfriends." The joy on Sasha's face made JD relax. He put his arm around Sasha's shoulders and kissed her head.

Logan lowered his voice. "You good with this, Ian?"

JD appreciated Logan's concerns for Ian since the reality was that he was better friends with JD. And, JD had quite a reputation for his threesomes in the past.

"I'm dating a beautiful and amazing woman. My brother is finally in a great relationship too. So yeah, life is good." Ian's body relaxed a little.

"Well good." Logan paused but then the words raced out of his mouth like an unstoppable steam engine. "Holy fuck, do your parents know? They are like super religious. No offense."

JD laughed. "Our mom was the first to suggest the situation."

"No fucking way!" Logan threw his head back in laughter.

"Our dad was very encouraging too." Ian nodded as he laughed.

"Unbelievable." Logan shook his head.

Ian kissed Sasha on the mouth quickly. JD almost applauded Ian's initiative. It also reassured JD that Sasha was still breathing. He felt like he had just won a hockey game.

Ian ordered another round of drinks. *Did he need it to take the edge off?*

More players started to enter the bar. Most conversations steered toward hockey.

After the second beer, Sasha excused herself from the table to use the restroom. Emma joined her.

With a couple of extra open seats in the booth, Kurt and Samuel pushed their way in to sit.

Samuel harrumphed when he sat. "Your parents are nuts! I love them but they are crazy."

"What the fuck, dude!" JD barked. His hackles rose. Ian clenched his fingers in a fist on the table.

"Your parents called me and lectured me for an hour and a half on how getting a divorce was a terrible sin. They wouldn't get off the phone until I agreed to get counseling for a least six months. And then, called to verify that I was actually going to counseling. They're fucking crazy." Samuel shook his head and threw his hands in the air.

Logan laughed. "Your parents meddle in other people's marital affairs but approve of your threesome?

They are crazy!"

"What fucking threesome?" Samuel's lips twisted.

Ian cleared his throat. "JD and I are both dating Sasha."

"What the hell JD, I thought we were buddies. Why didn't you offer to share with me the other night?" Kurt punched JD in the arm.

"We aren't fucking topping her, dickhead!" JD seethed, pushing Kurt away. "We are in a serious relationship."

"Sorry man." Kurt held up his hands defensively, but then butchered his apology. "Do you guys alternate every other night or what?"

"Fuck off! She isn't a fucking puck bunny." Ian stood up. The knuckles in his fist were white. Was he going to take a swing at Kurt? The only thing that probably saved Kurt from a black eye was the fact that Sasha hadn't heard his fucking comment.

Kurt put up his hands in a surrender position. "Sorry. Sorry. I didn't realize. Listen, I really am sorry. I hope it all works out for you." He got up from the booth. Despite his apology, JD wasn't going to forgive him tonight.

"You realize that he's going to go tell everyone right now." Logan cocked his head in the direction of Kurt leaving the table.

"Shit, you're right. I should go check on Sasha." JD got up from the table and looked for her.

While JD got up from the table, Samuel added, "I can't believe your parents can encourage you but wanted to bathe me in holy water to protect me from the wrongs of life. And your mom still calls me Sammy." JD resolved many years ago that his parents were set in their ideas.

He noticed Sasha surrounded by Emma and Olivia, both of whom he knew were really nice. He kept a small distance, knowing that allowing Sasha to become friends with the women on her own would fortify her belief that this could work. He stood inconspicuously near the bar but in earshot of the three.

Olivia got in Sasha's face. "You lucky bitch! How in the world did you snag both O'Malley men? If you came here tonight to make us all jealous, it's working." JD smiled approvingly.

"Uh, thanks?" Sasha stammered.

Emma introduced them. "Sasha, this is Olivia, Owen's wife and one of the greatest women I know." Emma turned to Olivia, "I was telling Sasha, now that she's a member of the tribe, we all need to take her out to formally introduce her to all the WAGs."

"Absolutely." Olivia hugged Sasha.

Sasha smiled, which made JD want to high five his brother.

All was going great until a puck bunny shouted in Sasha's face. "Who's the whore now? I saw you give me the side-eye the other night. You uppity bitch! Now I hear you're whoring it up with both O'Malley boys."

Emma stepped up. "Trust me honey, the only whore here is you. She's one of us. You, on the other hand are nothing but a fucking puck bunny. You'll never be one of the WAGs."

"Go fuck off." Olivia stepped aggressively closer to the trashy woman. The puck bunny tucked tail and left.

Sasha blinked her eyes rapidly and gaped. "Uh, thank you, again."

"No worries, babe. We got your back. Those puck bunnies are nasty. It's our job to chase them away."

Emma put her hands on her hips.

"You okay, beautiful?" JD stepped in and kissed Sasha on the forehead.

"Yeah. With a little help from these two badass women and my two men, I'm good." Her willingness to refer to him and his brother as her men was great and fortified the feeling of security in the relationship.

"If you ladies, don't mind, I think we are ready to head out." JD wanted to go home and be with his girl. With his hand possessively attached to Sasha's back, he escorted her back to the table where Ian was still sitting.

JD caught his brother's attention. "You ready to go bro?"

Ian smiled broadly and stood quickly to leave.

Yeah, their little test was successfully complete.

Chapter 21

Ian

Ian opened the main door to his and JD's two-flat and suggested, "Let's go up to my place, I have the perfect bottle to open up to celebrate coming out to our friends today."

They ascended the stairs and entered his apartment. "I thought tonight went really well. You guys agree?" He waited with bated breath. If they didn't agree, there was no cause for celebration. If that was the case, he might need to down a bottle of hard liquor and drown his sorrows.

"I never really cared about outsiders' opinions. My concern was always about you two being able to handle the complications." JD stilled, turning to look toward Sasha.

Ian had already gotten over his issues at work, which was his biggest obstacle. He too, turned to look at her. Was she going to be able to commit to two men? He held his breath and waited for her response. The suspense was killing him.

Sasha placed a palm on each of their hearts. "I know I haven't handled things well since I agreed to try. Trying these past few weeks has been really difficult for me and I made a mess of things. And I apologize for hurting both of you in the process. In the midst of the debacle, I realized how much you both mean to me. You mean more to me than bragging rights about working at a top firm. I also realized that I'm strong enough to endure some flippant-negative comments. I don't doubt that there will be many challenges for us in the future. There isn't any reason to say we are going to simply *try*. I *know* we can do this together. I'm all in. I hope you both can forgive me for the past." A small tear fell down her smiling face.

Ian released the breath he was holding. He put a hand on the counter to steady himself.

JD picked her up and hugged her, burying his face in the crook of her neck. He kissed her and made room for Ian.

Ian took her face between both of his palms and kissed her soundly. "I love you." He felt her kiss throughout his entire body. Fuck, it felt good.

"Where is that bottle? We need to celebrate!" JD proclaimed, bouncing from foot to foot.

Ian pulled out the fancy gold box and set it on the counter. He snagged a few glasses.

"Woah. that is some fancy champagne! *Damn,* bro."

"You sure want to pop it open tonight?" Sasha smiled shyly.

"Absolutely, and you can thank our Sasha for it. She gifted it to me when I made partner." Ian kissed Sasha. "Thank you, again," he mouthed. She shared a half smile with him.

The memory of that day was bittersweet. Making partner had been a tremendous high, but Sasha's admission that she was dating someone else was gut wrenching. All that was history now. They had reason to celebrate and the rest needed to be put in the past.

"That's a very nice gift, Sasha. You know Christmas is coming up. I have a few things on my wish list, if you need suggestions," JD teased, elbowing her in the side.

She looked down. "Well, I think I'm going to seriously have to reassess my budget now that I'm no longer making bank at the firm," she said with a weakened voice.

"I was only kidding Sasha. I would never expect expensive gifts." JD hugged her. Ian caught sight of JD over Sasha's head. He shook his head at his brother, who then replied with an embarrassed eye roll.

"It's not that. I'm going to have to move out of my apartment and find something less expensive too. The thought of moving sucks. Actually, I was thinking maybe I could find something nearby to you guys." Sasha looked back and forth between the brothers.

"We are getting booted out of our place in a few months," JD bemoaned, rolling his head dramatically. Ian bit his lip.

In light of Sasha's complaint about income, it wasn't the ideal time to mention his intentions, but Ian didn't have much of a choice. "I was actually thinking about buying this building." When she didn't appear to be resentful or hurt, he continued. "I thought it might be a good time when rates are low and I figured I could argue for a good price from the owner since he could avoid hiring a broker and I could handle the closing for free."

"Bro, can I rent my place from you?" JD begged.

Sasha eyed Ian with reservation like she was sitting in a deposition taking in information.

"Actually, I was wondering, if maybe Sasha would consider moving in with both of us. What do you guys think?" Ian dropped the idea that he had been carrying around with him. He stared at Sasha and attempted to read her reaction. She didn't smile, but rather looked contemplative. At least she didn't look appalled.

"Oh hell, yeah!" JD emphasized his point with a kiss. "It could be great, beautiful."

"I thought that it would be great for our relationship," Ian doubled-downed on JD's point.

"Yeah, it could be great." Sasha's response lacked enthusiasm. She looked away.

Ian took Sasha's hand. "But?" Ian sensed there was something else she wanted to say. He abandoned the champagne and pulled her to the table. The tone of the conversation suddenly required sitting.

JD sat down with him and nudged her. "Sasha?"

"I don't want to move in with you guys because you guys feel bad about me needing to move right now. Moving in together is a big deal. It shouldn't be based on convenience." She hung her head.

"Listen, the property is about a real estate investment. Regardless of purchasing the building, I want to live with you. I have been thinking about this for a while. I dreamt about living with you during all the weeks we were apart. I researched the housing market well before you ever made a job change."

Ian took her hands and made her look him in the eye. "I know this seems like a quick decision, but I have been kicking around this idea in my head for a while. I have known I wanted to be with you for a long time. And, after tonight, I feel confident that we can make this work. I love you, Sasha. Please consider moving in with us."

"What, I bounce back and forth between each of your beds? Don't get me wrong, I love being beside each of you in bed, but bouncing back and forth is insane."

Sasha's mouth twisted.

"We'll figure something out," JD pressed. "I can't imagine anything better than living with you." JD's puppy-dog eyes that he gave Sasha almost made Ian laugh. Sasha didn't react.

"Actually, in my obsession over the idea, I already considered this problem. I was thinking that we could redefine the spaces. We could make the upstairs apartment where we all sleep and each of us can have our own bedroom. And, we can add an extra bathroom."

The corners of Sasha's lips turned slightly upward. "I love the thought of each of us having our own room. It is great to be with both of you, but it is also nice to have one on one time as well." Her cheeks flushed. "And admittedly, there will be days I probably would prefer to close my door and sleep."

JD pushed his fist into Ian's shoulder in a friendly way. "That's an awesome idea, bro. I could do most of the construction work myself and get a lot done during winter break."

"That's what I was thinking. It could help save a lot of money." Ian knuckle-bumped JD.

"Do you plan to rent out the lower apartment?" Sasha asked tilting her head to the side.

"I was thinking we could use that as our living space. Maybe convert some space into an office and an art studio." Ian eyed both Sasha and JD cautiously.

JD unexpectedly enveloped Ian in a real hug, not the one-armed bro hug. "An art studio?" JD choked up. He didn't let go of Ian. "I think I always worried that I might get pushed out of this arrangement." Ian felt the depth of JD's vulnerability in the hug. The admission disoriented Ian. His brother was always so calm and collected.

Sasha hugged JD. "I told you I would never choose one of you over the other."

JD held Sasha's hand, but looked at Ian. "I think the fact that you are both attorneys, on some level it felt like you two might belong together more."

Sasha pulled JD's head so that he was looking at her. "JD, I love you both. Equally. It has nothing to do with careers. It's about how you treat me and how you both help make me a better person. I can't imagine being without either of you." She kissed him.

Ian nudged Sasha. "You love both of us?"

"Yes, I love you Ian." She kissed him as well. Then turned to JD. "And, I love you JD."

This was a huge step for Sasha to admit. It wasn't lost on either man. JD scooped her up in a bear hug and whispered in her ear, "I love you beautiful. I've never told a woman that before and I've never felt more certain of my feelings than when I'm with you."

Ian stole Sasha from JD as soon as he put her back down on her feet. "Oh, hell yes. I love you too." He had dreamed of hearing those words from Sasha. Hearing them spill form her lips now was better than he ever imagined.

"Now this is something to toast to." Ian popped open the bottle and filled each of their glasses with champagne. "To loving each other and making this relationship work." They raised their glasses and enjoyed the bubbly.

"What do you think about moving in here, Sasha?" Ian pressed as they all enjoyed the champagne. He emptied the rest of the bottle into the glasses.

"I like the idea, but maybe we should consider trying this on a trial basis for like a month first? You both may find that you hate living with me." Sasha looked down.

Ian nodded to JD. "Go get the rope. I think we need to tie up our girl. She's trying to run again."

"I'm not trying to run." Sasha blushed and took another sip.

"Good, then you agree to live with both of us." Ian pushed for a commitment like a good lawyer and finished his glass.

"Do you want to be with us?" Ian leaned in closer to Sasha.

"Yes," she whispered and drained the last sips of champagne.

JD deepened his voice. "Do you like being with us?" He set down his empty glass and closed in on Sasha, too.

"Of course." Sasha's blush deepened.

"You love us, both?" Ian prodded. Sasha nodded as they were only inches away from her.

"Then say yes to moving in with us." JD kissed her neck. He kissed her shoulder. He ran his hand slowly up her side grazing the side of her breast. She moaned. "Wouldn't you prefer to stay here, with us?"

"Mmm." Sasha purred.

Ian kissed her deeply, preventing her from saying anything more. His brother unbuttoned her shirt.

The original anxiety of working with JD to pleasure Sasha had almost been completely eliminated. He worked seamlessly with JD and no longer needed to have every step vocalized. The awkwardness had waned, thank goodness. It felt much more natural. He even used his newfound power and asserted himself as well.

Ian slowly removed Sasha's suit pants. Inch by inch, he pulled them down along with her panties. He took a bite at her hip and she yipped in response. The sound made his cock jump.

JD peppered her neck with kisses as he removed her bra. Sasha shivered.

"Let's take this to the bedroom." Ian grabbed her hand and led her to the bed. "Hop on up."

He lustfully admired her gorgeous body, sending all his blood rushing to his cock. The thought of touching her made him sweat. He removed his offending shirt.

JD grabbed a stashed bag from under the bed and pulled out a coil of rope. Sasha's eyes widened. He wrapped a bit of rope around each of his hands and pulled the one-foot section taut between his fists. A thudding snap resounded loudly. She gasped. "Are you good with a little bondage tonight?"

Ian looked for any sign of fear in Sasha's eyes. The only thing he saw was heat and desire burning in her brown eyes, which set him on fire.

Sasha nodded yes. "Can you please use your words? I don't want there to be any misunderstanding," JD skated the rope along her skin.

Sasha blushed deeply and responded in the affirmative.

"I love it when you blush," JD said in a low voice. She coyly dipped her head. "I picked this crimson-colored rope specifically to match the blush in your cheeks." Sasha nipples tightened into pert little buds.

Ian gawked. The color looked magnificent against her skin.

A throaty rasp escaped Sasha's lips, "Yes."

JD helped move Sasha's hands so that her palms were together as if she were praying. He began winding the rope in an intricate pattern keeping her forearms together. Ian respected JD's artistic desire to apply the

Shibari techniques that he had been honing over the years. Ian knew enough about the art form to know that JD wasn't going to truss her up like an animal in a rodeo. It was one of the ways JD used his specific skills to worship Sasha. Ian wanted Sasha to feel adored.

Ian positioned himself beside Sasha and whispered in her ear, "Told you we would tie you up so you couldn't leave."

"I still could run," Sasha challenged with a mischievously look. Damn, he liked her cheekiness. He kissed her, tugging on her lip with his teeth.

Ian countered her argument, "Really? Opening the door would be rather difficult with your hands tied together. But you are correct about running. I think I have the perfect answer to that dilemma." Ian pulled a spreader bar from under his bed. Sasha didn't make any motion to move. "This will keep you from running and give me the unfettered access that I'm craving right now." Sasha watched as Ian locked both of her ankles into a spreader bar and stretched her legs wide open.

JD continued to lace the rope into a beautiful pattern down Sasha's arms.

Kneeling behind her, Ian leaned next to Sasha. He started with a line of kisses from her bare ass, up her spine, all the way until he nipped at her ear. "Still want to run?"

"Never," Sasha moaned. The ankle attachments to the spreader bar clanged as she tried to bring her legs together.

JD took a momentary break to kiss her, holding the back of her head carefully. With her hands and legs bound she was at their mercy for maintaining balance.

Ian ran his finger along the inside of Sasha's thigh.

He was pleased to find her opening wet as he slipped a finger inside. He stroked in and out, moistening his fingers then circled his slick finger around her clit. She squirmed.

"Oh god, Ian. Aaah!" She started to lose her balance.

JD caught her. "I've got you beautiful."

JD finished the last of the knots and gazed at Sasha's tied hands between her lush breasts. "Fuck, you are so beautiful." She blushed. "Tell me Sasha, are you blushing because I can't keep my eyes off of you or is Ian fingering you driving you crazy?"

"Mmmmm." Sasha's eyelids drooped.

Ian continued toying with Sasha's clit as JD lightly stroked a single finger along the side of her breast. "Do you enjoy being with us beautiful?"

"Yessss," she moaned and panted loudly.

"Do you love both of us?" Ian stopped circling her clit and waited for her answer. His brother brushed a thumb over her nipple.

"Yes, I love you both." Sasha panted.

"We very much love you Sasha and we want you to move in and live with both of us." Ian went back to fingering her but then stopped just before she was about to orgasm. "Will you agree to move in with us?"

JD kissed her and pinched her nipple. Ian began fingering her again. JD broke the kiss and pressed her for an answer, "Will you agree to move in with us?"

"I need to come," Sasha begged.

Good thing that JD had tied up her hands, because if she had a hand free, she probably would have finished herself. Ian grinned as he took her to the edge and back several times. He didn't want her to think. He wanted her to feel, to listen to her gut, and go with her heart. Ian stroked her again.

"This is coercion," she whined. Her jaw went slack and her breaths came in deep bursts.

"Yes, and isn't it fun?" Ian rumbled, giving JD a conspiratorial glance.

"Agree to live with us beautiful." JD whispered, "We love you. You love us. I honestly believe that living together is going to make this relationship even better. Agree to live with us, please." Sasha threw her head back with her eyes closed and JD kissed his way up her lush feminine curve.

"Yes?" Ian stroked much more purposefully, adding in an additional finger, while managing to use his index finger to put some pressure near her clit. He repeated again, "Yes?"

Sasha hesitated. "I…" Her breathing came faster.

Ian persevered. "You must be confident in the love that we share together." To sweeten the deal, he offered, "JD and I can share one bathroom and you can have the other all to yourself."

JD pinched her nipple. She cried out, "Fuck."

"All in due time beautiful. Say yes." JD pulled at her hair and her jaw went slack.

Ian placed his mouth next to her ear and with a desperately deep voice he prodded, "Say yes, baby."

"Yes," she screamed her approval. "Please!"

JD kissed her deeply. His brother came at her boldly and knocked her onto her back. He shifted out of the way, giving Ian plenty of access. Ian dove between her legs and had her flying over the edge. JD swallowed her screams with his kisses.

JD stripped off his clothes. "I fucking need to be inside you."

Ian was more concerned with getting a firm answer. "Now that the tension has eased, do you still agree to move in here?"

"Yes, Ian. I love you both and would love to live with both of you—Ohhh!" Sasha shouted as a guttural grunt escaped from JD's mouth. He was inside her before she'd finished her sentence.

Ian kissed and touched Sasha as JD hammered in and out of her. JD shoved Ian out of the way.

Ian knew JD was close because he usually lost control like that right before his release. Ian stroked his own cock listening to Sasha's cries for more. Her whole body flushed as she came with JD. Finally, his brother maneuvered out of the way.

Ian needed to be with Sasha. He wanted to hear the words while inside her. Waiting and watching had him close to edge. He pumped hard and furious into her. He wanted to be buried in her. "I love you, Sasha."

"I love you." She wailed and her channel clamped around his cock.

Ian came in a tremendous roar with Sasha following him.

All three laid unmoving on the bed. Sasha placed her head on Ian's chest and JD spooned Sasha from behind. It had been an emotional week. But now, they were sated and content.

"Tell me again, beautiful," JD whispered. Ian wanted to hear the words again, too. He knew the sentiment in his brain, but hearing them soothed his heart. Even when Sasha directed those three words towards JD, Ian felt his heart expand.

"I love you JD." He kissed her shoulder.

Then she turned and kissed Ian's chest. "I love you,

Ian."

"Your shoulder needs some new artwork." JD drew on Sasha's back with his finger.

"Wait, I thought I saw something a few weeks back. The day I spilled the coffee on you. What was that on your shoulder?" Ian didn't like focusing on that period of time when he was apart from Sasha, but that was a moment that had piqued his curiosity.

"JD had drawn a white snow leopard with a marker." Sasha hid her face in Ian's side.

Ian turned her face toward him. He didn't want to make her feel insecure about her previous time with JD. "Would you consider getting a real tattoo?" Ian didn't currently have any tattoos.

She twisted her mouth. "Probably. With JD's creativity, I bet I could finally commit to a design for life."

"Thanks, beautiful." JD kissed her shoulder again.

"Hmmm. I think it would be hot," Ian added. The idea completely turned him on. "It would be cool if we all got matching or related tattoos."

"I would be down with that. I'll start drawing up some sketches and see what you guys think." JD started tracing on Sasha with his finger. Ian supported putting JD's artistic skills to work.

Sasha maneuvered herself and faced both JD and Ian. "Are you guys sure you want me to move in here?"

"Fuck yes," they said in unison.

"What if purchasing the place doesn't work out?" As an attorney, she considered every possible obstacle.

"Then we figure things out together. Just like we will figure everything else out. Together," Ian offered and beamed. "Between you and I, we are going to kill this real estate transaction. I almost feel sorry for the seller." Ian had researched the hell out of the project and knew all the price points for negotiation.

"You have the next few days off of work, yeah?" JD clarified, "You don't start your job until Monday?" He bit his lip.

"Yup." She nodded.

"How about we get you moved in here this weekend?" JD suggested flashing her a toothy smile.

Ian spun on Sasha and kissed her hard before she made some kind of objection. He thought the idea was great and wasn't going to give her any wiggle room. His tactic was near laughable as he lacked any subtlety. He finally allowed her to come up for air.

"For the record, I was going to say yes," Sasha mocked.

"A good attorney doesn't allow someone to offer an answer they don't want to hear," Ian countered.

JD squeezed her tightly and buried his head in her shoulder. His breath hitched and he sniffled.

"I love you both." She squeezed JD.

"Goodnight, beautiful. Love you."

Ian placed a kiss on top of Sasha's head. "Love you."

Sasha provided Ian with comfort and stability, which served as the basis of love between them. And, the fact that Ian and JD loved and respected each other as brothers, made it possible for Ian to share her. With a contented heart and mind, Ian fell asleep.

Chapter 22

Sasha

Anxiety woke Sasha from her sleep. Moving was bad enough, but doing it on the spur of the moment was crazy. She put a pot of coffee on out of habit, not out of need. Her leg nervously bounced as if she already had a few too many cups.

"Morning beautiful," JD greeted her with a kiss and a huge smile.

Despite her best effort she couldn't return the smile. She gnawed on her cuticle as she sat at the table and made a list of things to do.

JD put a hand on her leg. She glared at him. "Please! Do not try to distract me right now."

"I was only trying to get your leg to stop shaking before all my hot chocolate gets jostled out of my mug." He squeezed her leg.

"Oh. Sorry." She went back to her list.

"We got this all under control. Ian found a twenty-four-hour postal store to purchase boxes. I brought down extra suitcases to pack your clothes. Ian and I will go get a moving truck while my parents help pack up your kitchen stuff. And my cousins are going to help unload everything when we get here. So you see, everything is under control." JD kissed her on her forehead.

Sasha took a deep breath through her nose. Her lips

remained in a thin line.

Ian came in the kitchen smiling and gazed at her. "Yup. I can't wait to wake up every day with you here."

"Hell yes to that," JD added, raising hand to high-five Ian.

The corners of her lips turned up slightly. She pulled her shoulders back and pushed up from the table. "Okay, let's do this."

As promised, the O'Malley family was a huge help. They even brought doughnuts with them when they arrived at her old apartment. Sasha's stomach growled at the sight. In the midst of her earlier panic, she had forgotten to eat breakfast and the doughnuts hit the spot. She also learned that JD not only had an obsession with pizza, but doughnuts too.

The O'Malleys had the moving thing down to an amazingly efficient system. Mrs. O'Malley packed like a pro, ordered food along the way, and gave Sasha the encouragement that she needed. Mr. O'Malley was in charge of keeping an eye on the truck, which on the ticket-obsessed-cop-filled and thief-riddled streets of Chicago was an essential role. JD and Ian did all the heavy lifting. And the extended younger cousins got everything into the two-flat in a blink of an eye. They were more than happy to help as Ian and JD gave them a load of extra furniture and kitchen supplies that they had in duplicate and triplicate.

Sasha stood in JD's apartment overlooking the sea of disarray of furniture and boxes. She grinned. The dread she felt at the beginning of the day had vanished. The chaos of moving was not nearly as bad as she expected, because she had never had the benefit of an entire family supporting her. Not only did she have two amazing men in her life that she was going to get to live with every day, but she also gained an entire loving family.

She caught Ian's scent as he approached her from behind. His strong hands wrapped around her middle and pulled her close against him and he kissed her on the top of her head. "Don't worry about this mess. We will get it all figured out in due time."

She spun around in his arms and gifted him a warm smile. "I'm not worried. I know we will all figure it out together."

"Yes, we will. But for now, it's been a long day, let's go to bed." JD led her by her hand to his room.

She snuggled between Ian and JD. Damn it felt good.

"I'm so happy you are here." JD kissed her goodnight.

"You aren't thinking about running?" Ian playfully gripped her wrists like handcuffs.

"No. You may need to pry me out of this bed tomorrow. I'm tired enough to sleep for days. I love you both."

"Love you too."

She had the greatest night of sleep.

The next day, Ian woke exceptionally early and hopped in the shower. She pulled her body out from under JD's warm cuddles and went to the kitchen.

Alone, she stared at the percolating coffee machine. Goosebumps sprung up along her arms. A fluttering in her belly made her nauseous. She crossed her arms over her chest and rubbed her arms in a soothing motion.

She startled at the sight of Ian appearing in the kitchen. "I'm sorry. Did I scare you? I was trying to be quiet and not wake JD." Ian kissed her on the top of her head.

"No. You're fine. I was feeling a little off. It's weird that you are going into the office and I'm not." She bit her lip.

"You moved yesterday and are starting a new job tomorrow. It's okay to feel a little uneasy." He hugged her. "JD and I are here for you and we love you very much. Give yourself a break today and take some time to get settled here."

"I love you, Ian." She nuzzled into his chest.

"Now that is something I will never tire of hearing." Ian gave her a peck on her lips. "Okay, I better get out of here and get to work. The sooner I get into the office, the earlier I get to come home to you."

The thought of seeing him later eased some of her anxiety. She kissed Ian goodbye.

JD joined her in the kitchen while she was sipping her first cup of coffee. "Morning, beautiful. Did Ian leave?"

"Yes, and good morning. Can I get you a cup of hot chocolate?" Sasha got up and grabbed a mug.

JD intercepted her. "Yes, right after this." He kissed her until all the butterflies were quieted in her belly. "Now I can check off kissing you in *our* kitchen off my bucket list."

"What else is on that bucket list?" Sasha blushed.

"A whole lot of things I plan to do to you." JD kissed Sasha's pink cheeks. "But we have a lot of other things to do today and I have to teach the last class of the semester."

Sasha stirred the hot cocoa and then sat the mug in front of JD. "Would you mind terribly if I skipped class today? I really would prefer to use the extra time to clean up here and get ready for my big day tomorrow."

"Only naughty girls skip class. I may have to punish you later, which I'm sure will be enjoyable for you and me both." JD dragged a finger back and forth across his lip. Sasha really enjoyed being the beneficiary of his salacious antics.

Hours later, he kissed Sasha before heading off to class. She admired his ass as he walked out the door like she had several times while he taught. She smiled. His ass looked perfect in the jeans. Her mouth watered at the thought of him without jeans.

All day long, up and down the stairs, carrying heavy boxes, felt like an exercise class taught by Satan. Her thighs ached. She climbed those stairs between JD and Ian's apartment over and over. Until Ian closed on the building, there wasn't any real reason to prepare for the renovation phase. She decided to keep all of her clothes upstairs as the downstairs was crowded with everything else.

By the late afternoon, she collapsed in a chair with a bottle of water. She chugged it in one big guzzle. Her dehydrated body desperately absorbed every last drop. Her shirt clung to the perspiration on her body. She wanted to grab a shower and get dinner together before either Ian or JD returned.

She removed all her clothes and walked into the bathroom. She pulled back the shower curtain and realized none of her bath supplies were there. Ian smelled great in the shampoo he used, but she wanted to smell like herself. She fell against the wall.

"Ugh." She grunted. With a heavy sigh, she pushed herself off the wall. She wrapped herself in a towel and went off to search for her missing bath supplies. She checked every bag upstairs. Nothing. She checked under Ian's bed. Nothing.

Fuck! She was going have to go down to JD's apartment. The corridor that separated the two apartments wasn't heated. It was as cold as a refrigerator. The cool wind drafted through the front door frame. Her bare feet registered the bone chilling stairs. She skipped down the stairs as quickly as possible. Upon entering JD's apartment, she was struck by the state of disarray. Dammit! Where was the bag? She looked all over until finally she found her bath supplies packed in what must have been JD's gym bag, in JD's closet.

One more time, she faced the staircase. She froze on the first step as a blustery breeze smacked her from behind. She turned to see Ian walking in the main door. Shivering, she held the towel to her body tightly. Ian shut the door, none too quickly.

"What are you doing running around in a towel? You could get sick," Ian fretted. "Don't answer, let's get you upstairs out of the cold." He pulled her by her arm to the warmth of his apartment.

Through chattering teeth, she explained the situation to Ian.

"Let's get you in the shower to warm you up. You have everything you need now?" Ian hugged her shivering body.

Sasha nodded as her teeth chattered.

Ian didn't waste time taking his jacket off. He took her hand and led her to the bathroom. A low moan seeped through her chattering teeth and a stern line formed between his lips. He cranked the water temperature to high.

"Hopefully it will warm up quickly for you. Jesus, your lips are blue." Steam started to billow out from the shower stall. Ian reached under the stream with his hand. "It's hot; get in."

"Ow." The hot water on her cold skin hurt. She slowly stepped into the spray. Within seconds the discomfort morphed to bliss. Her teeth ceased clanging together. She bent her head backward, enjoying the feel of the warm water trickling down her body.

The rattle of glass reverberating was quickly followed by the bang of a closing shower door. She smelled his masculine scent. And then, she was encircled within his embrace. This was all she needed.

"I'm not complaining about coming home to a naked woman, but maybe next time you should wait someplace warm. Like my bed." Ian laughed.

Her frozen brain cells defrosted. "What are you doing home so early? You are normally the last one leaving the firm."

"It's amazing how efficient someone can be with the right motivation. I plowed through my work and rushed to come home to you." Ian kissed her.

"Welcome home," she murmured between kisses. His length grew thick and large between them. She stroked him. The intensity of his kisses heightened. He kissed with a burning passion, just like how she wanted to be fucked.

"We don't have to worry about the pain-in-the-ass neighbor complaining about our time in the shower." They both laughed. Now that they were in a good place together, it was easier to laugh about the past.

"Good. Then let's not rush." She dropped to her knees. She took Ian into her mouth, stretching her lips around his large girth. She tightened the suction in her mouth slowly pulling up on his cock. She tongued the tip and toyed with him, then took him deep into her mouth once again. Sasha loved giving Ian head. The act turned her on as much as any directed toward her. Ian empowered her in many ways, but giving him head was one of the fun ones.

"Oh fuck, Sasha. It feels so fucking good." Ian lightly played with her hair.

She held his balls in her hand, rolling them like dice. They tightened in her clutches, closer to his body.

She stroked his length again. His fingers entwined in her hair, pulling at the roots more than pushing himself deeper down her throat.

His moans turned her on. She was high on the power of making him feel incredible.

"I'm close," He moaned.

She fisted him faster as she sucked, and her tongue lapped at him furiously.

"Sasha!" He shouted as he came.

Sasha swallowed his release, then rose to a standing position. Ian squeezed her tightly. She felt his chest beating against her own. "I love you."

"How much?" She looked at Ian as the drops of water streamed down her face.

"Um." He stammered and narrowed his eyes at her.

"Enough to go grab the gym bag near your door that has all my bath soaps?" *How had she forgotten the bag?* Oh right, the sight of Ian and the prospect of shower sex distracted her.

"Heh. Yes. I don't want you chilled again. Let me go grab it for you." Ian wrapped a towel around his waist and fetched her things.

One by one, Ian handed her all of her bath products while she stayed in the warm shower.

"Now I know you love me." Sasha said before sticking her head out of the shower and kising Ian.

"Love you too."

Chapter 23

Ian

A couple of weeks later, Ian was thrilled to finally have an evening where he got home at a reasonable hour. While he had the chance to spend many hot nights in bed with Sasha, they hadn't had much time to talk other than texts and quick words over coffee in the morning. He was excited to share the news that he had negotiated a great price for the building and looked forward to discussing details about the renovation with JD and Sasha.

The lights were dark in his apartment. He assumed that JD and Sasha were downstairs. They'd put a kibosh on knocking before entering after they learned quickly that being relaxed about the little things facilitated the more complicated logistics of their relationship.

Ian opened the door and heard Sasha in the thralls of ecstasy. The sound instantly made his cock hard. He loosened his tie and belt and headed to join the fun in the bedroom. Sasha had a vibrating dildo in her core while JD was pounding her from behind. The two of them neared climax. Ian had never heard either of them scream so loud. Sasha's orgasm lasted substantially longer than Ian had experienced with her. Ian watched the two of them collapse in a heap.

He bent to kiss Sasha while she was trying to slow

her breathing. JD hopped up from the bed and disappeared out the door.

"I'm happy to see *you*." She said as she kissed Ian with renewed energy. He liked knowing that his presence was able to inspire such a reaction. "I want you."

Those words touched him deep inside. Not only did she love him, but she wanted him. It made him feel ten feet tall.

Her skin was already flushed, but he teased her nipples playfully. He rubbed his finger across her lower lip. He wanted her lips wrapped around his cock. The intimacy of the act enhanced the bond between them.

She tugged him closer as soon as his pants hit the floor. Her impatience was sexy as fuck. "I want to suck your cock. Come closer." She knew exactly how to use her mouth on him to drive him crazy. It wasn't just her skills that drove him mad but her enthusiasm was electrifying. From the position that he was in, he was able to touch Sasha at the same time. He felt her core convulsing around his fingers as he came.

"I like when you get home early from work." She kissed Ian one more time. "I'm going to hop in the shower."

Sasha passed JD exiting the bathroom as she entered.

Both dressed in sweats and t-shirts, JD and Ian hit the refrigerator in search of something to eat. Ian shuffled his feet and commented, "Seemed like that was a pretty intense moment for both you and Sasha earlier." His voice came out strained.

JD looked him square in the eyes. Ian diverted his eyes and shied away. "Hey is something wrong?" His brother took a step towards him.

"Have you and Sasha used the vibrator before?" Ian stepped back and swallowed.

"Yeah, she really gets off on it," JD noted and focused again on the contents of the refrigerator. "And, it feels great for me too. Everyone wins." JD shrugged.

"Was it her idea? She and I have never tried using it like that." Ian's neck felt impossibly hot. He grabbed at it and wiped at the droplets of sweat clinging to his skin.

"Not really. Before the three of us got together she asked me if I had ever had a threesome. One thing led to another and she admitted to wanting to know what it felt like to be double penetrated." JD pulled some cheese out.

"Has she said anything about it since we have been together?" Ian fidgeted back and forth.

"Have I said anything about what?" Sasha asked as she entered the kitchen in a long t-shirt.

Well fuck. He didn't expect Sasha to walk in on this conversation. Sweat trickled down his back.

"I told Ian how you had asked about DP."

Sasha turned deep pink. "Oh."

"You never mentioned this to me." Ian didn't want to put her on the defensive. He was worried that she felt more open with JD than him.

"Um, I'm not sure what to say right now. You seem angry about something and I don't understand." Sasha's brow furrowed.

JD intervened. "You know, we haven't really had any discussions about sex, other than the desire to stop using condoms. Which I'm very pleased that we are done with them." JD winked at Sasha. Ian's lips turned upward. "Other than that, we have been generally winging it as we have gone along. If there is something that we need to discuss, let's do it."

Ian ran his fingers through his brown hair, "I haven't been jealous that the two of you get to spend more alone time together. I know that both of you accommodate my crazy schedule and make sure that I get time with Sasha. I think tonight was the first time that I worried that maybe because you two have more time that you feel more open with each other."

"JD and I had the conversation before the three of us were together," Sasha qualified, crossing her arms in front of her.

Suddenly, Ian felt a divide between Sasha and himself. "Why didn't you mention it to me? Is it that you feel one way toward JD and something different towards me?" Ian whispered. He feared the answer.

"I love you *both*." She stepped closer to Ian and put a hand on his chest.

"I'm not trying to keep a tally here, but do you see us differently?" Ian was having trouble getting his message across completely. This was extremely difficult for Ian to express his insecurity.

"I love having sex with both of you. It isn't that I prefer one of you to the other. I'm so sorry if I made you feel that." Sasha hugged Ian and he leaned in to her for reassurance. She continued, "And a bit selfishly, I really enjoy being with both of you together."

"If you being selfish means more sex for us, please be selfish!" JD winked, which caused Sasha to blush.

"Is this about the double penetration question?" JD put it out there.

Ian nodded.

"I'm not following." Sasha looked between Ian and JD.

"Ian and I had originally had a discussion before we

got into this relationship that he had no desire to share you in that way," JD mentioned.

"I'm just not comfortable being in that close of proximity to my brother," Ian admitted while looking away. He felt bad, knowing that it was something that Sasha wanted, but he was uncertain if he was able to conquer the mental hurdle.

"I kind of assumed that. I mean I can understand why both of you wouldn't be interested in that type of connection. I would never expect either of you to do something that you weren't comfortable doing. I want everyone happy." Sasha kissed Ian. JD came up behind Sasha and held her.

"You do make us happy," Ian murmured as he held Sasha's hand. He realized he was making this conversation unnecessarily difficult. "After hearing you come tonight like I've never heard before, it made me think that I haven't been satisfying you *fully*."

"Bro, I've seen and heard her come with you. She's not faking that."

Sasha laughed at JD's comment and of course blushed.

"I didn't realize that I was keeping you from getting something you wanted. It was me preventing that." Ian hung his head.

"Ian, it's okay. I will be fine if we never do that. More importantly, *we* will be fine. And if you want to incorporate more toys in our play, I'm good with that too." Sasha winked at both Ian and JD.

Her sincerity made Ian believe her and that was all the reassurance that he needed.

"Look who's all sassy now." JD kissed Sasha. "More sex. More toys. We all win."

Sasha took both of Ian and JD's hands in hers. "I know I'm winning here. I have two men in my life that respect and support me. Ian, you make me feel good about my career change, where I can be proud of my work and my choices. JD, your encouragement for me to seek out what makes me happy has dramatically changed my perspective on life. And, with my new job, I have a lot more energy to focus on things that bring me happiness. And, you two are at the top of that list. This is not where I expected to be, but I couldn't be happier. Having you both in my life and in my bed, makes me the luckiest girl in the world."

Ian kissed Sasha on the head. JD repeated the sentiment.

Ian turned to face both Sasha and JD. "I can't believe that I found a situation where I can have everything that I wanted. My career is going really well. I finally made partner. I get to come home to this beautiful woman that respects my long hours at work, but also makes me feel adored as a man not just as an attorney. And I'm thankful for my brother that makes all of this work. He isn't just someone I share a woman with, he makes our relationship work. I don't think I could have any of this pleasure without him."

JD hugged Ian. "Thank you."

Sasha squeezed Ian's hand and smiled sweetly at him. She wiped a stray tear from her eye.

JD took a deep breath. "When I lost my hockey team, I thought I had lost everything. But now, I feel like I am part of a much stronger team with the two of you. Thanks to Sasha seeing that article about the arts foundation, I contacted the college. I may be able to run their new art program for the community as well as work as a voluntary hockey coach for the men's team. I may not have yet found a permanent career path, but I feel like with both of your support that I can get there in a way that is most fulfilling. It will be a process, but you both help me feel confident about my decisions and I truly appreciate it."

"We are behind you, one-hundred percent." Sasha hugged JD.

"Thank you. You know, originally, I wasn't sure if I would be able to share Sasha, but that isn't how it feels now. I don't think in terms of mine, yours, and hers. Through our process together, everything feels like ours. And I feel like I have more happiness in my life than I could have ever hoped."

Sasha kissed JD while pulling Ian closer to her. "I need you both. Now."

"Let's see what fun toys we can use on our girl," Ian suggested.

"Great idea. We all win," JD noted like a sportscaster.

A word about the author…

Liz Ellyn strives to nourish people's cravings for the irresistible. Like the decadent desserts she delivers, she creates alluring characters deserving of happy endings.

With degrees in both engineering and law, she argues that the positive energy gained by indulging in one's guilty pleasure appropriately counterbalances the serious forces of daily life.

When she isn't writing or devouring steamy romance books, she spoils her family, including her two dogs, Boomer and Tanner.

Bon Appetite and Happy Reading

Thank you for purchasing
this publication of The Wild Rose Press, Inc.

For questions or more information
contact us at
info@thewildrosepress.com.

The Wild Rose Press, Inc.
www.thewildrosepress.com

www.ingramcontent.com/pod-product-compliance
Lightning Source LLC
Chambersburg PA
CBHW051137030726
47504CB00004B/911